I EXIST
Prince Charles Louis
de Bourbon

Trafford Press Victoria B.C.

Cover shows Louis XVI and Louis XVII and the author, Charles de Bourbon. Graphic design by Holly de Bourbon of The Puddleduck Co. Contact: hdebourbon@rogers.com

Note for Librarians: A cataloguing record for this book is available from Library and Archives Canada at www.collectionscanada.ca/amicus/index-e.html
ISBN 1-4120-5299-8

Printed in Victoria, BC, Canada. Printed on paper with minimum 30% recycled fibre. Trafford's print shop runs on "green energy" from solar, wind and other environmentally-friendly power sources.

TRAFFORD

Offices in Canada, USA, Ireland and UK
This book was published *on-demand* in cooperation with Trafford Publishing. On-demand publishing is a unique process and service of making a book available for retail sale to the public taking advantage of on-demand manufacturing and Internet marketing. On-demand publishing includes promotions, retail sales, manufacturing, order fulfilment, accounting and collecting royalties on behalf of the author.

Book sales for North America and international:
Trafford Publishing, 6E–2333 Government St.,
Victoria, BC v8t 4p4 CANADA
phone 250 383 6864 (toll-free 1 888 232 4444)
fax 250 383 6804; email to orders@trafford.com
Book sales in Europe:
Trafford Publishing (uk) Ltd., Enterprise House, Wistaston Road Business Centre,
Wistaston Road, Crewe, Cheshire cw2 7rp UNITED KINGDOM
phone 01270 251 396 (local rate 0845 230 9601)
facsimile 01270 254 983; orders.uk@trafford.com
Order online at:
trafford.com/05-0194
10 9 8 7 6 5 4 3

Dedicated to to Louise, Michael and Edmond, in the hope I have lessened the burden on you.

Magna Carta of 1215: Clause 40: To none we will sell, to none deny or delay, right or justice.

Emile Zola: "J'accuse."

TABLE OF CONTENTS

FOREWORD

In 2004 the Spanish branch of the de Bourbon family
tried again to bury the story of Louis XVII. With great
fanfare and publicity they buried a heart, which they
claimed was the heart of Louis XVII. Just where this
heart came from I do not know but their representative
in France had access to all the hearts of the French
Royal family. What we do know is that even if Dr.
Pelletan had removed a heart from the body of the boy
that died in the Temple that still does not prove that
the heart is from Louis XVII. Of course the French government continues to claim that boy was Louis XVII
but over 100 false dauphins demolish that theory. No,
he definitely escaped, everyone knew. The strange
thing is now the Government claims we cannot test
that body, to which this heart belongs, because everyone knows it is NOT Louis XVII.

When my great, great grandfather died in Delft
Holland and was buried as Louis XVII in a grave now a
National Monument, the French government made
strong objections but to no avail. Ever since the push
has been on to bury not the heart but THE STORY.

Between 1910 and 1927 Georges Pinet de Manteyer,
historian to the Princes of the Spanish de Bourbon-
Parma researched all the archives of Germany to see if
he could shake the story of Louis XVII. He published
numerous articles and books, of course against my family. But Mr. Escaich, the famous French lawyer wrote:
"Contrary to what the author wrote, he reinforces the
theory of the Mystery of Naundorff". His theory that

Naundorff was the soldier Berg was disproven by the exhumation of 1950.

Many years ago I decided to write a book about my great-great grandfather since almost all the material that existed was either in French, Dutch or German. I wanted my children to know the story. I decided later to bring the story up to date by adding some chapters on my own life. I have left out the hundreds of days that I happily spent with my family and at work. They were the best days of my life but a bore to the reader. But the main story remains as close as possible as I lived it and in some ways strangely similar to the life of my ancestor.

I am not an historian and I may have a date or two wrong, I am also not unbiased but I will gladly look at any proof against our claims. So far I have not seen anything that has shaking my believe in the truth. I have done the best I could to give the straight story as I see it, but the last chapter has not yet been written.

I am most grateful to all those who have helped me with this book. Mrs Eileen Bos, who so carefully went line by line and made many corrections. My sister Amelie de Bourbon-Koning, her husband Steven and her sons Maarten and Peter have all had a hand in the revisions. Then Holly de Bourbon, who helped make the manuscript and the family trees what they are. My thanks also to family friends Tom and May Fitzpatrick and family, Lorne and Isobel Emmerson, Cees Bos, Lloyd, Kay Barthau and Taher Gnaba. In France Philippe and Claire Mac'Rel and Madame A.M. Mercier-Derôme. In Spain Stephan and Cornelie Schoor and Felix Hes. In Belgium there are two families without whose support I would have long ago given up this project, they are the Marquise Marthe de la Hamaide, Dr. Rudy Meganck and his wife Lea de la Garde. And most of all in Holland our lawyer Dominique Rijnbout, who for the last 4 years has worked so hard for us and who has started the Foundation de Bourbon. I am leaving out many, many others and I thank them as well.

Finally, I appeal to the French government to correct the error which now stands in French history for over 200 years. The Revolution killed Louis XVI and Marie Antoinette for political reasons. Please now let the young son live! There is no longer a need to keep pretending that he died June 8, 1795. You have always known that he did not die that day, you know the death certificate was false. My family belongs nowhere until you let us live in honour with our name. I carry it in honour but you have never given me the courtesy of making it official and we will keep on fighting until we get your agreement.

Charles Louis,

Markham, Ontario, Canada, November 5, 2004.

Chapter 1.   EARLY MEMORIES

"He has the loudest voice in the whole maternity ward," said the nurse to my mother, "He can really yell."

"Maybe I should comfort him here" said my mother.

"I will go and get him," said the nurse.

My mother had to wait a whole day before I arrived from the ward. She kept asking for me but there was always a new excuse. Finally I arrived, my mother noticed I was wrapped up very tightly and she thought that they were choking me. She unrolled the blanket and then noticed a bandage around my leg. She wondered why and asked the nurse.

"We had a slight accident" the nurse explained, "The hot water bottle cover came off and he burnt his leg."

I still carry a 5 inch scar and sometimes I still yell loudly. My parents had married earlier that year and lived in Nijmegen in Holland, where they had both attended the University. My father Louis had a law degree and my mother Gudrun had a degree in French. A friend to both had introduced them and she became my Aunt Mary, although she was no family. My brother Henri joined us a year and a half after my arrival.

Father preferred writing to legal work, he had worked on the University's paper and after graduating became a reporter. A group of well-known Dutch writers formed a literary magazine "Roeping" (Calling in English) and they remained friends for life. They included the well-known Dutch writers Anton Coolen, Jan Engleman and Anton van Duinkerken. In 1935 my father accepted a post in the Dutch Indies (now Indonesia) and we moved to Surabaya. I remember little of our stay there, just that my mother claimed that the little girl next door was my first girlfriend. I do remember a little red pedal car that I loved.

Some evenings we sat on our front porch and listened to the bell ringing from the small kitchen on wheels that came by and sold us local delicatessens. I remember the large green trees and the beautiful neighbourhood, but after my sister Amelie arrived, my mother found the climate too hot and humid for herself and the children so we returned to Holland in 1938 just steps ahead of the Japanese invasion.

Father had already applied to become a town mayor, in Holland. It was an appointed position, which he accepted and became mayor of Escharen and Langeboom, two small villages in the province of Brabant. Gassel was added later and we moved to Heumen to a stately house across from a famous restaurant, which lay along the highway from Nijmegen to Maastricht. The owner had, I believe nine children among which a set of twin boys who became my friends. There was also a daughter who I pined for her in my dreams. Later during the war there was a bombardment on Nijmegen and one of the twins was killed by shrapnel while standing in a doorway. His twin brother survived.

We then moved to a larger house in the town of Mook, this property lay on the edge of the Mookse Heide, a large forest that runs from Holland to Germany. We had this forest at the back of the house and a lovely view of the countryside at the front. But not for long; World War II broke out for us in Holland when the Germans invaded and we had the odious honour of being the first to be occupied. At 4:00 in the morning of May 10, 1940 there was a lot of noise outside and there they were. The Germans thought that my mother was trying to hurt them. She had put up a clothesline and it interfered with the men on horses. Father had to explain that it was not on purpose. They stayed till sun up and then they advanced on the main road running north to the bridge that connected us with the rest of Holland. Holland lasted three days against the overwhelming hordes of Germans and then it was all over. Soon life returned to some normalcy.

In early 1941 my father became town mayor of Oss, an industrial city just south of the large rivers that cut Holland in two. The north of Holland was busy and industrial; the south was more rural and friendlier.

Life was becoming difficult as the Germans made more and more demands, especially from the town mayors. They needed food for the "Fatherland". They needed workers for the war factories. They placed restrictions here, there and everywhere. No portraits of the Queen, no killing of your own livestock for food. The NSB was the National Socialist Bond, a political party that aided the Germans.

My father was a great actor, always trying to impress children and adults with tricks and jokes. It was how he survived the two years he was in Oss. During the day he did the best he could to work with the Germans and at night he worked with the underground to help those hiding from the Germans.

Bob Zadok Blok tells the story of his family. His father was arrested in Amsterdam, not only because he was a Jew but also because he had helped people and that was noticed by his neighbour, a member of the NSB. He died in a concentration camp. Pastor Cox of Maren hid the mother and her two children but again a NSB neighbour called the Germans. Father arrived in the middle of the night and picked up the family and brought them to Oss. From there they were separated and moved around to keep them safe. Bob told me later that they moved him forty times before the war finally ended.

Many people had a story to tell. The Dutch newspaper "Parool" tells the story of October 2nd, 1942 when the Germans demanded that all Jews present themselves for a trip to Germany. That evening Louis went to the school to see how many had arrived. There were 143 persons at the school and they were put on trucks to the capital of the province—Hertogenbosch. Louis followed them and that evening in the station there were 143 persons and one policeman and one mayor. Louis complained to the head of the German detail that one woman had passed out, she was seven months pregnant. "Give her some water, it will help" said the commander, "I cannot do anything. They will be transported to Germany at 4:00 in the morning."

Louis knew the head of the Sicherheit Dienst, a Sturmfuhrer Samel and decided to call him. The phone rang and rang and finally Samel answered:

"There is a woman here who is seven months pregnant, surely she is of no use to you in Germany," said Louis "and there is also an old man well over the age limit that you required but the commandant here won't let him go. Another old man is here with three children whose mother has died. You do not want those."

"What are you doing there?" answered the Sturmfuhrer. "You have no business there."

"I am the mayor and these are my people," replied Louis "You should come over and see for yourself."

Louis realized then that maybe he had asked for too much but he had guessed right that this stiff German was an honourable man and the Sturmfuhrer promised to be there within an hour.

"All right then, make a list of those and I'll come over."

Due to those efforts several lives were saved.

Louis managed to hold on for almost two years until the situation became too much and he resigned and he went underground because he heard from friends that the Germans were going to pick him up. He moved from one to another safe house until he hid in Mook where he had lived before the war and where there was an artist's colony of mainly painters but also sculptors and writers. My mother and the children had to vacate the mayor's home and we all were dispersed. Soon I was in a boarding school run by Catholic brothers and Henri went to the family Koning, Amelie moved in with a young family and then shortly after with the family van de Hulst. I did not like boarding school but I managed it for a year. The twins I had known in Mook were there and I spent a weekend with them during the holidays.

On March 17th 1944 the Germans sentenced Louis to death, fortunately they could not catch him. He had become involved with the underground and was in charge of 5 groups of other patriots. My mother had moved to Oisterwijk and lived with her brother Svend and his family and I came out of the boarding school I do not know how we all fitted into that small house but we did for almost a year and it was one of the best years of my life. Many days there was no school and we hung around in the forests that surrounded Oisterwijk. We had a climbing tree that we climbed better than monkeys. In front of our neighbours was a small lake where we could go fishing. What else did you need?

One day I remember visiting my father when someone was hiding him in a little house in a forest far from any town and we spent a weekend there with my mother. We had not seen Father for a year but we did not mind too much because he was much stricter than mom.

Then on a sunny day the allies came over in planes and gliders. There were hundreds, no thousands. It was operation "Overlord". We had shelters built in our back yard, each person had his own. We spent the whole day there watching them all pass by. Nearby an ack ack gun fired at them and one plane pulling a glider behind was shot down. The following day the Germans were driving around town in an American jeep.

Shortly after we went looking around to see what trouble we could get into. I was the oldest, my uncle and aunt had two sons and I had a good friend who lived next door. Together with my brother and sister we were six. We all walked through the woods to a main highway. There we noticed a large old mansion, it seemed to have been a building the Germans had occupied but now the doors stood open and there was not a soul around. So we sneaked through the whole place, they had abandoned the furniture, papers were spread all over and junk was piled high. It was an adventure.

The following day there was a lot of shooting nearby and suddenly there was a loud rumbling and then a large tank came out of the woods and the guys on top were Americans. What a dance we did. Uncle Svend had his first real cigarette in two years and Mom got some real tea. We had lived for the last two months on apples from the garden and bread made without yeast. And now it was all over. We walked by the empty house where we had been the day before. Now there was a big sign on it. "German Headquarters—Booby Traps!" We must have lived right.

Father came a week later on my birthday, the second of November. What a birthday present. He had liberated his own town. The allies had reached the large rivers in Holland and had attempted to jump over them with the attack called "Overlord." But the Germans were waiting for them in Arnhem and they had gone "One bridge too far." The roads—Hertogenbos to Nijmegen—had been won from the Germans but the towns between the road and the rivers were still in German hands. Father and his five groups had advanced on Oss themselves and with the help of two tanks commandeered from the highway, they had liberated Oss. Dad was back as mayor and he received a great welcome.

So we went back in the mayor's house, which had been occupied by the NSB town mayor Apeldoorn, who had been killed by the resistance. So it was back to school for me. Under the Germans we had dropped French and had studied German. Now we dropped German and started with English plus French in the first year high school. The following year it was German again. The country is quite small and only Dutchmen speak the language so we needed more than one language.

The war had been strenuous for my father and while he was living with the painter Jacques van Mourik in Mook he had started an affair with his daughter Ity. The affair soon meant the end of the marriage to my mother and father had to resign from his position. As a catholic he could no longer serve in a catholic town and he promised Ity that if he came out of the war intact he would marry her. She made threats of suicide if he did not but it was my mother he really loved and some years later he remarried her. He was also ill from all the pressure during the war, a sort of reaction to all he had endured and he wanted away from everything. He went back to writing and completed several romantic novels and much poetry. But he survived on articles for papers and magazines. It was difficult to keep head above water and the family had a difficult time. We again had to leave the mayor's house and Mother moved to The Hague.

I had known for some time that I descended from the royal family of France. My name was "de Bourbon" and my father had always told us to be extra good because we had a reputation to uphold. It did not really impress us. We grew up as ordinary children and with the war there was no time to worry about that.

Then Father came to visit because he was to meet a group from France. They had come to pay their respects to what they considered to be the Head of the Royal family de Bourbon. My great great grandfather was Louis XVII, he had settled in Holland after the revolution and we had lived there since. But father was sick and asked me to accompany Mr. Begeer, the owner of the large Royal Begeer Silver Factory. He was Father's best friend and a great supporter of our family's claims, so I had to go. I was only 16 and frightened of what was expected of me. We were introduced and sat down and soup was served. I waited for the gentlemen to start eating; I knew that was the rule. But they all waited for me. In the meanwhile the soup got cold until Mr. Begeer broke the ice and told me to get started. He spoke to me in Dutch which no one understood.

My father and I would sometimes make trips to towns in the north of Belgium to give lectures on my family's history. I acted at times as his secretary and I typed his manuscripts and his letters. One evening in Hasselt there was a large audience; the Governor of the Province of Limburg was present. Father promised to have dinner with him at the end of the speech. Thus he was in a hurry to leave when the speech was over. He spoke to a few of the people who approached him when an older lady asked for a few moments of his time. He tried to put her off but she was quite insistent. He took her to a small office next to the lecture hall.

"Do you remember when you were very young, you and your parents lived in Henegau in Belgium?" asked the lady.

"Yes, said my father," we had to leave in a hurry when the Germans came in the beginning of the First World War."

"Yes" said the lady "Your family fled to Holland, which stayed out of the war. My father was a bailiff and the Germans were mad at your family and ordered all your belongings sold. He did as the Germans wanted but he called the family together and told us that he had kept two paintings belonging to the family in his attic and if ever after the war one of us would meet a member of the Bourbon family, they were to return the portraits to them."

And so the following day Louis retrieved the portrait that now hangs in my living room from the lady's house. It had been missing for 40 years.

The clearest memory I have is that of the opening of my forefather's grave. He was buried in Delft, Holland. Just a few miles south of The Hague. His tomb, surrounded by a heavy wrought iron fence, lies in the corner of a small park. His single tombstone is marked:

ICI REPOSE

LOUIS XVII

CHARLES LOUIS DUC DE NORMANDIE

ROI DE FRANCE ET DE NAVARRE

NE VERSAILLES LE 27 MARS 1785

DECEDE DELFT LE 10 AOUT 1845

This stone had cracked and needed repair. My father and Mr. Begeer had decided to exhume the body after opening the grave and to perform some up-to-date forensic tests on the body.

I remember the day very well. It was near the end of September and fall had set in. It was cool and damp. In that sombre atmosphere we stood for a long time, I remember the shivers running down my spine when they finally brought the casket up out of the grave. The little doctor looked out of place in his white apron among all the dressed up onlookers. He had a long white beard, wore a rubber apron and resembled a small fairy dwarf. My brother Henri and sister Amelie were there with my father and his great supporter Mr. Carl Begeer.

There were several police officers, the town mayor some other officials and a few reporters. Finally the casket was taken to the police station for the research and it was opened in the large room set aside by the police. Inside were a skeleton, some hair and a brown residue. The little doctor, Dr. Hulst was a forensic specialist and we all stood around not knowing what to say to each other. The skeleton was of a 60 year old, which agreed with my forefather's story. He could not have been Werg, the soldier. Werg had been the boarder and lover of Mrs Sonnenfelft in Berlin in the same rooming house where Louis XVII had lived. From the marks that were found on his skeleton the doctor made out that he had been stabbed and that he could not have self inflicted these marks on his back.

It still gives me a strange feeling to have been so close to my forefather and his mysterious past. How did a French King end up in Delft? What had happened? I had many questions back then and somehow they took a long time getting answered.

My mother had met a Canadian who urged her to go to Canada. She convinced her brother, my uncle Svend that this was the land of the future. He left after a few months and then the Canadian boyfriend died in Hamilton from a bad case of pleurisy that had hung on since the war. So I promised Mom I would go to Canada and get settled and then bring her and my siblings over. So a few months after reaching 18 I left for a new adventure in Canada leaving my forefathers behind.

Chapter 2.   LOUIS XVI

The death of Louis XV was a long, drawn out agony which lasted 10 days. Smallpox in an older man in the 18th century was fatal and he knew it. He called for the Duchess of Berry, who had been his companion for the last few years, and bid her farewell. When she left, the rest of the court knew the end was imminent.

He made his peace with his God, he confessed his sins and said his goodbyes. On May 7th, 1774 at 3.30 in the afternoon a loud cry was heard: "The King is dead, Long live the King". A very reluctant Louis XVI stood by. He was only twenty years old and had had little training to take on this heavy burden. His father had died nine years before and now his grandfather was gone. He had a great fear of what lay ahead and would never be completely at ease with his position.

But he was the most sincere king that France had ever known and a most loyal husband and father, one of the very few de Bourbon's without a mistress. Of course the king's actions are often judged by the work of his ministers and there is no doubt that Louis XVI was much better served by his foreign minister than by all the other ministers. Louis XVI still has not received the full credit he deserves for many of the things he did. In particular his role in the American Revolution was substantial as he personally, influenced and financed a large part of it.

Many Frenchmen early in the conflict accepted the ideals of the American Revolution. Under the influence of the writings of Rousseau, the young people of France became very excited about the establishment of a new nation and the King himself still young and very intrigued by such a prospect.

Young men like Lafayette and Noailles eagerly followed and listened to a strangely dressed Benjamin Franklin, who strode around Paris in his cotton pants, his half powdered wig and his rustic jacket. He was a living incarnation of the dreams of Rousseau. There was a rage to serve this new nation and enthusiasm fired the imagination of many, including the King.

The King's foreign minister, Vergennes, was hesitant. He wanted an agreement from the Spanish to back the French in their support of the Americans. But the Spanish did not care for this idea which made Vergennes very nervous. On September 7th, 1777, Louis XVI made his decision, without the advice of his ministers. He, by himself would support the Americans. A few months later he signed, on his own stationary, the conditions for the basis of negotiations between France and the United States.

Hopefully credit will eventually come to him as new historians re-examine his external policies and his life. This period in history is now being re-examined without animosity and Louis XVI is being judged a far better man and king than previously recorded.

Among the many accomplishments of his reign were: the free trade of grains, wine and meat, the reformation of the army and especially the navy, which became very strong during his reign. He also abolished feudal rights, slavery and torture. Several laws which were humiliating to the Jews were wiped from the books and a Treaty with the United States was signed. Louis XVI 's government also established the rights of women and children to receive their own pensions without needing authorisations of their husbands or guardians. Finally and not to be forgotten, he signed the bill, which declared The Rights of Man.

Louis Charles, later Louis XVII, was born in Versailles on March 27th, 1785. His father was Louis XVI and his mother was Marie Antoinette, Archduchess of Austria. He was their third child following his sister Marie-Therese and his brother Louis Joseph Xavier Francois, the Dauphin or Crown Prince. His godfather was his father's brother Louis Stanislas Xavier, Count of Provence and his godmother, his aunt Marie Charlotte Louise de Loraine, Archduchess of Austria, Queen of the two Sicilies.

Unfortunately he could not have picked a worse godfather. Instead of looking out for the boy's well being once his father died, the Count of Provence did his utmost to harm him and in the end he even denied him his name.

It had started earlier at the baptism of Marie-Therese, the future Duchess of Angouleme. Again the Count of Provence was the godfather. In the middle of the ceremony he asked the officiating priest: "Aren't you going to ask whom the parents are?"

This cynical remark was aimed at Louis XVI who had had a barren marriage for seven years. A malfunction of his reproductive organs, which by this time had been corrected by a small operation, was the problem. The Count of Provence resented very much that he was not the king and now soon he would not even be the Dauphin any longer.

He had written to his friend in England, the Duke of Fitzjames, that of the three brothers he was the right choice to reign and that he was going to get the evidence to prove that his brother's children were not his and, therefore, he was not fit to reign. He became indignant when Marie-Antoinette presented Louis XVI with the first son, a new Dauphin. As Dauphin, the Count of Provence had for ten years occupied the Dauphin's quarters, which he now had to vacate, since he lost that title to the new prince.

The fierce determination to reign made the Count of Provence a vicious man and his scheming aided the revolution. His accomplice was his younger brother, the Count of Artois, whose children would inherit from the Count of Provence, once the main branch of Louis XVI was eliminated; the Count of Provence had no children.

The Count of Provence, who later became Louis XVIII, was a member of the Free Masons, a secret society started in 1717 by the Protestant Reverend Anderson, the historian Payne and the puritan minister Desagaliers. Their ideals were the same as the French philosophers Rousseau and Voltaire. They dreamed of a Utopia with every person having his individual rights. They were against religion and the monarchy. Although they used Louis XVIII, in the end it was he who succeeded to the throne.

One of the earliest and most influential Free Masons was the Duke of Choiseul, who disbanded the Jesuits. He let parliament ignore the bills issued by the Popes

Clemens XII and Benedictus XV condemning the secret society of the Masons.

The Masons held their first international conference in 1771. A second conference followed in 1781. Then at the conference in Frankfurt in 1784 it was decided to eliminate the Kings of Sweden and of France. The King of Sweden was later assassinated and Louis XVI was beheaded.

Nearly all the ministers of Louis XVI were Free Masons and inevitably, they steered the government and the people towards the destruction of the monarchy and of the country.

When Louis Charles was born, his father appointed for him, a staff of forty people under the Duchess of Polignac, who was governess of the royal children. The Duchess of Tourzel later replaced her. There was a sub-governess, and three chambermaids, one of which was Madame Rambaud. There were also several teachers, cooks, butlers and footmen. The child was strong, cheerful and friendly. He called his serious older sister "Madame" and his mother "Mama Queen" and she called him her "Choux d'Amour", her love cabbage. The boy loved to work in his own little garden every day and he always brought back a flower for his mother.

The family was actually quite different from what has been portrayed in some history books. The father was courageous and steadfast, attentive and conscientious. He was very religious and had the best of intentions. He had inherited a bad system; which had gotten badly out of hand. He believed that he was a servant of the people wanting only what was best for his country and his people. He liked to work with his hands and gave his son an avid interest in watches and miniature armaments. His main fault was that he tried to be popular, giving in to many demands instead of leading and sticking to his own good ideas.

Different political groups and governments made silly demands which Louis XVI allowed. Slowly but surely this led him down the garden path. He trusted in the ultimate goodness of humanity believing that, in the end, everything would turn out all right and that everyone else also worked towards the same virtuous goals.

Marie Antoinette was majestic and graceful, having both courage and spirit, but she did not like the pomp and ceremony of court life, preferring to live a simpler life with her family and very few friends. She never said those famous words that for decades have been attributed to her: "Let them eat Cake."

Life in France at this time was heavily influenced by the philosophers of the time. The words of Diderot, Voltaire and Rousseau were on everyone's lips. Their books, plays and thoughts were quoted by everyone, but especially by the wealthy and the educated, although much of the satire and irony was aimed at themselves. It was fashionable then, to laugh at oneself, at the King and at religion. Everyone wrote poems and pamphlets, which eventually became especially vicious against Marie Antoinette and the Catholic Church.

The financial state of the country was dreadful. It cost a fortune to keep the kingdom with its palaces, aristocracy and servants. Any good deed done for the King was rewarded by a life pension. This list was a long one and the Queen had her own list.

The costs were enormous, bringing France to the verge of bankruptcy. In this period, most Frenchmen lived comfortably and enjoyed a high standard of living, the highest in Europe. The farmers owned 50% of the land, a very high percentage for that day. Paris was affluent and the port cities bustled as trade increased with the colonies. But the tax system needed overhauling and there was much opposition to change as no one wanted to pay more. The burden of the taxes lay with the poor; nobility and the religious orders were almost completely exempt. The system dated back to the days when the nobility supplied the armies for the king and did the policing. Which exempted them from taxes.

However these duties had long ago been taken over by the army and the police and paid for by the state. The taxpayers paid the costs and the nobility were still exempt. The weight of all these taxes and their unfair distribution eventually brought on the revolution. In England the rich always carried more of the burden. The religious orders were exempt because they looked after the education of the population.

Then it was, that Louis XVI made one of the worst mistakes of his reign. He called up the General Estates. This consisted of three chambers, each with one vote. The first chamber was the aristocracy, the second was the clergy and the third was the rest of the people or about 97% of the people. Each chamber deliberated on its own but now the Third Estate; the people, wanted a vote for each representative. They invited the other two chambers to a common meeting, which they did not want at all, although a few aristocrats and a few priests did support the idea. The King suddenly decided to enlarge the hall where the Third Estate met and the members arrived to find the hall closed by workmen. The members agreed to meet on the tennis courts instead. They passed a resolution that they would remain there until a new constitution was made.

The king then called all three chambers together and declared that each had its own rights and that things would remain as they had been. He lowered the salt tax, to pacify the Third Estate, but that was not enough. The Third Estate objected and finally the king yielded. A whole series of confrontations followed which the king lost and which caused the whole system to collapse.

The king lost his power gradually and the bold revolutionaries continued making new demands. Now they had the initiative and soon they had the power. The sad part was that the king had the right ideas and his opponents had no idea where they were heading. They talked of equality and liberty, but their policies were not working.

Meanwhile, in Paris, the political clubs had become very active. Some met once a week, some three times per week; discussions were held on how to run the government. They argued all night long and started to resemble political parties. They published their own pamphlets stating their policies, often listened to paid agitators and foreign spies, who urged them on. Little by little as the talk got stronger and more aggressive, the actions became more vehement. The conservatives, frightened by what was occurring locked themselves in their homes. No one had the courage to stop what was happening.

In the centre of the city stood the Royal Palace, which belonged to the Orleans family, a junior branch of the de Bourbon family. It was at the centre of the worst abuses. Prostitution flourished inside the palace, everyone had a mistress and daily pamphlets were printed attacking the king, the queen and the Roman Catholic Church. Paid informers and agitators made up half of the palace courtiers.

The Duke of Orleans was a descendant of the brother of Louis XIII and one of the worst intriguers of his time. When he was 18 years old he said he was sad that he could not slap God in the face. He later dragged his brother through a life of debauchery, which cost him dearly. In 1771 he became a grand master of the Free Masons lodge in France. Having financed the attack of the palace of Versailles he later paid his agent, Danton, to prosecute the Princess de Lamballe because he owed her 300.000 francs which took care of that. He then had his mistress assassinated and openly sold her jewellery.

At one time he even managed to persuade the future Louis XVIII to aid him in his efforts to upset the current monarchy. He convinced him to appeal to Marie Antoinette for the hand of her daughter Marie Therese for his son the Duke of Chartres. Marie Antoinette answered; "I, during my reign as queen, have seen several of my projects cancelled because of a stroke of bad luck or because of deliberate snubs. I have seen myself insulted, my honour attacked, my life threatened, scoundrels have followed my family into the Tuilleries where we are today. I have had to put up with the rudeness of City Hall, with the slander of people without honour but nothing hurts me as this. There is no more king of France, no more majesty of the throne, no more respect of human life because the Duke of Orleans, my assassin, the enemy of my husband and my children, he who for years has made me the object of all his cruel jokes, he expects me to consent to such an audacious request! Who! Me! To give my daughter to such a man, a foolish Jacobin. I should give her away to usurp the throne from my son! Better that my son, my daughter, my husband and even myself succumb to a hurricane than that man succeeds. And you my brother, how come you agreed to act for them, that I do not understand."

The king continued to tolerate everything, and optimist that he was, he believed that all would end well, because after all everyone was working towards the same end!

The king and the government had no power to stop anything because the same troublemakers had infiltrated the police and the army. Many of them also belonged to the clubs. Even the army had a club where their superiors were ridiculed. There was no discipline and morals were almost non-existent.

In June some troops mutinied and were jailed. On June 30th 1789 a group marched on the prison, forced the door and freed the mutineers, who then proceeded to have a party to celebrate their release. This was now pure anarchy with gangs roaming the streets, throwing stones and tearing down statues. There was no controlling the crowds. Some of the police and the troops joined the mob instead of stopping them.

Most ordinary people were at home, barricaded in. It was the riffraff who were in charge and now overran City Hall. They cleared out a police station and freed the prisoners. On the morning of July 14th, 1789 a mob assembled near the Invalides, led by the Duc of Orleans and his group, who grabbed people off the street and paid them 10 francs to join the fun and then

34

march to the Bastille. This prison had the reputation that it held the political prisoners of the king, brought there on the King's "Lettres de Cachet". It was an old reputation and no longer true but it served as a symbol. The Bastille also contained a large number of guns and ammunition.The mob had just found a large cache of rifles but they needed bullets and powder.

The governor M. de Launay had some troops and some Swiss Guards, enough to defend himself and his buildings but his philosophy was to side with the people and he did not want to make a stand. He negotiated with two members of the mob but the rest climbed over the first two towers looking for something with which to set them on fire. Finally, someone hacked through the drawbridge rope and it rattled down. The multitude started towards the first courtyard. The mob had its first taste of victory.

They faced four cannons, but the garrison was afraid to act and a subaltern promised that no one would be hurt. The troops convinced de Launay to give up and he surrendered. In spite of all the promises and the arrangements de Launay was immediately massacred. A kitchen boy, who knew how to handle meat, cut off the head and put it on a pike. He paraded it around, covered with blood, for the rest of the day. The major, his aide and a lieutenant were killed also.

Inside the Bastille, the mob found only seven prisoners. Four were convicted frauds, one was a sadist, a follower of the Marquis de Sade, and the last two were mental cases. There were no political prisoners after all.

This then is the famous "Bastille Day", which is still the major holiday in France for Republicans; a shame really in a country with such an illustrious past, and so many memorable days, that this day of horror has become its major symbol.

Once back at City Hall, the mob sent its demands to the king. They wanted the government leader, Necker, returned to his post; they wanted the troops pulled back and they wanted the king to come and talk to them in Paris. Finally, here was a moment when events should not have been allowed to continue; people cannot take the law into their own hands and ransom the government to obey. They had, through public opinion, already gained more than they would for years to come. People cannot be allowed to murder freely, set prisoners free and create panic in the streets. These were not the French people, these were hooligans and paid agitators. The real French people had no leaders and were hiding in their homes. The king gave in again, in hopes that these people would give up but instead of course, all they wanted was more.

The king travelled to Paris and was given a tremendous welcome. He was still very popular but he had allowed anarchy to take over. Many aristocrats were moving out of the country. The king's younger brother, the Count d'Artois, had left and the king and queen were constantly urged to go too. But that was not Louis XVI's way; he wanted to save France and his people. He took his job very seriously and he knew he had to stay and do his best. He was still the only steadying force to hold the country together, and once he left, all hell would break loose and the Terror would begin. The Terror was that phase of the revolution when the worst crimes were committed.

Meanwhile the Dauphin Louis became very ill and died on June 4th, 1789. His younger brother, Charles, now became Dauphin.

In September 1789, the government severely curtailed the powers of the king. He could only veto major new laws and then only for 3 years. By now, the economy was starting to fall apart and there was a shortage of food in Paris. Then in October 1790, the army gave a dinner in Versailles. The Duke of Orleans paid for agitators to form a new mob to go to Versailles for food. The Duke's secretary was seen leading the first group.

The following day they arrived at the gates of the palace where Louis XVI spoke to a delegation. They had come for bread. They had a wild night in front of the gates of the palace, drinking and carousing and then they regrouped in the morning.

La Fayette had arrived during the night with his troops who then surrounded the palace. But the gates had been left open and the mob paraded in early. They reached the doors and forced them open. The Duke of Orleans was seen taking the mob to the queen's quarters and she, just steps ahead of them, managed to get to the king.

The mob was crying: "We want the queen's head. We want to cut the head off and cook her liver."

La Fayette was awakened and the National Guard raced to the palace. Some order was restored, the king and queen appeared on the balcony. Now there was the cry: "The king to Paris. The king to Paris."

There was no longer any direct fear for the royal family. The king was surrounded by his troops but not wanting to see blood flow, he promised to go.

A dreadful procession now left Versailles on its way to Paris. First came a gang with pikes held in the air and on the pikes, the heads of some of the guards. Next, a bunch of the worst riffraff, prostitutes and gangsters marched drunk, yelling vulgar remarks, singing filthy songs.

Then came some wagons with flour, followed by some drunken soldiers and then, finally, the royal coach surrounded by pikes and bayonets. Along the road, one of the men carrying a head on a pike noticed the young Dauphin Charles looking out of the window of the carriage.

He stuck the head right up to the window and scared the boy so badly he had nightmares about this trip for the rest of his life.

On arriving in Paris, there were wild celebrations, everything was lit up, cannons were firing and everyone ran wild in the streets.

The royal carriage went to the city hall where there were speeches. Then the royal party settled into the palace of the Tuileries, which had not been used as a residence for over thirty years. The government followed a few days later. The royal party was now the hostage of the city.

Paris was now the dominant factor in France. The city government became stronger than the national government with city representatives louder and fiercer than their counterparts. Fear reigned almost daily and those who yelled and screamed the loudest got their way. It was a government of fear.

For the royal family, however, there were some days of peace and quiet. The Abbey of Avaux had not given the dauphin any lessons for a while because of all the excitement. Now the lessons resumed in the presence of the queen. When it came to grammar, the Abbey said: "We were doing the three degrees of comparison, the positive, the comparative and the superlative, but you probably don't remember?"

"But I do", replied the dauphin, "When I say my Abbey is a good Abbey, that is positive. When I say my Abbey is better than any other Abbey, that's comparative. And when I say my mother is the most tender and loving mother of all the mothers, that's the superlative."

The queen pressed the boy in her arms and a tear escaped from her eye.

The dauphin worked daily in his little garden. He had a little troop of his own soldiers, boys his own age, called the royal dauphin troop. One day the mother of one of the boys was sitting in the park waiting for the dauphin to pass. When he did, she stopped him and said: "Monseigneur, I wonder if you would make me as happy as a queen?"

The dauphin responded with: "I know a queen who is not happy".

The next morning he had a couple of gold pieces that he had received from the queen, wrapped up in tissue and a few flowers for the lady.

Another day, he was leaving the garden after practising with his gun. The guard at the gate said: "Sir, you had better surrender your gun before you go out."

The boy said: "No."

And Madame de Tourzel, his governess said: "That is not very nice, Monseigneur, you must act and speak better than that."

"Yes," said the boy, "I would gladly have given him my gun if he had asked me for it, but surrender, never!"

Chapter 3.   THE TEMPLE

The story of the diamond necklace is an excellent
example of how the enemies of the Royal Family used
public opinion, against them. The main players in this
game were the Cardinal de Rohan and his lady friend,
Jeanne de Saint-Remy. The Cardinal came from a
famous French family, the de Rohans, who were
Princes often opposed the Royal Family. In fact one of
his forefathers was sentenced to death, under the reign
of Louis XIV, for plotting against the Royal Family.

Jeanne de Saint-Remy was the daughter of a poor
farmer who had such a meagre existence that she often
lacked enough food to survive. She was an illegitimate
descendent of one of the last Valois Kings who had
reigned on the French Throne before the de Bourbons.
Jeanne managed to get an aging Marquis to take her in
and he then arranged a pension from Louis XVI for
her. That success spurred Jeanne on to press her
claims to all the formal Valois properties that had long
ago been dispersed. One day, while pursuing her quest,
she met the Cardinal who, after hearing her story, gave
her a small sum of money.

Jeanne continued to circulate around the Palace of
Versailles and after a while managed to convince the
Cardinal that she was the confidant of the Queen.

De Rohan felt that the Queen constantly snubbed him because she, who greatly disliked anyone who was against her husband, had therefore not spoken to the Cardinal for eight years. He desperately wanted just a word from her or a gesture to show that she still acknowledged him. Jeanne told the Cardinal that the Queen did care for him, and that she would show this by a movement of the head the next time they would meet. The poor Cardinal wanted so badly to believe Jeanne that every time Marie Antoinette moved her head it was a sign to him that she was fulfilling the promise. Jeanne, having married a "Count" Nicolas de la Motte, had also added a lover, Riteaux de Vilette, to her circle of friends. This gentleman had a very tidy hand and could write beautiful lines. Jeanne made him write little letters on expensive notepaper. These she showed to the Cardinal and implied that they had come from the Queen.

Meanwhile the Cardinal had also come under the influence of the famous charlatan, the so-called "Count di Cagliostro". Di Cagliostro, who claimed to be in touch with the ancient Pharaohs, told the Cardinal that he possessed special powers. Soon this fraud became the Cardinal's private prophet. He, however, saw through Jeanne's little scheme, but played along with her letters, thereby helping to convince the Cardinal that his future looked bright and that the Queen would see him in a much better light. He was so eager to believe all this, it was not hard to convince the Cardinal.

While this scam was unfolding there were many pamphlets distributed around France about the secret love life of the Queen, about her affairs with many people at court including even her brothers-in-law. There was not a word of truth in it yet still many people believed the printed word or believed that with so many stories around that there must be some truth to some of it. This way it became possible for Jeanne to convince the Cardinal that Marie Antoinette was in love with him. She also managed to persuade the Cardinal to pay her well for her job as intermediary between the two lovers.

When Jeanne decided that the time had come to entangle the Cardinal, she located a prostitute who had a fleeting resemblance to Marie Antoinette. A meeting was arranged and one dark evening, in the gardens of Versailles, the Cardinal met a lady he thought was the Queen. He threw himself on the ground, kissed the hem of her gown and the blond imposter passed him a rose which he then kept for years. Jeanne then told the Cardinal that the Queen urgently needed 50,000 francs for a needy family and a couple of months later she asked for twice that again.

Then one day Jeanne met the King's jeweller, Charles Böhmer, who wanted to be known as the maker of the most luxurious jewellery in the world. To acquire that reputation he had slowly started to buy up the largest precious stones that he could find. These purchases had put him in great debt but he still wanted to make the most spectacular necklace in the world. He finally created his enormous necklace and was ready to offer it to the famous Madame de Barry, who was the mistress of Louis XV. However, he died just then and Madame du Barry had to retire. Now Böhmer offered the necklace to Marie Antoinette who refused it because it cost too much, plus her husband had started a serious campaign to economize on his personal expenses. Also, she liked simple things and the necklace was heavy and ugly.

In all Marie Antoinette bought only two expensive items from the jeweller, having told him already years before that she wished for no more. Böhmer then tried to sell the necklace in Spain, in England and elsewhere, but had no luck. He feared that if he did not sell it soon he would have to declare bankruptcy and thus threw himself before Louis XVI begging him to buy it. When the King checked with his wife she remained adamant so the necklace returned to the jeweller with the advice to break it up into smaller pieces.

When Böhmer heard from the Cardinal that Jeanne de la Motte was a confidant of the Queen, he made it a point to meet her. He told her that he still wanted the Queen to buy the monstrous piece. Suddenly Jeanne saw a way to make the fortune that had always escaped her. She had to try to get the necklace no matter what the cost and started by getting her lover, Titeaux, to write another letter to the Cardinal. This time the letter asked the Cardinal to act for the Queen. He was to arrange the purchase of the necklace for her and the note spelled out the terms that the Queen wanted. The Cardinal did not question the letter for a minute. He did what she had asked him to do. The jeweller was, of course, ecstatic and gladly agreed to the four instalments that she requested. He also asked for a signed contract and in due time received one back signed, "Marie Antoinette de France". The Cardinal should have known that Marie Antoinette never signed her name in that manner, because she used only her first names, but still he accepted the contract as signed and gave it to the jeweller.

The Cardinal received the necklace and gave it to Jeanne to pass on to the Queen. Jeanne and her husband quickly followed the earlier advice of the King and broke up the necklace into smaller pieces and, after having saturated the market in Paris, took the remainder to London. Soon the first payment was due and, to remind Marie Antoinette of her obligation, the jeweller sent a note thanking her profusely for accepting his greatest work. Of course, he did not mention that the payment was due. Marie Antoinette destroyed the note thinking that the poor jeweller had gone out of his mind. When no payment came and no answer to his note, the jeweller could no longer contain himself and travelled to Versailles. Marie Antoinette was thoroughly surprised by his demands and quickly summoned the Minister of the Household and Louis, her husband, to tell them this strange story. The King then called the Cardinal de Rohan to Versailles. The Cardinal was told to write down his involvement. Having done so, they charged him with trying to defame the Royal Family and promptly jailed him. Warrants were issued for Jeanne, her husband and for the famous Count di Cagliostro. The scandal hit the streets and, in no time, due to the busy printers, the whole affair became the juiciest piece of gossip in the country.

First the rumour was that some clever scoundrels had defrauded the King and Queen, but then, due to the pamphlets, the opinion of the people changed and everyone started to believe that indeed Marie Antoinette must be the guilty party. In the end, because the findings of the court were that he was duped, the Cardinal was given a "not guilty" verdict.

Jeanne received a jail sentence but, because she had so many influential friends, was free again in just two years, and then settled in England. From there she wrote a damning biography in which she blamed Marie

Antoinette for the whole affair, this although Marie Antoinette had never even spoken to her. The Count di Cagliostro left for England and spent the rest of his days there in exile and, when asked if he would ever return to France, he answered,

"I shall not return to France until the jail, called the Bastille, where I rotted for such a long time, has been torn down and a park made of its lands."

So, it was a false count who was among the first to call for the destruction of the Bastille, an event that did occur.

The Royal Family was by now a virtual prisoner in the Palace of the Tuilleries, the guards surrounded the castle as much to keep the King and his family in, as to keep the populace out. From time to time, the church bells rang. That was a sign for the gangs to get together because there was a new "event" taking place or a new "parade" to see. Marie Antoinette was so afraid that sometimes she sat all night at her son's bedside.

Finally, even the King and Queen became convinced that they must try to leave Paris because life was getting too dangerous. The King refused to leave France as so many exiles had already done. He thought that if he could reach a large city where he still had supporters that he would find some loyal troops to help him restore law and order, and thus regain control of the country.

The Royal couple made plans to leave for the castle at St. Cloud just outside Paris, where they had spent the summer the year before. This year the Convention would not permit them to go. They then planned to escape from Paris in the middle of the night. Since the "émigrés" who had escaped the country insisted that the King was no longer in charge, and, because he allowed them to pass under duress, his laws and edicts were not to be obeyed, the situation had by now become a vital turning point for the King. He kept trying to insist and prove that he was free to move and act, but now that he could not even go to his summer residence, it became obvious that he was no longer a free man.

On July 20, 1791, the arrangement was completed and they were ready to go. Just before midnight, the Royal Party, in little groups of two and three, sneaked out of the palace through a door left open by La Fayette. They had disguised themselves as a party of a Madame de Korff (Madame de Tourzel) and a Madame Rochet (Marie Antoinette), the governess, with the King dressed as a servant and the Dauphin and his sister dressed as girls. They also carried proper travel papers signed by the King. The small party assembled some distance from the palace, where a large coach was waiting for them, and thus they fled Paris. The trip was full of delays as the King stopped here and there to talk to people, thereby risking exposure.

They passed towns and villages, changed horses and stopped for something to eat. At Chaintrix, the son of the Postmaster, having been in Paris the year before, recognized the King, but, being a Royalist, said nothing. At Chalons, all the townspeople came out to see the King. Somehow word had got out that the Royal Party was on its way.

An escort was to be waiting at Pont de Somme-Vesle, but it was not there. It had been earlier and announced that it was there to guide and protect a treasure but, after several hours, the villagers had become suspicious. Afraid that the truth would become known, the commander had thought it best to wait at the next stop.

It was too dangerous for the Royal Party to wait, so they had to continue. At Sainte-Menehould, it was again the son of the Postmaster, Drouet, who recognized the King, and because he was a revolutionary, this time their luck ran out. Drouet rode ahead to the next village to warn the inhabitants and to set up a roadblock. It was now the middle of the night. At Varennes, the Royal Party had to change horses but, without being aware of it, the relay point was changed. The coach stopped at the centre of town, the Mayor came out to meet it and to check its occupants' passports. He invited the party of Madame de Korff to descend from the coach and to spend the night with him in his home. Everything would be sorted out in the morning. Then a local judge recognized the King and fell on his knees before him. The King embraced him and the Mayor. When the escort finally arrived, they proposed to clear the road by force, but the King would not hear of it. The Mayor again promised that all would be fine the following morning. The opportunity to escape had now passed, for during the night, troops from Paris caught up with the Royal Party still asleep, at the Mayor's home.

The ride back was long and painful. The population was waiting along the road—some cheering, some jeering. The Royals were now real prisoners and under the control of three members of the Government who had been sent out especially to retrieve the King. At a small village on the way back the young Dauphin looked out of the window. He noticed that in this village many roof tiles showed an unusual pattern that looked as though there was a large 'S' shape on the roof. The Dauphin remarked on this to the King and remembered this discussion many years later when he told his sister about it.

At another village a friend of the King tried to approach the coach but the mob grabbed the poor man and killed him. His head was carried along on a stake and for several hours the situation looked very dangerous. The mob could have taken over at any given moment. Eventually the party reached Paris where the leaders took the King and his family to the City Hall.

Meanwhile the King's brother, the Count of Provence, who later became King Louis XVIII, had left the same night. It was he who had in fact arranged both of their escapes. His plan was successful and he reached Belgium without any problems. Whether his brother's problems were due to this planning never became clear, yet the Count did write his aunt, Madame Adelaide, some years later:

"As I recall the period October 7, 1789, and June 21, 1791, it is impossible not to thank God for the best luck in the world; because from that moment on everything went in my favour."

It was the beginning of the end for his brother and his Godson, but it left the Count as the heir to the Throne.

In Paris life became more difficult every day, the political factions were jockeying for position. Every day brought new laws and ordinances while the economy slid into yet further disarray. For the Royal Family there were no major problems until almost a year later. Their life had again become routine. In the Tuilleries Palace they were prisoners, but could still move about the Palace and its grounds without much trouble. The King occupied himself with the running of the Government, but his only power now consisted of a veto on new laws passed by the Government, and even his veto could only hold up legislation for a while.

Then on the June 20, 1792, there was an assault on the Palace and a crowd of rowdies, spurred on by the revolutionaries, tried to enter it. The King went out, stood in the middle of the crowd, yet, because he still had the respect of many, they did not touch him. There was an investigation to find out who had started this riot and the Mayor of Paris lost his job over it.

The King and his family were not injured, but it again reminded them that any day now the situation could get out of hand and so the King decided to begin preparing for the worst. He called his son into his study and showed him a wooden box with a complicated double lock that he himself had made. Louis XVI explained that there were some papers, precious jewels and gold coins in the box, and that, if ever circumstances became really bad, Charles could come and take it. He showed him how to open it and where he was going to hide it. This was to remain a secret between the two of them and played a great part later on.

Louis XVI had written to his brothers several times and begged them not to interfere with his handling of the Government in France. Since he was not free and they were, he was in a very precarious position; and, because they had other plans, the brothers ignored his requests.

An army was poised outside France to come to the rescue of the King. The Duke of Brunswick led it, and the brothers now supported the Duke in issuing a Manifest to the French people. This Manifest stated that any French-man found helping the revolution was guilty and would be sentenced. It also stated that the King was not free to act and that his support of some legislation of the new Government was therefore meaningless. When Marie Antoinette heard of the Manifest, she recognized it to be a threat to the Royal family, tantamount to a death sentence.

The Manifest arrived in Paris in the first days of August and immediately the City Hall began to plan a large demonstration at the Tuilleries Palace. In fact a massacre was planned as the brothers had foreseen.

First the revolutionaries ordered some of the troops loyal to the King away from the Palace of the Tuilleries. Then, on August 10, the church bells rang and the crowd headed for the Palace, the part of the large complex that we today know as the Louvre. Inside, the Royal Family heard that the troops could not guarantee their safety, and their advisors thought it better to move them to a hall in another part of the immense building, where the National Assembly was meeting. They hoped to find a safe haven there under the protection of the Government. Surround-ed by friends and some loyal Ministers, including the Minister of Justice, Mr. Joly, the Royal Family arrived at the Assembly unscathed. Outside the slaughter had started. The Swiss Guard had been overrun, while some had managed to escape; but the rabble was not satisfied, followed them and then started a house-to-house search. Henri Lescot, a Swiss guard whose wife played an important part later, was among those killed that day.

The rabble murdered the whole staff of the Palace and then ransacked it completely. Again, there was a parade with heads on pikes and much blood dripping. Many clergy had been locked up because they would not swear allegiance to the state. Now the guards entered their prison and murdered them in a frightful fashion. Kan-garoo courts sprang up to dispense rapid justice. One could file a complaint against a personal enemy who would then be picked up, judged and sentenced all in one day.

The Royal Family remained in the Assembly for a couple of days while the Government and City Administration argued about where to put them next. The City won and locked the family up in the Temple, formerly the old headquarters of the Templiers in the days of the Crusades. The Templiers had been disbanded several years before and the City of Paris had now taken over the building. It was a solid building, about sixty feet square, with a tower on each corner. Each floor had a centre hall with four small rooms and there was one room in each tower. Two more towers were later connected to the main building by walls. The floors of this addition were not as high as the floors of the original building and, as a result, the fourth floor of the new tower was on the same level as the third floor of the older structure.

The Royal Family first went into this annex while their permanent quarters underwent repairs and only then did they move into the main building. The main floor consisted of the administration of the building. On the second floor were the guards and on the third the quarters for the King, the Dauphin and their one manservant, Cléry. On the fourth floor were the Queen and her daughter, Marie-Thérèse, and the King's sister, Madame Elizabeth.

Outside the slaughter continued. A court found the Princess of Lamballe, a close friend of Marie Antoinette's, guilty. She went out through a door, designated for the guilty, which led to a narrow street where the revolutionaries were either lined up to wait to carry out the sentences of the court, or ready to watch. A man jumped out at her with a sword and, with two or three strokes, cut off her head. Her body was then violated and dragged through the streets toward the Temple. Halfway there, the mob took the head into a hairdresser to have the hair powdered. They stopped off here and there for a drink. When they reached the Temple, they called for Marie Antoinette. Marie Antoinette went to the window to see why they were calling her name and there, on a long pole, was the head of her friend!

One day the King, with the Dauphin at his side, received Joseph Paulin who had come to cheer him up and who then slipped him three rolls—each containing fifty gold Louis coins. These would greatly help in getting little extras from the guards, and only Charles was witness to this act of charity.

Towards the end of the year, the trial of Louis XVI was to begin, it would be held in the Assembly, although it did not have any judicial powers. It was more "a duty", as Robespierre called it, a duty to kill the King because in a Republic there was no need for a Monarch. He could have been banished from the country, but they decided that would be too dangerous. Besides the Convention needed a victim, a dupe, to make up for all the misery that they themselves had inflicted on the people. The Convention made the charges, and it appointed lawyers. There was a defence, but no real trial and no proper judges. When it came to a vote, a majority found the King guilty. When it came to a vote for punishment, the chamber split down the middle. When the roll call came to the former Duke of Orléans, a Freemason who now called himself Philippe Egalité (the Equal), there was a hushed silence. When he voted to have his cousin killed, even some of the worst rabble present there could not believe their ears!

The King lost the vote by one, and his cousin had cast the deciding vote! They granted him a couple of hours to say good-bye to his family. These were tearful hours, yet the King remained surprisingly calm. The next morning, January 21, 1793, he was placed in a coach and driven to the Place de la Concorde. Although a group of supporters, under the Baron de Batz, made an effort to rescue him, they never managed to unite because, the security being solid, traffic was unable to move between one area and another.

The King prayed and asked for forgiveness for his people. When his head fell, the executioner picked it up and showed it to the crowd. But this was France. Here the King does not die. "The King is dead, long live the King!"

Louis-Charles, now seven years old, became King of France and Navarre. He reigned as Louis XVII. The revolutionaries did not of course, recognize him, but he was King to the loyal people of the Vendée, to his relatives in Austria and Spain, and to many Heads of State in Europe.

Chapter 4.   ARRIVAL MONTREAL

I arrived in Montreal on a cold day in March 1952. An old aunt had given me $10, my parents had paid for the trip but could give me no more. Because I spoke some English the guide asked me to sit up front with the driver and translate anything he said. We were on our way by bus to the rail station in downtown Montreal. I loved American and English movies and had learned not to watch the Dutch translations on the bottom of the screen. My English was not too bad and most of the farmers on the flight understood very little English. Only farmers were allowed in at that time and I had a job on a nursery farm waiting for me. So here I am on the front seat behind the driver, the first Canadian I met in Canada. He starts: "This f__ weather has made the f__ roads just very slippery. And these other f drivers don't know what the   f__ they are doing." I did not translate all that, I just told the rest of the group that the trip may take a little longer than expected. Today one could expect that language perhaps but in 1952 it was exceptional and did give me a very strange impression of my new land.

My first stop was to be in Montreal. A captain in the Canadian army had been bivouaced in our home in Oss at the end of the war. We also had a pair of nurses staying with us; soon the captain was courting one of the nurses. A few months later my parents attended their wedding in Germany. When I arrived in Canada Captain Lorne Patrick was now a Lt.Colonel and Chloe, his wife and he lived Montreal. Lorne had been posted with the peacekeeping forces in Crete. Chloe picked me up from the station and soon I was having a rest in her apartment because the flight had been a long one. Chloe wanted to do some shopping and wanted to leave me in the apartment but I wanted to see my new home country. I saw the strange looking houses with metal front steps to the second floor where two doors led to two apartments, an arrangement that still impresses me and is so typical of Montreal. I also saw the two story sheds behind the houses. I remember how we almost walked into the grocery store door, which opened automatically as we came close. That was a shock, the first of many.

The following day it was off to Beamsville where my uncle and his family had received a house for their use while he worked for Prudhomme's nurseries. My uncle Svend had arranged a job for me and again my knowledge of English soon stood me in good stet as I was made manager of the nursery sales station. The growers were mostly Dutch gardeners and I could translate between them and the clients that came to buy seedlings and plants. We worked 60 hours per week, from 7 am to 6 pm and 5 hours on Saturday morning. The nursery was then right on the Queen Elizabeth highway between Toronto and Niagara Falls. A lot of traffic went by but many stopped so business was pretty good.

By using "farmers" who in real life were really carpenters, plumbers and other tradesmen the Prudhomme's soon built themselves a motel and then a barn theatre and soon a playground. My job was not going to last because in the summer they sold few plants and so after a few months I started to look for something else to do. One Saturday afternoon as I sat with two friends in the local drugstore, behind an enormous milkshake a young man started to speak to us. His English was atrocious but half speaking in French he told us that he was on his way to Timmins, 500 miles north to find gold. He had been told that it was easy to find and you could make your fortune there. That was for me, the fortune in my mind grew with his every sentence, I was sold. I had bought a car 50-50 with my uncle, it was an old wreck but it still ran and I made a deal with him that we could drive it to Timmins if someone would bring it back to him. My Canadian friend Bill was married and wanted to come to see if he could find work up there. Then he would drive back and get his family and return the car. My other friend a Dutchman called Eddie wanted to come as well and so we went to Timmins. I remember the trip with me speaking Dutch to Eddie, French to our new friend and English to my married Canadian friend. I had a headache that lasted for days but we got there and started to look for jobs the following day. It turned out that the goldmines were closed for their annual summer vacation and so we had to look elsewhere.

Eddy was a typesetter by trade and found work at the Timmins Daily Press, our Canadian friend found no work and left with the car. The Frenchman found a job with a French Canadian survey gang that was looking for minerals in the bush and I decided that with my languages I might get something at the local hotel and I was lucky, they needed a desk clerk and I got the job. We worked three shifts, from 8 am to 4 pm, then from

4 to midnight and a third shift from midnight to 8 am.
Every weekend we would switch and once every three
weeks you had a 24-hour gap between shifts. It was a
good job; I liked it and met a lot of interesting people.
The nightshift was boring, we did a little book work
and made our rounds and spent the rest of the night
talking to the operators at the phone company and the
provincial police. The phone operator could hook us up
to the long distance operator and various other people
but the basic group was three or four. We listened to
the calls to George's, the local girlie dispensary and to
any emergency calls and that was the most excitement
we had. One night I divulged that we had an elevator
in the Empire Hotel and the girls all wanted to see that
so we met at 8 am and I gave them a ride to the top.
None had ever been up in an elevator.

One of the girls was very quiet and I liked the looks of
her, we made a date and we became a steady affair.
Arline was a steady night telephone operator, she preferred that shift and so we met at odd times because I
was constantly on different shifts. I longed for a family
life and her family was very pleasant and I got along
with the whole gang although her brothers liked to
tease me. I was quite able to defend myself. After a
year without a single day off, we worked even Xmas
day, I decided to try the goldmine again because they
got a much better pay. I was hired as "crew", which
meant any dirty job going was ours, but only in the
mill, not underground. Cleaning between the huge vats
of gold solution was the worst job. The solution contained cyanide and the overflow would build up to 5 or
6 feet high. Then it was our job to wash it down with
high pressure hoses, but if you got cyanide in an open
cut or wound you could get cyanide poisoning in which

case you could no longer work in that mine and it went on your miner's card and that took care of any other mine that used cyanide. Not that you got a pension or compensation, no you just lost your job. In the end I was the sole member of my 8-man gang who did not get the poisoning. I was now promoted to tipping carts of sand into a shaft for backfilling once the ore was removed. The carts came at a fair speed on a long cable from across the street, once the cart came close to the platform where I stood a lever tripped the locking bar out of the back of the cart and several tons of sand plunged down the shaft. Then I had to grab the swinging edge of the basket give it a push and swing it back in the upright position and slam the lever back in. I worked with a partner because you could do no more than 20 minutes on and 20 off.

In the meanwhile I had proposed to Arline and I was lucky, she accepted. In April 1953 we had a small wedding, no use spending a lot, everyone said it was not going to last. After a few months at the mine the miners decide to strike. I did not like strikes and found they seldom resulted in any advancement. (The strike there lasted 9 months and they went back to work owing huge sums and they received the 5 cents an hour that had been offered in the beginning). So Arline and I decided to go and try for our luck in Toronto. I left with Bob McManus, who had married Arline's best friend Isobel 3 weeks after we got married and we soon all settled in Toronto. I found a job as a shoe salesman at Owens and Elms on Yonge street in Toronto. That lasted only a few months I was no good at it but then I got an Xmas job with the Robert Simpson Company just a block further north on Yonge Street.

Simpson's was a large department store in Toronto with Eaton's department store across the street. I was put in their warehouse along the beautiful Toronto harbour and I convinced Arline that we should look for an apartment on the island. I went to work every day starting with a boat ride across the harbour, what a wonderful start. Arline was pregnant and stayed at home.

Our first-born was a little boy Philip. We lived on a quiet cul de sac with only our small apartment building. The island had only two cars, one for the police and the milk delivery wagon. The milkman came almost daily and used to back out because there was no circle to turn. The baby was tied at the front of the house but unfortunately crawled under the truck. It had not a chance. Fifty years later it still hurts.

Simpson's gave us a week off and we went and visited Montreal, on the way back we visited Chloe and Lorne Patrick, he was now back and in charge of the depot at Cobourg. They had built themselves a small house right on Lake Ontario. Xmas went and Simpson's kept me on, that was lucky because most Xmas staff was laid off. I was even promoted to stock keeper in the main store. After a couple of years I found out that Simpson's had an executive course that you could try for. Only six or seven were chosen each year and if you had family in the executive offices your chances were much better. But I tried and did not get on the first year but the following year I had success and was chosen with 6 others. The executive course consisted of a short period with all the non-selling departments in the store, that lasted 6 months and then two 3-month assignments in selling departments. We had to do reports on every department and on Tuesday afternoons we received lectures by the top executives in the store. So I spent a week in an order office in Welland, 3 weeks in the credit department, one week with the drivers delivering merchandise, which in those days was free.

It was one of the most exciting years in my life and I learned a lot. At the end they asked you to choose which direction you wanted to take. Everyone wanted the selling departments because that was where the money was made. But I had been warned about the fashion departments, there was a lot of infighting going on so I mentioned that. They promptly made me assistant manager for the ladies coat and suit department in the bargain basement. I was extremely lucky because the manager was Bob Shapiro an Englishman. He was a real happy fun loving character and we got along like a house on fire. He had been a furrier in England and started in that department in Simpson's but he was now in the larger Ladies Suits and Coats department.

He was flamboyant and looked after the purchasing, I was good at figures and did the paper work and budgets. It worked great. He took me on my first buying trip to Montreal where we had great friends in the large garment districts and to Winnipeg were it was hot in the summer when we were buying winter coats and ice cold in winter when we went for spring coats.

As assistant manager I got an executive account card, it meant you received an automatic 25% discount on everything you bought, I also received the key to the executive washroom. Talk about class.

When Arline went shopping she was asked who her father was because surely it was her father that qualified for such a card. We had married when we were 19 and now we were barely 25, but we had Louise and Michael by now and the salary allowed us very little in extras.

We had borrowed $750.00 from her parents and bought a little converted cottage in Fairport Beach, Pickering along Lake Ontario. We had been kicked off the island; the houses on Centre Island were destroyed for a park. We hated to leave but after a few months in the centre of the city we had found our cottage. Now we were back near the lake.

Chapter 5.   LIFE IN JAIL

Louis XVII was a good-natured boy and life had not yet been very hard on him. The first few months in the Temple he spent with his father, who instructed him daily and had no doubt spoken to him about the great responsibilities that lay ahead. During these months the family ate their meals together and saw each other every day.

The manservant Cléry, who looked after the young boy and Louis XVI and slept with them on the third floor, remained with the family until after the death of Louis XVI. The Tissons, a husband-and-wife team, served the ladies on the floor above. The services provided by the Temple included cooks and service staff, so life there had some semblance of normalcy. The only major change that occurred was that Charles moved upstairs with his mother after Louis XVI was charged, and this gave the King a chance to work on his defence uninterrupted.

There was also some contact with friends on the outside. Everyone spent a lot of time discussing escape plans; Marie Antoinette always insisted that she would not leave unless her children went with her. There were still many monarchists in France, and even some republicans, such as the guard Toulan, who became convinced that the Royal Family deserved some help or that otherwise they would all perish.

The first escape plan included Toulan, who undertook to get the Royal Party out of prison. Marie Antoinette put him in touch with Field Marshall Jarjayes, who would arrange for financing and a way out of France. Toulan managed to talk two other guards into helping him. They were going to dress up the Princesses as guards and Madame Royale as a helper of the lamplighter. Turgy, who by now had replaced Cléry, would carry the young King out in a basket.

On March 8, 1793, they were all ready to go, but the day before there had been a big scare about an invasion by the Duke of Brunswick who, being poised on the border with an army, was preparing to liberate France. The Government, being alarmed, cancelled all passports, closed all the borders, and the escape plans fell through. The Duke of Brunswick had 60,000 Prussian troops with whom he planned to rescue the country from the revolutionaries. He had against him only 5,000 French troops, yet just when the French were ready to surrender, the Duke gave up the fight and fled. The Duke, who had been near bankruptcy just before this defeat, was suddenly able to pay his 8,000,000-franc debt in cash, while the real losers continued their imprisonment in the Temple. The defeat paid off for the Duke but many believed that it had been arranged.

A second plan concerned only the Queen. Toulan again offered his services to Jarjayes, but, because she was not going to leave her children behind, the Queen wanted no part of it. Toulan, a true friend, gave Marie Antoinette several items from Louis XVI's room after it had been locked and sealed. He also brought mail in and out. Other guards who helped the Royal Family were Lepitree, Cortey, and Michonis.

The third plan came from the Baron de Batz, the monarchist who had tried to rescue the King on his way to the guillotine. He tried various plans and almost succeeded a few months later in getting the young King out. Once again, a last minute interruption interfered and they had to hastily cancel the plan.

Meanwhile the Count de Provence, who had escaped to Bruxelles the same night that the rest of the family tried to escape via Varennes, had been busy. From there he had been scheming to overturn the French Government. On January 27, 1793, he wrote to his younger brother the Count of Artois,

> *"We have done it, Louis XVI is dead. I under-*
> *stand that the Dauphin is going to die. They do not*
> *understand how good this news is for the state."*

On the following day, January 28, he announced formally to all the Governments and Courts of Europe the death of his brother Louis XVI and the reign of his Godson, Louis XVII. He proclaimed himself regent while Louis XVII remained a minor and appointed his younger brother, the Count of Artois, as Lieutenant General of France. Of course they were not in France, they had left while the going was good.

Europe was reluctant to receive his announcements, and many countries did not accept them. Austria did not accept him as Regent since the Regency normally belonged to the mother of an underage King and Marie Antoinette was after all still alive. Even four years later, King Charles IV of Spain was calling Louis

XVIII, "the Count of Provence". Eventually there was some acceptance, notably by the Czar of Russia. This was very significant as will be shown later.

In May, the young King had a fever and the prison doctor for Paris, Dr. Thierry, visited him and gave him some medication. At the end of May, Charles received an injury while he was playing very roughly with his hobbyhorse. The Queen asked for the specialist, Dr. Pipelet, who checked Charles and found him in excellent health, except for a hernia. This was cured with further medication and rest.

Suddenly the Commune of Paris decided that Charles should be separated from his mother and sister. On July 3, 1794, the commissioners came to take him back up to the third floor. Marie Antoinette put up a terrific fight, but after an hour of pleading and shouting she had to let go of her son. Charles was now eight years old, still much too young to make it through life on his own, but this was the last time he saw his family.

The separation from his family was a deep psychological shock that stayed with him throughout his life. It is no wonder that, from time to time, he was completely withdrawn, and that throughout his life he sometimes showed signs of psychological disturbances.

The Commune had appointed the shoemaker, Simon, and his wife as guardians of the young King. Simon was a friend of Chaumette, a revolutionary leader, who in turn was also the son of a shoemaker. Simon had been an active member of the revolution for about two years. He had been in and out of City Hall so often that he had finally been elected to represent his section. He was a rough character and his instructions had been to raise the young Royal as a "sans-culotte", which was what the revolutionaries called themselves. Although a difficult expression to translate into English, it literally means "without pants"; but one could, in referring to the fiction that none of them owned anything, not even pants, also call it "bare-assed".

Simon has often been described as a monster, but he was not as bad as that, although in public he liked to make out that he was very tough on the boy. He was full of revolutionary ideas, which often changed from day to day. At ease on the streets of Paris, he knew many people and liked his drink. He bought the boy many toys and in private, treated him like the son he never had.

Simon married a fifty year-old widow late in life. Although no great beauty, she did receive a pension and this made her more attractive. She was a soft-hearted lady and, since she had no children of her own, she enjoyed having young Charles to look after.

Simon did his best to teach the young King how to live and speak as he did and as he thought revolution-aries should. There were no titles and thus everyone was "comrade". The language ranged from rough to vulgar. There were plenty of licentious songs around and Simon tried to teach them all to Charles. He also encouraged him to drink wine and hard liquor and taught him to swear and curse.

Occasionally some noise carried up to the ladies on the fourth floor and it shocked them to hear the young boy behaving so badly, but there were also periods when Simon's better side showed. He gave the King a dog with which to play and together they kept some birds on the roof balcony. He often took the boy out to give him some fresh air.

In April 1793, the Assembly established the Committee of Public Safety, of which its nine members controlled everything that was presented to the Assembly. This meant that they in fact controlled the Assembly. The committee's leader was Chaumette and his assistant was Hébert, also known as the columnist Père Duchene.

The other very powerful committee of the Assembly was the Committee of General Security, which was responsible for the security and protection of the State. Its wide range of activities included lying, substituting, withholding, confiscating, destroying, or anything else that would convert the truth to whatever it perceived was in the best interest of the State.

The Tissons, who looked after the ladies on the fourth floor, had a daughter called Pierette. The prison authorities caught her carrying pen and paper for the Queen while visiting her parents in the Temple and she was therefore interrogated and thrown into jail. This then panicked her parents into giving evidence to the Committee of Public Safety. They said that the guard, Toulan, brought in messages for the Queen, and that their daughter was not half as bad as the guards and visitors. Because others had received the guillotine for much less, they were understandably hysterical. The Committee deliberated and decided to keep the Tisson family in the Temple as prisoners. They were still there when Marie Thérèse, the last member of the Royal Family to live there, left in the fall of 1795.

Now the Commune of Paris again needed a new victim to stir up the population. At the beginning of August, the Committee of Public Safety brought Marie Antoinette to the Conciergerie, so that she would be close to the Government Buildings where her trial would take place. Hébert had thought up a terrible scheme to bring charges against her. He arranged for Simon to bring Charles out for walks to observe the ladies on their strolls, talking to the guards. Charles was to make a big issue out of this and to report the prisoners' behaviour to the Committee.

Hébert made out a statement for the eight-year-old to sign, and for good measure also inserted some vile accusations against Marie Antoinette who, according to him, had been playing sexual games with her son. He claimed that Charles' injury from the hobbyhorse was actually an injury inflicted by his mother. They interrogated the boy for several hours and tried to make him sign this "confession". He refused so they forced him to drink wine until he became intoxicated. Finally someone forced his hand across the page, and this broken-up signature is still today, quite noticeable on the confession.

Handwriting experts later testified that the signature was fake or forced, and Charles wrote in his memoirs that they had forced his hand to sign it. The "confession" caused many problems, because it was then shown to his sister and aunt, and they in turn were forced to sign it as well. This was the last time Charles remembered seeing Marie Thérèse and Elizabeth. Many believe that this was the cause for all the bad feelings that Marie Thérèse held for him. Although the boy was now barely nine years old, and thus did not understand what was happening to him, she felt that he was spoiled and had grown into a monster. Marie Thérèse and Elizabeth had also succumbed to the dreadful pressure and signed the same confession, so therefore in truth, they had little for which to blame young Charles.

Marie Antoinette had an English friend, Mrs. Atkyns, who now attempted to help her escape. Being an actress who had lived for a time in France and had married a rich Englishman, Mrs. Atkyns spared no expense in trying to aid the Royal Family. She managed to get into the Conciergerie to see Marie Antoinette by bribing the guards with 10,000 francs. (Since he was in on the plans, Hébert took a large share of this money.) She begged the Queen to exchange clothes with her and to escape in disguise Marie Antoinette did not want to leave her children behind, and therefore she again refused.

Mrs. Atkyns employed at least two full-time spies to report to her on the situation in France, and especially on the affairs of the Royal Family. She had to pay for bribes and for escape plans, and in all spent more than 2,500,000 francs over a period of several years. Yet she never had the satisfaction of knowing whether it was to due her efforts that the young King was freed.

On October 14, Marie Antoinette stood before the Tribunal, pleading for her life and that of her children. She appealed to all mothers everywhere to stand up with her against the ridiculous charges that had been brought against her. Although she received a great deal of sympathy from the audience, her case had been decided long before the trial began. She was sentenced to death, and the following day it was her turn to visit the guillotine.

This period was a very tumultuous one in the reign of the revolution. There was much infighting between Chaumette, Hébert, and Robespierre who had now become the dominant figure of the revolution. Robespierre called himself "the Incorruptible". He was a lawyer from the south of France, where his practice had been barely successful enough to keep him going, but, having been an early revolutionary, he corresponded with the various Jacobin clubs across the nation. He became Club Secretary of one of the largest Paris clubs, and thus was the most influential Jacobin of his time. He also kept a secret correspondence going with the Count of Provence, who was never above making a deal with even the devil, if it helped his own cause.

There was now much discussion about the fate of the remaining prisoners. Hébert wanted to kill them all, but Robespierre voted against that plan. He wanted to keep the prisoners because he realized how valuable they were in negotiations with the Vendée, the monarchist province, and the Spaniards. The former Mayor of Paris, Bailly, wanting to save his own neck, came up with some accusations against Charles's aunt, Elizabeth, a complete innocent. Yet she received the same treatment as the rest, and was also sentenced to death. The accusation, the trial, and the execution took place in only twenty-four hours. Today there is a serious movement in France to have Elizabeth declared a saint.

At this time the Baron de Batz uncovered a scandal involving the Company of the Indies, and several deputies of the Assembly were given their trip to the guillotine as a result of his disclosures.

In January 1794, Mayor Poche of Paris noticed that fewer and fewer members were showing up for the meetings of the Commune of Paris. He passed an ordinance that members must not hold more than one

Government position, and that they must choose between their membership and their regular job. Simon was one of those affected, and although he did not want to give up his job of looking after the young King, he preferred to hang onto his membership as a deputy.

Charles now entered the saddest period of his jail term. Left all by himself on the third floor, he had no one with whom to chat and no one to pay him any attention. He decided to punish his guards by refusing to talk to them or to speak only when spoken to. He spent much of his time in bed. He had no one to play with, no chores to do, and very little exercise. His clothes were not changed and his bed was not made. As a matter of fact, he didn't like his bed and slept instead on a cot in the middle of his room. He saw his guards only when they handed him his meals and at night when they yelled at him, "Capet, leve-toi" or "Get up, Capet, we want to see if you are still there."

Marie Thérèse wrote in her memoirs that she saw her brother once in this period and that his condition was very bad. Charles himself could not recall seeing his sister, but he remembered that they had during the period, tried to pass someone off as his sister. At this time he was very withdrawn and hardly aware of what was going on around him. This encounter is important, however, because some historians believe that the young King died when Simon left the Temple, while others think that he escaped the day Simon left, on January 19, 1794. The encounter would disprove both theories. Up to this point, the official history and the real story are the same.

For six months, from this date onward, nothing is known of the young King, although when Simon left he had received a receipt that the young King was in good health. There was no reason that he should not be in good health, because the Simons did look after him well and he had his daily outings.

In March, it was the turn of Chaumette and Hébert to visit the guillotine. On March 14, Hébert had been accused of paying bribes and of trying to arrange an invasion of France, which, if successful, would result in Hébert becoming Regent for the young King. Some of the accusations, as always, were very frivolous and some were never proved; but they were almost always good enough to convict the victim. Seven others were arrested with him. It showed how important the young King still was, and many of the Assembly deputies, including Hébert, Robespierre, and Danton, dreamed of a return to the Monarchy with themselves as Regents.

On March 30, Danton was accused of dealing with the "émigrés", the Frenchmen who had left the country to sit out the revolution. Delacroix, Fouquier-Tinville, and six others were also arrested. They were tried and sentenced to death within three days, and executed on April 5. It was a great way to take care of the competition, for there was a great struggle going on, to be in control, to be the leader and thus the survivor. The pendulum swung from one group to another as accusations flew left and right. It was so important to be rid of this leadership that the Police went to the effort of concocting a "conspiracy" in the prison, giving them a reason to pick up even the widows of Hébert and Chaumette, with twenty-one others, including two Generals. They all died on April 13, with their widows following their husbands, by only eight days.

Robespierre took over as leader of the Assembly and the Committees. In May, there was a report that Robespierre had freed the young King for a week to take him to a town called Meudon. There is no confirmation, but it is an interesting theory. There is another story that Robespierre wanted to marry Marie Thérèse and thus become Regent or even the King of France.

The Government was holding meetings with Spain where the de Bourbon family was, after all, on the Throne, and they demanded the release of the young prisoners. Negotiations were also going on with the insurrectionists in the Vendée, who wanted to re-establish the Monarchy. The release of the Royal prisoners was also their first demand.

Baron de Batz was still trying to start an escape plan. He met with forty people early in 1794, supported by funds from Mrs. Atkyns, who was now a widow. She had even placed a large mortgage on the famous Atkyns house in Ketteringham. When all her efforts were exhausted, she had gone through her entire fortune. Unfortunately nothing resulted from these new plans. There must have been a traitor who exposed the plan, and because the Baron de Batz saw that his plan was exposed, he escaped; but all his friends died on the guillotine on June 17, 1794.

The revolutionaries now began in earnest an attack on the Church. They suppressed Sunday services, Saints, the clergy, the churches, and anything that even hinted at the old values. The Priests had to marry and were no longer permitted to wear clerical garb. The revolutionaries tore down all the statues and crosses along the roads, and any signs of religion were purged.

Robespierre now took less and less interest in what was happening. He returned to the Assembly one day after a long absence and made a long speech attacking all whom he felt were against him. He cried out, that the revolution was going in the wrong direction, that there were more celebrations than victories, and that the Government was corrupt, but he refused to give names. In the following days, there were noisy sessions at the Commune of Paris and at the Assembly. Slowly, a group opposing the current leaders began to grow and then one day a fight for leadership seemed imminent. Robespierre left with his brother and a member named Saint-Just, to meet with them and see how they could thwart this fight. Meanwhile the arguments in the Assembly continued until midnight, and finally someone made a motion declaring Robespierre and his cronies outside the law, which of course meant automatically death without judgment.

Barras, the new leader, and a few policemen started to look for Robespierre and his friends, and located them at the City Hall. Robespierre fired his gun and in the return fire, received a bullet in the jaw from a police agent called Merda. Robespierre's brother jumped out of a window and broke his leg. Saint-Just surrendered without a fight, and the rest of the group also surrendered during the night.

The following night, Robespierre and twenty-one friends, including his brother, Saint-Just and Charles's former jailer Simon made their own final trip to the guillotine. Before leaving the jail, Robespierre begged for a pencil and paper because he had an urgent message to give and he could not talk with a broken jaw, but the jailer said to him, "We are no longer interested in what you may have to tell us."

It is really too bad that he took his secrets with him. The following day seventy members of the Commune of Paris received the death penalty and on the July 30 there were twelve more on their way to the guillotine. Historians call this period "the Terror".

We are able to study some of the very secret deliberations of the Committee of Public Safety because the For-eign Secretary of England had a spy inside the Committee and he, therefore received regular reports of its meetings. These were later published as the 'Dropmore Papers' of Lord Grenville.

CAPET, LEVE-TOI is the title of a 1987 book about Louis XVII by Robert Ambelain, and it answers a few of the final questions remaining in this story.

Chapter 6.   ESCAPE

On the day of Robespierre's defeat, a new leader,
Barras, emerged—conqueror of the Terrorists. He was
named General of the Forces of Paris and became the
leader of the National Assembly and of the two
Committees. He spent his first day inspecting all the
important posts in Paris, and it ended with a visit to
the Temple, which was probably the most important of
his new responsibilities.

He found Charles in poor shape but not as bad as he
later remembered in his memoirs:

> "I visited the Temple and found the boy sound
> asleep in a crib in the middle of his room. He woke
> with difficulty, and was wearing trousers and a
> gray cloth jacket. I asked him how he was and why
> he slept in the cot instead of in the bed in the corner
> of the room.
>
> He replied, "I have swollen knees and ankles and I
> ache when I walk. The crib suits me better."
>
> I inspected his knees and ankles and his hands
> and wrists as well. His face was pale and drawn. I
> gave the commissioners orders to clean up the room
> and scolded them for the way they had looked after
> the boy. I ordered them to get Dr. Desault and to
> take the boy out for walks outside."

Barras wrote these memoirs many years later and obviously he was making sure that his description of the boy at the beginning of his reign, tallied with the boy at the end. There were no swellings mentioned in anyone's reports or in the Temple records. Dr. Desault did not receive orders to visit the young Prince until a long time after and there are no records that Barras ordered any changes.

Indeed when two members of the Convention visited the Prince a month later, the conditions were exactly as described by Barras and they were responsible for the cleanup. When Barras returned that first evening to the Committee responsible for the Temple, he learned that the Committee had appointed two new guardians for the young King. Barras had other plans and he canceled these appointments. He preferred to have his own man in the Temple because he wanted full control. He asked his secretary, Borot, to suggest a reliable young man and Borot suggested Christopher Laurent.

Laurent was a mulatto from the island of Martinique in the Caribbean. He was a member of a group, which promoted the rights of the blacks. Borot was a member of the same club and so was Barras' mistress, Josephine de Beauharnais, widow of General de Beauharnais and one of the most attractive women of her time. Being not beautiful, but alluring, lively and highly intelligent, she always attracted interesting men and later became Napoleon's first wife. She played an important part in the survival of Louis XVII.

On August 31, 1794, a huge explosion took place in the gunpowder factory at Grenelle. There was a death toll of some 1500 and a genuine fear gripped the heart of many Parisians. Was it treason? Was it a Royalist coup? Were the allies already that near that they could now be heard in Paris?

The Committee of Public Safety immediately sent two of its members to the Temple to see if everything was all right. This again proves how important the young prisoner was. The two members chosen were André Dumont and Goupilleau de Fortenay. They found that almost the same conditions existed as those reported by Barras at the end of July. Thus, no cleanup had taken place. Now they ordered that the room should be cleaned and that the boy be given fresh air. Within two days a maid had arrived who cleaned up the boy, gave him fresh clothes and his room a thorough cleaning. Laurent took him for a walk in the garden. Thus ended the bad treatment of the boy that had left him locked up by himself from the end of January to the end of July. A long enough time, but not long enough to make a complete wreck out of him.

Barras had carefully considered his position, because all his predecessors had lost their heads. He wanted to make sure that he did not lose his, and therefore selected a plan that would insure his future security. He realized that his best protection lay in having the young prisoner as his personal hostage. He could then play him off against whoever came to the top even if the monarchy should return. As so often before in history, it paid to protect ones back.

Many thought the young King should remain in prison to die there, but that did not help Barras very much. To hand him over to the Vendée or to the Spaniards also did not fit in with his plans because then he would lose control. If Louis XVII died, then

Louis XVIII, the young boy's uncle, would become the head of the family and, Louis XVIII being out of reach would not help Barras at all. No, the smart move would be to smuggle the young boy out of the prison and to hold him as a pawn. This would give the holder power over Louis XVIII and control in dealing with the Spaniards and the Vendée, both of whom had the boy on top of their list of demands for a cease-fire.

The main problem was how to get the boy out of jail, because over 500 men guarded the Temple. He had to get him out while nobody looked or perhaps accomplish the same thing by hiding the boy in the Temple and at the same time substituting the boy with another? The first step would be to get rid of anyone in the Temple who might recognize a substitute and he instructed Laurent to replace all the old help. Laurent suggested that the military force be cut back to save some money. He also asked for some help for himself, because he found that he worked long hours. After all this was a seven-day-a-week job.

On October 28 another commotion stirred the Committee. Two letters were received that must have contained some explosive remarks. Unfortunately no record remains of these letters, but from the actions taken by the Committee, it is obvious that they either showed that the boy was about to or already had escaped. The Committee at once sent two members to the Temple to investigate and to make sure that every-thing was in order. It was again Goupilleau de Fortenay who was sent, and this time with member Reverchon. Their arrival at the Temple at 1:00 a.m. in the morning shows that it must have been urgent. These two men were well chosen because they were close friends of Barras, and their report stopped any further inquiries.

That report is missing and so we do not know what it contained. It is as if someone systematically searched through all the papers that concerned the young King, and removed those that pointed to his escape. Most of the laundry lists, much of what happened in the Committees, and everything else of no interest still exists today, but neither these two letters with the report of Goupilleau, nor the report of Dr. Desault, nor the ledger of the Temple itself, are available.

In France, and especially in Paris, the rumors were now abundant. Everyone had heard of how Louis XVII had escaped. Everyone either had helped, himself, or knew of someone who had helped. There were many versions and it was the talk of the town. Certain historians maintain that such rumors did not exist and they claim even today that no plans were ever made or carried out for the escape of the boy. Yet these rumors alone are the reason that over fifty pretenders to the Throne came forward later and claimed to be the escaped Prince. No pretenders ever claimed to be the first Dauphin who died peacefully in his bed, but fifty came forward to claim to be Louis XVII.

Reverchon and Goupilleau de Fortenay did suggest the following new regulations and the Committee passed them the same day:

Article 1. The commandant of the Paris army is, with this, given the most severe orders to stop not only the escape of the prisoners from the Temple but also <u>*the appearance of a possibility of an escape.*</u>
(The underlining is mine.)

Article 2. The police of Paris have two days to find and appoint an additional guard, of good republican standing, to help Laurent.

Article 3. The Paris Committee of Administration is to select one member of the Civil Committee per day to do duty at the Temple.

Article 4. No member of the Civil Committee should be called upon to do duty at the Temple more than once a year.

The horses had bolted and now they were closing the door. Yes, the missing letters were all about the children. Yes, they carried frightful news. Yes, someone had in fact smuggled Louis XVII out of his cell and brought another boy in his place. This young boy had been very carefully chosen, for, although he was taller and older, he was a deaf mute who looked similar to Louis XVII. This boy was in the Hospital for the Incurable and suffered from a fatal case of rickets.

Young Charles escaped from his room with the help of Laurent, but because Laurent had not found a way out for him, he was not yet out of prison. Laurent had hidden Charles on the fourth floor of the small tower among a pile of furniture. He had cleared a small area in front of a cupboard and, since no one else ever visited this area, he hid Charles there. It was very difficult to reach the hiding place and Laurent had to crawl in on all fours when he visited him and brought him food.

He had explained to Charles that his life depended on his being quiet. Charles, very happy to play the game, promised to be silent no matter what happened. He was now almost ten years old and a game such as this was very appealing. Years later he did complain about the cold because he had to spend most of the winter by himself. The substitute should have died quickly and once gone, it would have been easy to smuggle Charles out. But some time passed and Charles needed to stay hidden.

In his memoirs Charles wrote that he had hidden on the fourth floor and many historians claimed this could not be true. They claim that he was wrong and that the Princess was on the third floor and that the fourth floor was empty. It was sometimes used for the children to take a walk.

Then in the 1950's the clever historian, Jean Pascal Romain, discovered, while pouring over the plans of the Temple, that there was indeed a passage from the third floor of the main building to the fourth floor of the small tower. This area contained used furniture and no one ever entered it. The guards watched the ground floor of the main building, they stood at the bottom of the stairs and an official of the Temple administration checked everyone coming in or going out. There were more guards at the entrance to the second floor, both inside and outside the door. It was thus very difficult to get out that way, but upstairs there were no further guards and this was the way that the boy was smuggled out. Jean Pascal Romain also was the historian who discovered that Charles was telling the truth about the date of his escape at the end of March 1795. Charles had written March in his memoirs, but his lawyer, advisor and good friend, Gruau de la Barre, changed this to June, knowing that that was the date of the death the boy in prison. He should not have changed that date because Charles was in fact correct.

On October 31, 1794, Mrs. Atkyns received a letter from her agent Cormier in Paris and it included:

"I want to assure you that the master and his property are saved."

This was how she found out about the substitution and she was instantly aware of a very basic problem. She wrote back that she did not like this plan because if anything ever happened to the substitute, how would they prove that the escaped boy was Louis XVII. She was very perceptive because this is exactly what happened. Her agents had abused Mrs. Atkyns very badly; and had derived a fortune from her for some of the strangest expenses. At one moment she was paying for three different boats to stand by to take the Royal Party from France to England!

In December another delegation of the Convention visited the Temple to see how the children were and if the staff treated them well. The delegation consisted of Harmand de la Meuse, Reverchon and Mathieu. Harmand de la Meuse later wrote a report on what he saw:

The Prince sat beside a small table on which lay scattered a deck of cards, some were standing on their edge to make squares, and they looked like someone was building a castle. The boy continued playing with these as we came in and did not stop after we entered. He was wearing a sailor suit of gray material; his head was not covered and the room seemed well lit and clean. His bed consisted of a little box of wood but the sheet and mattress were reasonably good.

I approached the Prince but the movement seemed to make no impression on him. I told him that the Government only now had been informed of the sad state of his health and also of his refusal to take any exercise or to answer either the questions that were put to him or to take the medicine that were prescribed for him by the doctor. We had come to confirm these rumors and to repeat these proposals in the name of the Government.

We were here to get hopefully an affirmative answer to our proposals and to advise him and to warn him against keeping silent any longer and refusing to exercise. We had the authority to let him extend his walks and to let him have whatever he desired to help him regain his health. I begged him to answer me.

While I was making my little speech, he glared blankly at me without movement, he seemed to listen to me, but he gave me no answer. Therefore I repeated my questions as though he had not heard them the first time and I explained to him, that I might have explained myself badly or he may have misunderstood.

"But I have the honor to ask you whether you would like a horse or a dog, a bird or a toy of any kind, or some companion of your age, who you could choose yourself. Would you like to go up now to the tower or down into the garden? Would you like some candy, cake or anything?"

I tried in vain to suggest to him something that a boy might want, but I got not a single word or answer from him, not even a movement or a sign, although his head turned to me and he stared at me with great intensity, but he seemed completely indifferent.

I was therefore more determined and went on to say to him: "Sire, to be so stubborn at your age is a bad mistake, it is especially so since we visited you to make your stay here more agreeable and to provide better care for you so you will improve your health. How can we help you if you do not answer us? How can we make you understand? Is there anything else we can do, please tell us and we will do what we can?"

Again the same fixed stare, the same attention but no answer. I began again: "Sir, if your silence only concerned yourself, we would wait, not without concern, but with resignation, until it pleased you to speak, since you must be less affected than we had assumed, you do not seem to wish to leave the Temple. However you are not your own boss. All those around you are responsible for your person and condition. Do you wish to compromise them? Do you wish that we should compromise ourselves? What answer can we give the Government, whose agents we are? I beg you, answer me or I shall be forced to order you."

Not a word, always the same pose. I was on the verge of desperation and my companions as well, that look especially had an extraordinary expression of resignation and indifference, as though to say: "What does it matter? Leave your victim in peace."

I repeat, I could not go on, I was near to tears of sorrow, but I took a couple of steps up and down the floor and I regained my composure and I want-

ed to find out what a command would do. I sat on his right side and said to him, "Please, Sir, give me your hand." He gave it and I felt it up to the armpit. I found a knotted swelling at the wrist and at the elbow. These swellings did not seem to give him any pain; the Prince seemed not to feel anything. "The other hand please, Sir." He gave me that too, but there was nothing there. "Please allow me to inspect your legs."

He got up and I found the same swellings on both knees at the back in the hollow. The Prince showed symptoms of rickets and deformation. His thighs and legs were long and thin, the arms were the same. The upper part of the body was very short, the breastbone was high, the shoulders high and narrow, the head was handsome in all details, the hair was long and fine, well kept and light brown. "Now, Sir, please walk a little." He did so at once and walked to the door between the two beds, came back and sat at once. "Don't you know, Sir, that is not exercise? Can you not see that this apathy is the cause for your illness? Believe in our good will and in our experience. You cannot regain your health if you do not follow our suggestions and advise. We shall send you a doctor and we hope that you will answer him. Please give us a sign that at least you will cooperate." Not a sign, not a word." Be so kind, Sire, and please walk and this time a little longer." Silence and no movement. He stayed on his chair with his elbows on the table, with no change in the expression on his face. There was no movement to be seen in him, not even the slightest surprise in his eyes, just as if I were not there and had not spoken.

My companions had kept silent, we were looking at each other in astonishment and we were about to discuss the matter when his dinner arrived. A pitiful scene followed, one should have been there to have any idea of it. We gave orders in the anteroom that the disgusting diet should be changed in the future and that from that day forward something fresh, such as fruit, should be added to his meals. I wanted him to have some grapes even if they were rare at that time of the year. We gave the order and immediately thereafter we returned. The Prince had eaten everything up. I asked him if he liked his dinner. No reply. Did he like fruit? No reply. Did he like grapes? No reply.

A little later some grapes were put before him on his table. He ate them without saying a word. "Would you like some more?" No reply. "Do you want us to leave, Sir?" No answer. After this we left.

This report clearly shows that we are now dealing with another boy. A boy, nine years old, may try to keep silent for a few minutes if he is very angry, but how long would he have held out? Say nothing to the gift of a horse or a dog? Say nothing to the threat of being kept in jail? His whole demeanor shows that we are now dealing with a deaf and mute boy. He sometimes guesses what he thinks they want from him, especially he recognizes a medical examination, but his other responses are completely negative or non-existent.

The shape of the body also is completely different from that of the young King. This boy had rickets, a disease that takes a long time to develop to this stage and even longer to kill. There was never any question of Louis XVII having rickets. This one matches Barras' report, also written later, and on both it matches concerning the long legs and arms and the knobs. This body matches to the detail with the boy who died in the Temple in June of 1795, and it also matches perfectly with the skeleton found and inspected twice in the cemetery of St. Marquerite.

Harmand de la Meuse and his companions decided to keep their report to themselves, for they did not want to upset the public.

There are, from this period, copies of three letters that many believe Laurent wrote. They all show the signature L.

The originals are probably in the 202 papers seized by the Police from Louis XVII in 1836. The historian Bourbon-Leblanc, the illegitimate son of a de Bourbon Prince, was the first to publish these letters. Some historians have called him a spy against Louis XVII, and they consider these letters to be false. This cannot be ruled out. Yet still they have helped, for they show clearly what happened or what probably happened.

The date on the first letter is November 7, 1794, and the letter reads as follows:

My General,

Your letter of the 6th has arrived too late. As your first plan had already been executed, the time was right. Tomorrow a new guardian will start, he is a republican called Gommier, (Gomin) a good man says B but I have no confidence in men of that sort. It is difficult for me to get food to our prisoner; but I shall take care of him, you can rest assured. The assassins left and the new municipal guards do not question the little mute that replaced the D Now we only have to get him out of that horrible tower; but how? B has told me that he cannot start anything because of the strict supervision. If it is necessary for him to stay there a long time than I worry about his health because he has little air in his hiding place, where, if He was not all seeing, even God would not find him. He has promised me that he would prefer to die than give himself away, and I believe him. His sister knows nothing and I am guarding the little mute as if he was her real brother.

However, that poor little soul is happy and plays his role so well that the new guard thinks that he does not want to speak; there is thus no danger. Send your porter back quickly because I need your help. Take the advice that he takes with him verbally, because it is the only way to succeed.

(Signed) L.

Tower of the Temple, November 7, 1794.

Laurent has the name of the new guard wrong. It is Gomin and not Gommier, but that is understandable because he has not yet seen the man but only heard his name, and he has not yet seen it written.

The main reasons that we believe these letters are true is that this first letter found confirmation in an entirely different letter which was not discovered until a hundred years later. This happened when the writer Frederic Barbey located the confirming correspondence of Mrs. Atkyns, which had remained almost intact at her lawyer's office. The date on this letter from Cormier to Mrs. Atkyns is almost the same day. It is the letter we mentioned earlier, and both letters also closely follow the exploits of Louis XVII as he describes them in his memoirs. Of course, if they were false, they could have been made to fit; but not a hundred years later! No one is entirely sure who "My General" is, but it is probably Barras; and B is Botot, Barras' secretary, to whom Laurent reported. There is a possibility that the originals were in code and that would then be why only copies exist.

In the middle of November, Mrs. Atkyns received another letter, and this time it was from her admirer, the Chevalier Louis de Frotte. He wrote:

"All is finished, all is arranged, and in other words I give you my word that the King and France are saved. All the measures have been taken. I cannot tell you any more at the present"

This letter was also part of the correspondence from Mrs. Atkyns, which was found a hundred years after the events had taken place.

Laurent now received his new helper Gomin, and when he arrived Laurent asked him, "Do you know the young King?" Gomin answered, "No, I do not know him." Laurent then explained, "It will take some time before he will speak to you, not until he gets to know you."

Let us now have a look at the second letter:

My General,

I have received your letter. Alas, your request is quite impossible. It was possible to bring the boy upstairs but to bring him down at this moment is impossible; the supervision is so strong that I feel that I have been betrayed. The Committee of Public Safety has sent the monsters Matthieu and Reverchon accompanied by Mr. H. de la Meuse to see if our deaf mute is really indeed the son of Louis XVI. General, what does this comedy mean I do not know what to think of the behavior of B Now he talks of taking the dumb child out and of replacing him with a dying child. Are you aware of this? Is that not a trap?

General, I worry about things, because we make sure that nobody enters the prison of the mute boy so that they cannot discover the substitution. If anyone should ever really examine the dumb child they would discover that he has been deaf and mute since birth. To substitute him for someone who talks will be the destruction of the half-saved one and myself.

Please send me your opinion when possible.

(Signed) L.

Tower of the Temple, February 5, 1795.

France was at this time in terrible turmoil, Spain attacked in the south, in the north she was threatened by the "émigrés" and Louis XVIII, and in the middle of the country the Vendée continued to fight. The republic was desperate to make peace and peace talks continued daily.

On February 17, 1795, Charette signed the Treaty of Jaunaye with the Vendée. A secret clause provided for the release of Louis XVII and Marie Thérèse to the Vendée on June 15, 1795. This really put the pressure on to either do away with the prisoners or to produce them.

Charette wrote the following letter to the Count of Province:

"Monseigneur, (this is the correct title for the Dauphin)

I lay my head in front of your majesty's feet, if he judges me guilty because of the act that I have just signed. I signed a treaty with the so-called National Convention. I have recognized them and I separate myself from your royal cause and that of my King, for whom I have fought and given my blood and I take with me in my defection my officers and men and I suffer when I see the tri-colored flag hanging over the territory where it never flew until this horrible defeat. That is my crime! I do not deny it. But here is my excuse. My King and yours is a prisoner of the killers of his father, who may do the same to him. His sacred life is constantly in danger; everything is thus permissible to give him back his freedom. Well, his freedom I have obtained.

A secret agreement between the commissioners and me, of which I show you the original, takes care of the exit of his majesty. They are going to place his majesty with the Commissioners I saw and they agree to turn him over to us, and once with us I have no doubt that a general uprising will serve him much better than the efforts we have made while he was in prison. With him we shall be invincible and now we are nothing without a Prince of the house of de Bourbon.

It is according to me useless to discuss the treaty that I signed, to worry about whether it promises a return of the monarchy. If I am to blame, I who has made it, then I shall be guilty, but see the motif

*that made me do it. It is for him that I give up my
reputation and my peace of mind, but it is for my
King that I have done it; he and God will forgive
me later. They have given me all the assurances
that they will follow this great condition. If they fail
I shall pay with the loss of my life after having lost
my creditability. This must remain completely
secret from the agents of Austria, England and the
branch of the family called Orléans; this is only for
your eyes. You must understand me when I say that
there are traitors everywhere even in the service of
your brother (The Count of Artois). I thought that
in the circumstances I must notify the Regent of
France, so that if something goes bad he will not be
blamed. Only his very devoted and respectful servant, etc.*

Signed Charette

A marvelous letter from a loyal honorable man, in a
period when honor was hard to find, but unfortunately
it went to the wrong party because the Count of
Provence, God-father of Louis XVII, had been busy
scheming to get himself on the Throne. Barras meanwhile was also planning and his plans did not include
handing over the young King who could demand such
loyalty.

The substitute in the Temple was not dying fast
enough, soon would come the date to hand him over
and as the second letter shows Barras was planning to
bring in a new substitute, who would die quickly. Many
believe that it was Robespierre's sister who found a
poor boy who was dying and she promised the mother
(a Miss Gonnhaut or Lenninger) that her son would, for
his last few days, be cared for in the Hospital for

Incurable. Instead the boy went to the Temple where he soon died, yet unfortunately the doctor who was called to make the death certificate refused to sign that this was the son of Louis XVI. Even so a funeral was all arranged. The body of the dead boy was buried in the garden of the Temple.

I believe that this happened in March 1795 and that this was the funeral procession that carried young Louis XVII out of jail, while the dead boy was buried in the garden.

In 1801, the General, Count of Andigné, was locked up in the Temple that was still being used as a jail. While working in the garden he came across the body of a child that had been buried without a casket in a quantity of lime. He covered it up again quickly and asked a guard standing nearby if that were the body of the Dauphin. The guard replied, "Yes." The guard did not know, he had only come to work at the Temple much later than when the Dauphin or his substitute had been there. The body that he found was the body of the boy who died in March, and for whom nobody wanted to sign a death certificate. It was in his coffin that the escape took place.

The General tried to tell this story to Marie-Thérèse, but Cardinal de la Fare, Archbishop of Sens, told him that she believed in the death of her brother, and that his story would only bring back bad memories.

This also explains why there exist pictures of two funeral processions for the young King, the first one where the coffin rested on a wagon pulled by horses and another where the guards carry the coffin to the burial grounds. Ste Marquerite's church was only a few steps from the Temple. Louis XVII was correct when he wrote in his memoirs that he escaped in a horse-drawn cart in March, while everyone had been looking at the June funeral when the guards carried the casket by hand.

Charles, in two letters written long after the fact, wrote that he left his prison in March. In his memoirs, his lawyer Gruau de la Barre, who really wrote most of that book, changed the date to June to coincide with the June date that he knew as the death date.

The first substitute, who had never left the Temple, returned to the young King's room and so that plan of Barras failed.

It was now the beginning of March and the third letter appeared:

My General,

Our mute has moved into the Temple and remains there to be taken for the Dauphin. To you alone, General, belongs this triumph. Now I am at ease, order me to do what you will and I will obey. Lasne will take my place when it becomes necessary We have done what we can to insure the safety of the Dauphin. So I will be with you in a few days and I will tell you the rest myself.

(Signed) L.

Tower of the Temple, March 3, 1795.

There exists another document that describes a secret meeting held in the Directory. It consisted of the Directory members Carnot, Rewbel, la Revelliére, Lepreaux, Letourneur and Barras and took place at approximately this time. The famous historian Lenotre wrote that it is very difficult to contest this document.

There they discussed the abduction of Louis XVII as an approved plan and an established fact. They spoke of the banker, Petitval, who had backed them with funds against Robespierre. Petitval was a banker of Louis XVI and still at this time held funds for Louis XVII. The plan was to send the young King to his castle at Vitry-sûr-Seine with the agreement that the boy, should they need him, would be available to Barras and his friends. The boy's deliverance was the price of cooperation that Petitval had demanded from the Directory. Here therefore was another sample of the demands for the boy. La Revellière said that the child should not suffer because of his parents.

On April 21, 1796, a band of murderers attacked the Chateau de Vitry. They crushed the skull of Petitval, cut the head off the banker's mother-in-law, slashed four other women to death with sabers; but they did not steal anything. The only survivor was a servant who managed to run away with a young son in his arms. Again the Directory met and they decided that what had happened was the action of the Convention of which they also were members, so they decided to hide their involvement with the banker. Barras told his fellow directors:

"The lady's maid, that you all know, who looked after the boy has been beheaded."

The Police closed the case, and nobody ever found out who killed the Petitval family. But many believed that the young King, who had escaped, had been in the Château until just days before the attack.

Meanwhile the war with Spain was causing much concern and the French Government wanted it settled. An interesting document recording this is the letter from the Spanish negotiator for peace, Yriarte, who wrote:

> *It is the intention of my masters in Madrid to see the prisoners of the Temple free, that weighs more than any other consideration for peace. On our side it is a creed, a religion, even a fanaticism if you prefer. We prefer it to a few departments of land along our border or any other considerations. My instructions refer to conditions and pensions but they are not the real question. We would allow for an order to be inserted in the peace treaty that would stop the children of Louis XVI from interfering with the French Government. The only answer I got in my negotiations was that the boy had suffered so greatly under Robespierre that mentally and physically he was in no condition to be handed over.*

We have seen that this was not so, that the real reason was that they no longer had the boy, and even if they had him, it was too important for them to hang onto him because of the threat that he posed to the republic.

The negotiator chosen by the French Government was our old friend Goupilleau de Fortenay, who had visited the young King in prison twice on instructions of the Committee of Public Safety and his friend Barras. Goupilleau's almost paranoid behavior is described in the books of Louis Hastier and Prof. Francq. He knew the boy could not be handed over and did everything possible to avoid the subject, but of course the Spaniards were adamant. In his memoirs, written years later, Goupilleau admitted that the boy in prison was no longer Louis XVII. Goupilleau was a friend of

Barras and had helped along with these plans from the beginning.

The boy was tremendously important to the moral of the cause in the Vendée as well as to the war with Spain, and there was a great need for Louis XVIII to be rid of the boy. I believe firmly that he was never in the hands of friends. They would have immediately hailed him, and they would have had the support of at least half the country behind them. They would have shaken the republic to its very roots because by now most people wanted an end to the revolution. The boy held in his person the power of several great armies, but because he was in the control of Barras and his friends, they used this tremendous power to its fullest extent. The members of Parliament who had voted for the death of Louis XVI could not return to France during the restoration. Barras was one of the few exceptions, and, because he held power over Louis XVIII even after the revolution, the reason for this is obvious.

In December 1794, Leguinio had asked the Convention to eliminate the last remnants of the Monarchy. He suggested that they expel the son of the viper and had to wait until January 22, 1795, to get a reply. It was Cambacéres who spoke for the Government:

> "Better to have them where we can control them than to send them out where they may get support and start up problems. Even should they stop to exist, you will find them everywhere and they will continue to be the hope of French traitors."

This is the Government trying to take the wind out of the sails of Louis XVII, and they with this statement admit that he has escaped and may reappear anywhere. Laurent had a final meeting with the boy at the home of Josephine de Beauharnais where the boy had been taken. Laurent had done his job and thus asked for his freedom. He used the death of his mother, although she had died years before, as an excuse to resign his job. At the end of March Lasne replaced him. Laurent's last instructions to the new guardians were:

"Do not let the two children meet or see each other, they must not know even that they are still both in the Temple."

Though Barras claims in his memoirs that he instructed the guards that the children could play with each other, it is obvious that something had changed. Laurent later had a brilliant career and ended as Vice Commissioner of the Navy and Secretary to the Governor of French Guyana. On his death the Governor seized his papers and locked them up in the office of the clerk for the Appeals Court of Cayenne. Now they are lost! The destruction of important papers to do with Louis XVII is practically complete.

Barras with Borot and Laurent had conferred about who should look after the young boy after they got him out of prison. They had selected Elizabeth Leschot-Himmeli, widow of Henri Leschot, a Swiss guard, who had been killed at the riot at the Tuileries on August 10, 1792. She was a member of the staff of the Temple and Laurent had observed how she really cared for the Prince and how the Prince liked her. She was the niece of the famous Dr. Barthelemy Himmeli, who had treated Frederick II of Prussia. The same treatment later helped George III of England. He specialized in mental health and it was hoped that he could help the young

King who by now must have had some mental problems.

Henri Leschot had a brother called Jean Frederic who was an inventor and watchmaker. He had brought his marvelous moving toys to the Palace of Versailles before the revolution, where he had showed them to Marie Antoinette and her two sons. He later moved to Geneva where, during the revolution, he helped "émigrés" coming from France. He used the alias "Lebas".

Elizabeth Leschot took the boy to her home at 6, rue de Seine in Paris and there, because he had to pass as her son, started him immediately on an intense full-time course in German. She told him to speak only German and not to speak any French until he was saved. Rue de Seine backs on to the home of Josephine de Beauharnais and there is testimony that the wife of Napoleon and lover of Barras stated that she saw the son of Louis XVI on the day that he escaped from the Temple.

On April 25, Commandant Bourlier was temporarily assigned to the Armed Forces of Paris. In order to satisfy himself that the prisoners were still in the Temple and that they received the proper care, he asked for a decree, which the Committee of the Military of the Convention then issued. He went to the Temple and showed his decree to Gomin and Lasne. Still they refused him permission to see the prisoners. This was highly unusual because no rule existed preventing officials from seeing the prisoners. The guards had received new verbal instructions that no one, even with proper papers, could see the prisoners.

There is a report that one Commissioner had asked to see the boy and received permission providing he did

not talk to him. This commissioner, who was a trades-
man, told a friend from England that he found a very
sick lad whose face was covered with ulcers. Yet at the
same time the Commissioner Bellanger, who had
received permission to see the boy, made a drawing of
him, which some years later formed the basis for a
medal. According to him there was no question of any
illness or even pimples. It was now May 31, eight days
before the death of the poor boy that was left behind.

At the autopsy less than two weeks later, there is no
mention of ulcers or any external signs of an illness. In
eight days, the boy went from being perfectly healthy
to being dead.

Surely the guards must have reported that the boy
was ill, because Dr. Joseph Desault received orders to
present himself to the Temple. The date is May 31. Dr.
Desault was about the fourth or fifth doctor to look
after the young King during his three years in prison.
We do not know why the revolutionaries kept changing
the doctors, but maybe it was because the leaders were
constantly changed and each preferred his own. Or was
it because the boy kept changing? Anyway, Dr. Desault
had seen the boy before and now, because he did not
recognize him, he became very upset at seeing him
again.

He filed a report to the Committee of Public Safety.
It is report #263, dated May 31, 1795, and accepted by
the Committee members This report has been missing
since the revolution. Following the report a couple of
the members of the Committee took the doctor out for
dinner. After dinner the doctor became violently ill and
died the following day, June 1, but not before he told
his wife and his best friend Dr. Chopart of his

encounter with the false Louis XVII. We also have the testimony of his niece, Madame Thouvenin, who confirms the story of the report, what was in it and about the dinner. There are thus three independent witnesses to this event. The official story is, of course, that the doctor died of some disease, but no one has yet come up with a disease that kills in twelve hours. It was not a heart attack or a stroke. It was poison, because only poison acts this quickly. Dr. Valetin, who knew all three doctors but was a particular friend of both Chopart and Doublet, wrote regular reports on the situation in France to the British Government. His report on this matter ended up with the historian Eckhart during the restoration, and it says:

> "The doctors Doublet and Chopart, just like Desault, have died, all within 4 days; there is no doubt that this is now a new manner of arrest warrant used by the Committees."

For historians who have wanted to ignore this death, it has always been a very difficult matter. One of the most recent books makes a complete study of these deaths—complete with medical opinions of modern doctors—but this still does not explain Dr. Desault's death. It was not only Dr. Desault who died in a hurry, because Dr. Chopart, his good friend and confidant, followed two days later, and also suddenly without a warning. Now there are two dead doctors, and a missing report.

It is amazing to see how many reports have been saved and how much we know of what went on from day to day. One historian wrote a book, which was mostly about the laundry lists of the Temple, and from the lack of socks in January of 1794, he concludes that the boy must have died then. But unfortunately for the writer too many people who knew him saw the boy after that day. The fact that this report is missing more than likely means, that it contained something that could upset the public.

Now on June 4 a third doctor dies. He is Dr. Doublet, a friend of both Dr. Desault and Dr. Chopart. This is a bit too much to be just coincidental. Even the most skeptic must now be convinced. Dr. Abeille, a pupil of Dr. Desault flees France for the United States and a few years later, in 1817, publishes in "The American Bee" which was edited by Mr. Chaudron, an article about the sudden death of Dr. Desault. He also relates how he himself had to escape, because he knew the truth about the boy in the Temple not being Louis XVII, and he feared that he too would be poisoned, which was a very common occurrence during the revolution.

There exist separate testimonies by a M.F.M. Estier of Camdentown and a Miss DeLisle of New York which confirm the article written by Dr. Abeille. Both had known him and had heard the story from his own lips. The writer, whose book dealt with the death of the doctors and who studied the deaths very carefully, does not mention Dr. Abeille; but then again it would have been very hard to debunk his story.

Meanwhile the Chevalier de Chatellier, who was appointed by the army of the Vendée, had come to Paris to pick up the children. The Government told him that they would be brought to the Palace of St. Cloud on June 5, but then Mr. Sieyes, a senior Committee man, told General Beaufort de Thorigny to break the

peace treaty, otherwise, if not, they would have to surrender the children; and that they were unable to do.

Chapter 7. SIMPSON"S

My brother Henri followed me to Canada a couple of years after I arrived and now my sister Amelie followed as well. In Holland my father had slowly recovered from his nervous breakdown and he divorced his second wife and remarried my mother. It would have been something to attend your parents wedding but they kept the news from us for a few years. Henri soon married and Amelie followed, her partner's name is Steven Koning, which is Dutch for King.

We now received one more blessing and we called him Jean Edmond. The little house in Fairport Beach was full and we were a happy family although we just scraped by. Lake Ontario was at the end of the street and all landowners in our little community had a deeded access to the lake and a share in the community hall. Arline and I were active with the hall and we arranged dances for the high school kids.

We had marvellous neighbours, the family Fitzpatrick and I talked them into going on holidays with us and we packed some tents. They had 7 children so with our 3 we had a total of 10. All this went into 2 cars with some of it on top and some dragging behind. The first year we drove to Maine with some lovely parks in between. To me there was no holiday if I did not see the beach and the ocean. The ocean in Maine was cold and the next year we tried the outer banks at Hatteras. Tom Fitzpatrick had complained about the cold in Maine, he never said anything about the heat but I think he burnt his feet running for the water. Everyone had a great time.

On buying trips for Simpson's we left Sunday nights and started at nine on Monday morning. We always stayed Monday night so we could have a second night on the town. Later we were told to leave Monday morning and be back Monday night. One day while I patrolled the floor I overheard the floor manager making some really nasty remarks about me to an executive of the store. The President of Simpson's Mr. Allen Burton had told us, when I was a trainee that we could always come to see him, he had an open door policy and so I booked an appointment. In no time I received a message to see the store manager. He told me that I should cancel the appointment because it would be terrible if I went to see the President over everyone's head. But I was young and stubborn and I had a nice interview. The result was a transfer to the drapery department and an early retirement for the floor manager. I did not care too much for the much larger drapery department where I was one of about four assistants. I had also been told that my future at Simpson's would now be very limited and so I looked for other employment. It was scary because I had been there 8 years and switching jobs in those days was not often done. But the owners of one of our coats manufacturers needed a manager for a small ladies wear store they had started. So I said goodbye to Simpson's.

The job of manager was one I enjoyed but the brother-in-law who ran the small store stole from the firm and I told the brothers that I worked for. They had planned a chain of small stores and I was sure they would not continue with this partner but blood is thicker than water. So soon I needed another job. John Northway's and Son was a small chain of clothing stores in Toronto and Hamilton and the family wanted to sell. They had a very good reputation and had been bought out by a stock promoter and needed a ladies wear coat and suit and fur buyer. There were only 4 stores but the main store had nine floors and they were right on Yonge Street only a block from Simpson's. They also carried a top line of merchandise. Certainly much better than I was used to. Soon they bought another chain of stores and combined them together. Now I had 40 stores to buy for so the job became more interesting. I bought elegant suits and coats from the best Canadian designers such as Auckie Sanft and Irving Samuels. Merchandise you could wear even today without being out of style. The future looked bright. Ruby Hamra a top lady manager and merchandiser was brought in from New York. She had been with Franklin Simon a large New York firm and we were flying high. But the stock promoter had bad luck, the economy was slowing down, the Diefenbaker government used Diefenbucks to finance the government and the stock market dropped badly. The stock broker's brother got caught in a scam with some nasty boys and one day he was blown up in his bed in an expensive Toronto hotel. He survived but our reputation was really hurt.

Arline and I had finally decided to have a long week-end holiday in the mountains north of Montreal and when we came back the chain was in bankruptcy. Most of the senior staff had already found other jobs or they were looking, but I stayed with the sinking ship. We had a hero who came to the rescue. Adam Eckhardt decided that with the help of several manufacturers he would be able to salvage the company. Adam owned Ruth Frocks, a very large and famous ladieswear store in the west end of Toronto and he had an excellent rapport with his suppliers. We were now a small group which helped getting the chain moving again. We fought hard and worked long hours because Adam loved working late into the night. Of course we had to open the store at 9 am and he arrived at noon, but I would not have changed a thing because we loved every minute of it. However the economy continued to be bad and we did not make it. After a serious struggle we finally went bankrupt for good.

I was the most senior manager left and the bankruptcy company asked me to stay to help with the liquidation of the stores and the inventory. Some of the leases of the stores were valuable and we got some excellent prices for them. Then another smaller chain went bankrupt. The Taffy stores were badly managed and the trustee asked me to work with them and report back to him if the chain was worthwhile keeping. There was a lovely group of girls running and operating the place but I do not think the owners knew the business. I recommended it be closed, which it was. Again I worked for a while with the trustee. Adam Eckhardt asked me to stay with him as he wanted to manage their store better and to open some smaller stores. So I finished selling the Starlite and Taffy stores for the trustee and joined Ruth Frocks. We soon opened three Franklin Simon stores and I made a deal with Adam that I would work for him for nothing. A nice John Northway store in Markham was still empty; I wanted to open it again with overflow inventory from Ruth Frocks. My salary would then be offset against the inventory debt and after a year the store would be mine.

Arline was ready to take a job, the children were in school all day. She helped me in getting the store open and we called it de Bourbon Fashions. The former manager stayed with us and taught Arline the business. And slowly but surely the years passed. Adam lost interest in running his stores, gradually they deteriorated and I became disillusioned and started looking for another job.

The Fairweather chain of ladies wear stores had been taken over by an aggressive Toronto family, the Posluns with Mr. James Kay at the head. I had dealt with Irving Posluns when I bought ladies coats, his raincoat line was very well known. They were looking for store managers and I was hired. I started as assistant manager in their main store on Yonge Street a few blocks south of Simpson's, where I had started my retail career. I got along very well with the manager and after a few months I was given my own store in Oshawa, which was not a bad trip from Markham where we now lived near our store. I was no competition to Fairweathers and they had no objections to my store. They did however expect a lot from their managers and brother Wilfred was overheard one day remarking that they hired young managers worked them to death and then they would hire more. I worked hard and I liked the large shopping centre in Oshawa and became friends with several of the store managers. One day the manager of Eaton's, a very large department store, asked me to join him in setting up a Kiwanis club in the mall. We got some members from the offices above the stores, some store managers and some others and soon we had a great morning Kiwanis club, the Durham A.M. Club. Unfortunately on the day of inauguration I was away on a course and I was not listed as a charter member. But I am still proud to have been there.

In January 1975 I received a call from a friend of my father's that my father had passed away during the night in a hospital in Holland. I had seen him just a year before but I did not know he was in a hospital. He had been dehydrated so they had taken him in for a couple of days and had been told that he would go home the next day. When his friend came to pick him up he was gone. His long fight with medication was over.

Arline and I flew over the same day and did what we could to sort things out. We hired a firm to dispose of most of the assets and we paid the bills, and some personal effects we sent to Canada. Now suddenly I was the head of the family, the bearer of the family name and I had to inform his friends and supporters in France and in Holland and Belgium. I had spent little time on the family's affairs and knew little of the problems. But now that I had brought over my father's books and papers I studied as much as I could. I had always had a nagging feeling about the claims of my family and of my great, great grandfather and I wanted to make sure I did not continue and support a fable. So I read most of the books and articles that I had brought and I became convinced that the claims were valid.

It was a proud inheritance, there was no doubt but I really did not need it. I had three wonderful children, a marvellous wife, my own home and a good business as well as a great job. I could hardly keep up with it and so the de Bourbon affairs had to take a back seat. I was now promoted to manager of the Fairview Mall store and it was the third largest store in the chain, only the main store downtown and the Yorkdale Mall did a greater volume. Our total sales reached close to $2.500.000, which was really something in the seventies. I had a shoe store inside my store, a bridal salon and a Big Steel division along the main store. There were 40 staff and we got along like a house on fire. There is nothing like a business that is rolling along at great speed. The feeling of elation is great, you cannot stop it, and it rolls along and takes you on a ride. Granted we worked like little slaves, the store was open from 9 to 9, only on Saturdays did we close at 6, but we never got out till about an hour after closing. Three or four times a year we would do inventory on a Sunday and no overtime was paid. However I did get a bonus at the end of the year and that was wonderful.

Arline employed a lovely lady, Renate Cook for the two nights we were open late. Her husband Fred was a real estate broker and so I asked him what to do with my bonus. He suggested I buy a five acre parcel that he had for sale, part of a 150 acre subdivision he had started on the north side of Lake Scugog. The 100 acres at the lake had been divided in lots but he had 10 five-acre lots. The price was $6000, just what I had received as a bonus. So we decide that could be our retirement parcel some day and we took the plunge. About a year later I received an offer of $21.000, which astounded me. If you could make money like that, what was I doing selling ladies wear. I should sell real estate instead. So I left Fairweathers, I was close to burnt out anyway. And I took my real estate exams, I got my license and I helped a lady classmate who had some problems with the English terms that were used. The first tests in the real estate exams were more based on proper English than on real estate. That weeded out a lot of people but you had to know English to write the proper sales agreements. The ladies name was Arlette Bolliger and her husband Heinz was a real estate broker who worked all on his own with clients from Europe who came to invest in Canada. The majority were Swiss and they bought apartment buildings and factories Heinz would look after and collect the rents.

One such an investor had bought a lovely home just north of Markham on a 30 acres parcel of land. The previous owner had worked for 20 years on making this his retirement home. He had made three large ponds with little bridges that connected them and a lovely round house, a design that started with two large circles. It sat on the top of a mound and gave a wonderful view of the acreage. He bought it as an Xmas gift for his wife in Switzerland but she was very upset. She did not want to live in the wilderness in Canada, no thank you. So that became my first listing, it had to be sold, the Swiss franc was going up and up and the investor was having a bad time. There was a tenant who had promised to vacate on a moment's notice if an offer was made. He was a school principal and so we were sure everything would go smoothly. I received an offer, the purchaser had sold his house in downtown Toronto but he needed possession in 30 days. I brought a notice to our tenant, he let me into the kitchen were the family was having dinner. He told me that he would swear in court that he had never received a notice, he had the right to a 60-day notice and his family would swear I was never there. Well we gave him 60 days notice and lost the deal but now they needed a new tenant because there was a lot of grass to look after. Also the driveway was about 700 feet long and needed ploughing in winter. So Arline and I moved in and my son Michael who had just got married moved into our home.

I had joined Fred Cook's office when I received my license and Fred told me that he had just heard of a new way to compensate real estate agents. He had been to Miami to a convention and there he met with someone who was promoting a new franchise called Re/Max. They paid their agents 100% of their commissions but the agents had to pay a monthly fee. This way the office knew their income and the good agents did not have to give up half their commissions. And so after two free months I started to pay rent plus expenses that soon added up to about $800 a month. You had to work, no question about that but I had worked hard before. I did not have any clients though and so I was in a bit of a pickle. The agent next to me was a friendly chap and we soon became friends. Jerry Paxton had been in the trucking business but had made a lot of money besides, in various land deals. He had one great client and friend Michael Wade and together they were working on a subdivision called Bristol Pond. They sold 3-acre lots for estate houses and Jerry had bought four lots and built the first house to get things started. Jerry hated the real estate business so he soon handed me his listings and I spent the next 6 months sitting in a converted log house in Bristol Pond Estates trying to sell lots and houses. We had a friendly Irish builder who would build for clients and business was good.

Jerry and Mike Wade now started on another subdivision near Musselman's lake and while working on it Mike showed me a large farm and former gravel yard he had bought which bordered on a little lake called

Island Lake. I asked for first pick and chose a lot on the water. Jerry picked the two on either side of me and we started to plan to build a new home.

In the meanwhile Jerry and I had decided to make a small subdivision out of the 30 acres and the round house. I bought an adjoining parcel of about 12 acres and we took in as partners the owners of a further acreage. All this took time, a subdivision took six to seven years to bring on the market. The same for Island Lake and our plans were postponed and postponed. No wonder the price of lots was so high. The rigmarole we went through was enormous but nothing compared to nowadays.

By now my children had grown up and I had more time to spend with my ancestors.

Chapter 8.   DEATH IN THE TEMPLE

We enter the nightmare last days of the poor substitute boy in the Temple. It is 1795 and if he were the real Louis XVII, he would have served almost three years in jail. He would have lost his father, his mother, his aunt and he would not have seen his sister for over a year, though she was only one floor above him.

Almost five days after the death of Dr.Desault, the government finally appointed a new doctor to look after the boy. He was Philippe-Jean Pelletan and he made his first visit on June 5th. There seemed little cause for alarm and he prescribed a mild diet, as follows;

"Breakfast at 10 a.m. consisting of chocolate milk and current jam with bread, dinner was meat and soup, boiled, roasted or grilled meat, vegetable soup and vegetables such as asparagus or spinach; supper was meat again but concentrating on vegetables and a little salad with lettuce or endive and watercress. He could have a little wine at meals. He was to be in bed at 9:00 p.m. and rise at 6.00 a.m. The only medication prescribed was a small tonic once a day.

The boy should move to a room overlooking the garden that should help his spirits."

The doctor does not state if the boy reacted to his kindness or how he felt, but the lad can play with his

116

toys and read books, statements that somehow do not conform to reports that this is a dying boy.

But he was dying just the same because that solved the problem about handing him over on the 15th.

The following day, June 6th the Committee held a large meeting. Attending were Sieyes, Tallier and Cambacérés and the subject was the treaty with the Vendée and the commitments they had made. They had to surrender the young king on June 15th and they could not; there was only one solution. Dr. Sigault, a member of the revolutionaries, went to the prison with some poison.

Fabre D'Olivet tells the story of how, later he was once walking with his friend Dr.Sigault, a surgeon and a fierce republican. They met a Madame de Liniere (or de Limay), who had just been to the office of the Police Director and who was well known as a police informer. Fabre tells of how he stopped and spoke to her while Dr. Sigault strolled on.

Madame de Liniere asked him:

"How do you know such a monster? How can you be seen with him on the street? Do you not know what he did? He poisoned the Dauphin."

Fabre says that this statement astonished him and he ran to catch up with Dr. Sigault. He asked him if it was true that he had poisoned the Dauphin. The doctor would not answer.

He asked him three times and finally the doctor turned to him and said;

"My friend, listen to me well; I was not alone, the moment was terrible, and we all did our duty."

On June the seventh there was no cause for alarm. The doctor checked the boy and seemed satisfied that he needed nothing further that day. He did request that the government appoint a physician to practise with him, since he was a surgeon.

All these different appointments of the doctors are a puzzle and the only real answer to this puzzle is the substitution of the boy. Dr. Thierry, the official prison physician was still on duty as the prison doctor. He had treated Charles in 1793 and into 1794, but after that he was not to see the boy again, not for identification purposes or for the autopsy. The same applies to Dr. Soupé, the prison surgeon.

On June the eighth, the newly appointed Dr. Dumangin visited with Dr. Pelletan at 11 o'clock in the morning. This seems like a late visit because the guards had summoned Pelletan during the night, when they felt the boy had taken a turn for the worse. The doctor had sent a message back saying the boy could not possibly have gone that badly, so quickly and he would be there in the morning since nothing much could be done at night anyway. By 11 o'clock the situation had considerably deteriorated, the boy was vomiting and had to go constantly to the bathroom. The doctors gave a series of enemas (?) and prescribed a new medicine. The boy suffered colics, bile, rattle, cold sweats and a slowing pulse. Typical of digital poisoning. Only a poison could have acted that quickly. The new medicine arrived at two o'clock and then the boy had Lasne in the room with him as well as the commissar Damont, who had come on duty at noon.

The boy showed that he wanted to go to the washroom and Lasne picked him up to carry him there. As he did so the boy expired. Lasne laid the boy back down on the bed and went out to look for Gomin, having told Damont to stay there and say nothing to anybody. Gomin then left to give the news to the Committee. He arrived there at about three. The Committee must have decided to sit on the news for a day because they had ample time to announce the death to the Convention, which sat till four p.m. that day. Gomin went back with the advice to act as if nothing had happened, to continue to order the meals for the boy and to hold anyone in the Temple that may have found out.

Strangely enough simultaneously, a message arrived for Dr. Pelletan, it was the answer of the Committee to the question of the nurse and it read:

"The 20th prairial of the year 3, (the date according to the new french calendar used during the revolution)– Houdeyer, (secretary to the Committee) brotherly greets the citizen Pelletan and sends him with this the authorization of the Committee to get a nurse for the Temple and he would like to inform the citizen Dumangin hereof as well. Houdeyer with this also confidentially informs citizen Pelletan that the Committee expects to see not a word, not a hint escapes to the public about the illness that he is dealing with. This is a warning, that the most silence be observed and that nothing must be left to chance so that not even the smallest bit of gossip escapes."

Of course the doctors did not need much advice about keeping their mouths shut. They were very well aware of what had happened to their predecessors.

The government ordered Dr. Pelletan to hold a post mortem with his associate and to bring in two other doctors as well. They were the doctors Jeanroy and

Lassus and they all assembled the following morning to perform this post mortem on the dead boy. It was Dr. Pelletan who did the work of cutting the body but each doctor took his own notes. Before putting everything back Dr. Pelletan removed the boy's heart, wrapped it in his handkerchief and stuck it in his pocket. Dr. Lassus also took some of the boy's hair.

The post mortem report that follows, contains one sentence that gives the game away. The doctors were under extreme pressure and in light of what had happened to three of their friends and in light of the warning they had received regarding keeping silent on the real cause for death, they wrote as follows;

"We arrived, all four of us, at eleven in the forenoon at the outer door of the Temple, where the commissioners received us, and they led us into the tower. In a room on the second floor we noticed the dead body of a boy *who appeared to us to be about 10 years old, and who, the Commissioners told us, was the son of the late Louis Capet.* Two of us recognized the child as the one to which they had to give their attention during the previous few days. The child's death must be ascribed to a scrofula of long standing."

Not a word about scars, birthmarks or anything that would suggest the identification of the boy or his age. Dr. Dumangin, years later, told a friend of Mrs. Weldon, who wrote a small book about Louis XVII in Braille, that the boy he looked after whose body was the subject of the post mortem in the Temple, was not Louis XVII.

Also Dr. Jeanroy, who knew the young king, left a testament that was not to be opened for 100 years. In 1916, Lt.Col. René Jeanroy, Chief of the Historical department of the Army, opened the testament of his ancestor, Dr. Dieudonne Jeanroy, who died in 1816. In the testament, Dr. Jeanroy wrote that the boy he attended in the Temple was not Louis XVII whom he knew before the revolution. He wrote also that the Dauphin could be identified by the following marks;

1. *A birthmark on the thigh.*

2. *A scar on the lip from the bite of a rabbit.*

3. *Vaccine marks on the arms.*

This was at the beginning of the art of vaccination and the royal children were very lucky to be the first ones to receive it. None of these marks were present on the body that the doctor saw at the post mortem. Dr. Jeanroy also told Madame Morel de St. Hillaire that should the Dauphin ever be found, he could recognize the body out of 10.000 persons by these marks.

For the Committee, in its deliberations with the Vendée and with Spain, they have now solved the big problem, they did not have to hand over the young King. On March the tenth 1796, Sénar, secret agent for the Committee of Public Safety and a secretary for the Committee, made a report in which he clearly states that the subject of the post mortem in the Temple was definitely not the body of the young king. Sénar died a short time later and his report fell into the hands of a historical writer named Eckard. Eckhard wrote one of the first biographies of Louis XVII, during the restoration and the reign of Louis XVIII. He ends his book with a story about how upset Louis XVIII was over the death of his godson. Louis XVIII was many things but never a hypocrite.

There are other witnesses to the opinions of the four doctors but I will not bore you with repetition. In the memoirs of Napoleon, edited by Mothe-Langdow, there is a remark made by Napoleon when he read the sentence; " We were shown a dead body that we were told was that of the young Capet." He asked for a copy of the post mortem and while reading, stopped and cried:" This is no proof positive that it is the Dauphin!" Napoleon became interested in the matter through his wife Josephine. He knew she had involved herself and had spoken to him about Louis XVII. But he preferred his own reign. Still later we will come back to him with another excerpt from this book.

Meanwhile, at the National Assembly, deputy Sévestre made the following speech:

"Citizens, for some time past the young Capet had been suffering from a swelling on the right knee and another on the left wrist. On the 15th Florial, the pain increased, the patient lost his appetite and grew feverish. The well-known physician, Desault, was appointed to look after him and take over his treatment. His talent and his probity were a guarantee that no care should be lacking that we owe to humanity. None the less the illness assumed a very dangerous character. On the fourth of this month Desault died; the Committee appointed to succeed him the famous physician, citizen Pelletan, with citizen Dumangin, head physician of the Hospital for Health, to assist him.

Their bulletin of 11 o'clock yesterday morning noted symptoms threatening the life of the patient. At a quarter to three in the afternoon we received news of the death of the young Capet. The Committee of Public Safety has instructed me to bring it to your notice. All the facts are duly noted. Here are the papers, which will be preserved in the archives."

With that he grabbed some papers from his desk and showed them to his fellow members. This last act was sheer showmanship, because no papers yet existed. No post-mortem report, no death certificate, nothing. The Archives also do not contain copies of the death certificate. Amongst those who have searched for this valuable document were Napoleon, Louis XVIII and Charles X. The writer Beauchesne declared that he discovered it in the City Hall but it burned in a fire in their files. Beauchesne did show a facsimile in his book but there has been no effort to certify it as an authentic copy. Beauchesne wrote the first thorough biography of Louis XVII under instructions of Marie Therese. He claims to have spent twenty years accumulating facts for his book but it is full of errors, some maybe by accident but some are definitely fantasies. Sometimes it is not just by what is in a book that it should be judged but also by what is missing.

Beauchesne published his book six years after the exhumation of 1846, when the body of the boy, who died in the Temple was found. The body that could not have been Louis XVII.

However the book does not mention the exhumation at all, though he knew the priest very well and had visited the graveside several times. But he did find many papers and they can be found in his book and he also interviewed Lasne and Gomin. We know through Beauchesne, that both Lasne and Gomin under different circumstances told different stories and were highly unreliable.

Gomin testified that he had known the boy before he started to work at the Temple, which was a lie. He had never met Louis XVII, not even in the Temple, he knew only the substitute. He said that he held the boy in his arms when he died, but he was not in the room. He said that he worked in the Temple since July 27th 1794., but he did not start until November 8th. He did get himself a wonderful job after the restoration of the Monarchy, so it must pay to bend the truth. Lasne told Beauchesne that he spoke daily with the prince over many serious subjects but then he told the sister Marie-Thérèse that her brother was an idiot, whose brain no longer functioned. He also got all the dates wrong about when he was a soldier and supposedly saw the Dauphin at the Tuileries, about his starting time and about how long he worked in the Temple. At an inquest held by the magistrate Zangiacomi later in the 1830's he says that the Dauphin spoke to him only once. Then he refused to sign his statement, saying he had already signed a statement once before. The two statements do not match.

The death certificate, which Lasne and Gomin signed, was not preserved as promised. According to a new law passed less than three years before, by the revolution-aries, the two nearest family members must sign the death certificate. It was of vital importance that the death of this prince be above suspicion and it was easy since the sister of the deceased was only one floor above. However she never received permission to see the body and was not even told that her brother had died. Why?

The common explanation is that she was too young to sign, which did not stop the revolutionaries when it came to sign against the queen, even a little ten year old boy was old enough then. However there were others who could have stopped the speculations. The old servants the Tyson's were still in the Temple. There was Mrs. Simon, living just down the road and not very far away were the old doctors who had treated the boy two years previously, Drs. Thierry and Soupé.

Instead, they made all the guards sign as witnesses to the boy's death, and all the officers, who walked past the dead boy wrapped up in blankets, signed. None of their witnessing is very worthwhile, because none ever knew the real Louis XVII.

Therefore there never was a proper identification of Louis XVII or whomever it was that died in the Temple on June the 8th, 1795.

There is overwhelming evidence it was not he, but officially the courts have ruled that the papers were all right and the state has never allowed the death certificate to be put aside.

Professor H.G.Franq in his book about Louis XVII states that Lasne and Gomin were definitely liars. He also states that the substitution of Bigot for Gomin, who signed the declaration of death for the police, is inadmissible as the same witnesses who signed the official registration should do this. Bigot could be a witness, but not a declarant. Thus the registration was invalid on two counts because it was also twelve hours later than allowed by law. These infractions were not serious enough for the French courts in 1874 and 1954 and they refused to set aside the death certificate.

The government now made preparations for the burial of the body. Voisin, the officer in charge of the funeral, made the arrangements and he ordered a wooden casket. According to Beauchesne, the funeral took place on the 10th, but according to the "Monitor" newspaper, it was June 12th. There were many spectators milling around the Temple, so much so that Voisin contemplated slipping out of a side door with the procession. The commander of the troops called for another squad of riders to help control the crowds. Four bearers picked up the coffin and carried it to the cemetery of St. Marquerite's.

Once at the cemetery, they buried the coffin in a common grave without much fanfare and then they placed a guard there for the rest of the night. The local gravedigger, Pierre (Valetin) Bertrancourt, who lived on the premises, noticed that his king lay in a common grave and he thought that he should change that. When the guard was withdrawn he took the boy's body out of the coffin from the common grave and reburied it in a lead coffin just to the left of the side door of the church, as you come out of the church toward the cemetery, along the outer wall of the church. He marked the spot with a cross on the wall of the church. Later he told what he did to his best friend, Decouflet, a sexton, and he also told his wife. Both survived him by many years and, in 1815, retold this story to the detectives who investigated the location of the grave. There is no reason to believe that these were lies since at the time Bertrancourt made these remarks, he had nothing to gain.

Bertrancourt was in the cemetery one day in 1804 when he encountered Mr. Pinon-Duclos de Valma and they struck up a conversation. Bertrancourt told Pinon-Duclos that the cemetery contained the grave of Louis XVII and they had a long discussion about the fate of the young king. Bertrancourt then told the story that someone had dug up the common grave and moved the young king to a single grave. With that he pointed to the wall of the church. Pinon-Duclos de Valma later stated in a letter to Decazes at the time of the investigation that he got the impression that Bertrancourt himself had done this, but that he never really said so. There are thus three independent witnesses to the tale of Bertrancourt.

Amongst those that attended the burial there was also a dispute over whether there was a common grave or a private grave. Voisin and Police Commissioner Dussan and Lasne all testified that it was a private grave. Mr. Bureau, concierge of the cemetery and Bertrancourt and Decouflet all agreed that only common graves were allowed and it was strictly forbidden to have a private grave. Perhaps they buried the coffin a foot or so away from the last burial, giving the semblance of a private burial.

Now begins an almost comic tragedy that has lasted nearly two hundred years, because the main point in the dispute over the survival of Louis XVII is that his body is not to be found in the cemetery. The first efforts made to find the body, according to the experts, were by Risher-Serisy, agent of Louis XVIII in 1797, only two years after the death and the coffin he found contained nothing but books. There is a story that the young king was smuggled out in a coffin and was exchanged for books in the church just before the casket was buried. Without any further witnesses to this I do not know if we should accept this story. The next person to dig up the same coffin was Napoleon, still fascinated by the stories from his wife, Josephine.

In his memoirs written in 1834, it states that they dug in the cemetery and that Fouché and Savary, his two most trusted assistants were with him. They found an empty coffin, which they took with them to the police station. It could have been the coffin emptied by Bertrancourt. I am sure that Bertrancourt did empty the boy's coffin rather than excavate the whole box, which would have been so much harder for just one man, even if he had experience. Bertrancourt had easy access to lead coffins, which he used often. He stored them on the church grounds, and would have wanted to give his king as good a resting place as he could. Then he reburied him in a lead casket as we shall see.

In 1816, during the restoration, Louis XVIII was on the throne of France and the bodies of Louis XVI, Marie Antoinette and Madame Royale, Elizabeth were exhumed and brought to the Cathedral of Saint Denis. Saint Denis has been the site of the burials of many kings of France for many, many years. Louis XVIII instructed his police to look for and investigate the grave of his godson Louis XVII.

On February 21st., the Count Decazes, Minister of Louis XVIII received a letter from Count Vaublanc, Minister of the Interior, to start the search for the grave of Louis XVII. The Count Decazes answered three days later that this had also been on his mind and that the investigation was under way. He then sent a letter to the Count Angles who was the chief of Police and he, in turn, called in two of his best men, Simon and Petit. They remitted a report on March 15th and another at the beginning of June stating that they had found the grave and that they had arranged an exhumation for June 12th.

On June 12th, a large gathering met at the grave, when the king sent a special order to call off the exhumation. Louis XVIII could not afford to have them find the body of a boy that might not be his godson. He knew from Barras that this was not Louis XVII.

Defenders of Louis XVIII claim that the king issued this order because the king had just received new information from a Mr. Charpentier. This new testimony is as follows;

"On the 13th of June, 1795, at 5 p.m. a member of the revolutionary council from the section Luxembourg presented himself at my place and told me to be at the Committee that evening, which I did. There another member told me that I should present myself with two of my workmen and shovels later that evening at 10:00 p.m. At the time indicated we three presented ourselves at the Committee where we waited till 11:00 p.m. when one member, clad in his cape, without any explanation made us enter a carriage that took us to the edge of the Garden of Plants. He made us get down and follow him to the cemetery of Clamart, while keeping completely silent. Here I began to think that we were part of an impenetrable mystery. No other escort led or followed the carriage, in which we came from the Committee. When we entered the cemetery it was about 11:30 p.m., the man that led us, asked the man that opened the gate to return home. The man, who probably lived in the cemetery did not need to be asked twice, he obeyed immediately. We, I mean my workmen and myself, waited and after a few moments the member of the Committee, after making sure that there was not anybody around, made us go to a spot to the right of the entrance but only 8 to 10 steps from the entrance. Here he made us dig a grave of 3 feet wide and 6 feet long and 6 feet deep. We followed his instructions but since two workmen could not work in 6 feet, we made the grave 8 feet long. We had already gone more than 1 foot deep when we heard the noise of a carriage that came quickly toward us. When we completed our work, the gate of the cemetery opened and we saw three other members of the Committee descend from the carriage, all dressed in capes just like the man that guided us.

We all saw, at the same time, a coffin of about 8 to 10 inches wide and about four and a half feet long, that the members of the Committee with the coachman brought out of the coach and put at the entry of the cemetery. After which they asked us to move aside. Still a few minutes later they called us back and we noticed that they had placed the coffin in the grave and now they had covered it by about five to six inches of soil. They told us to finish filling in the grave and then after to stamp down the soil with our feet. We concluded that they wanted us to leave it so that no one would notice that anything had happened. We did everything that they asked us to do and then they told us not to say anything about what we had done to anybody. They even told us that they would find us if any one us would even commit the slightest indiscretion. Finally they gave each of my workmen a note for 10 francs, me they promised a favour, which I never asked for, for various reasons that probably would not have received anyway, especially after I heard a Committee men say while laughing: "The little Capet will have a way to go to find his family."

This statement then made an excellent excuse to look no further for the grave of Louis XVII because the implication seemed to be that here was a new spot for

Louis XVII's grave. Many other writers seem to have interpreted this the same way. However I feel that it means that these Committeemen were aware that Louis XVII was alive and that he would look for his parent's graves, after all no dead boy is going to look for his parent's grave. It was the parents that the Committee reburied, if anything. It could not have been the boy, his body would not have fitted in such a small casket, but the parents were buried in an extra heavy dose of lime so that their bodies would be destroyed quickly and their remains would have fitted in such a small box.

The revolutionaries knew very well that Louis XVII had escaped. I feel sure that the boy was in the hands of his enemies, his friends would never have kept him in the way that he was treated. There was so much to gain to declare that he was alive. This is why no one ever came forth and said; "I did it, I rescued the king."

Not that his friends did not try, we all know of the efforts by the Baron de Batz and Mrs.Atkyns and there were others as well. It was the Barras group that succeeded and *it was their idea that it not become public knowledge.*

It also astonishes me that this new grave in the cemetery of Clamart was never exhumed. Charpentier gives an excellent description of the location and if Louis XVIII believed his story and called off the search because of it, why did he not dig up this grave?

There is a report, in 1816, that Voisin tried still another exhumation. He arranged the original burial and had a firm idea of where the burial took place but this attempt also brought no further solutions. The attempted exhumation in 1815 had raised the curiosity of a historian named Simian-Despréaux, who had investigated thoroughly what had happened to the young king. He interviewed Dr. Pelletan who told him how he had cut the head to examine the brain. How he had lifted the cap of the skull and placed it back on and how he had covered it with a piece of cotton. The doctor told him that he would recognize this skullcap because of the way he had cut it, which was not the normal way of opening the head.

Simian-Despréaux had studied the report made by Simon and Petit. He made a nuisance of himself with his questions but slowly and surely he got closer to the truth. He made real noises about exhuming the body because he knew that with Dr. Pelletan, it would be possible to receive a positive identification.

The government became upset. Not wanting any inquiries made, it sent Simian-Despréaux a letter telling him to cease his inquiries. The letter explains that the government knew all it wanted to know about this affair and it instructed him to stop immediately.

The next exhumation took place in 1846 and the abbey Haumet, who was in charge of the St. Marguerite's church instigated it as he had heard about the famous grave in his cemetery. Haumet decided that he wanted to put a small addition to the church, just where Bertrancourt had reburied the body. Since his addition needed footings, he had a perfect excuse to exhume the grave that lay there. He arranged to have doctor Millicent there to observe the body and also doctors Gabalda, Tessier, and Davasse, the abbeys Bossuet and Serre joined them. They located a coffin in the correct place as suggested by Bertrancourt but it was made of lead instead of the wooden box they expected. Bertrancourt had not said anything about exchanging coffins but then he had not said that he dug up the coffin, only the body. He had told his wife that when he found the body he discovered the head, wrapped in bandages. He left the wooden box in the ground which would be the one, found later on the exact spot where the burial took place. The doctors thoroughly examined the body, which turned out to be of a boy of fourteen years or older. It had long legs and arms and there were signs of growth on the knee and wrist just as described by Dr. Pelletan in the autopsy. Also the skull was exactly as described by Dr. Pelletan for the post mortem.

The description also matches with that given by Harmand de la Meuse in the Temple in December 1794 and it matches with the description of Barras. There is no doubt that this was the boy who died in the Temple on June 8th, 1795. There is also no doubt that this was not Louis XVII.

There are three witnesses on the location of the grave, we have full descriptions of the post mortem by Dr.Pelletan and of Harmand de la Meuse, and everything fits. Yet there are still historians who have found objections. They say there were extra bones, they say that the body could have been of a ten year old, it was smaller in proportion. Many claim it was still the body of Louis XVII though these doctors have testified that the body was of at least a fourteen year old. The bit of extra bone may have fallen on the body when Bertrancourt moved it from one coffin into another. Not one doctor felt that this was a body consisting of various parts or female as some have suggested.

They reburied the body further along the church wall in the same garden area of the church as the first grave.

In 1894, due to the efforts of George Laguerre, they exhumed the body again. He was a lawyer, greatly fascinated by the case. Dr. Felix Bacher was present and he wrote a brochure about the results of this new examination done by him and doctors Bilhaut, Magilot and Marronvrier. Again they confirmed the results of the earlier examination. It established that the boy, who died, had a long history of scrofules, which is a disease that eventually kills but only after a long illness. There was never any report that Louis XVII had this decease and he had received doctors care all along as we have seen. Another interesting observation made by these doctors was the asymmetrical shape of the head. That meant that the right side at the forehead slightly protruded and also the right side of the chin. Later portraits show this asymmetrical view of the boy in prison just before his death. It is not part of the physical attributes of Louis XVII.

Time Magazine's article on the burial of the heart of Louis XVII shows a painting of a boy with an asymetrical face. Not only did they get the story wrong, the picture is not Louis XVII but the substitute.

The doctors who took part in this second exhumation did not agree on the age of the body. They agreed fully on the beginning of the report and it states;

   1.The body was that of a male human.

   2.The subject was at least fourteen years old.

   3.There existed a small case of scrofules in the body.

Signed doctor Felix de Becker and Dr. Bilhaut.

4.The skeleton was that of a boy of at least 18 to 20 years.

5.The body could not have been that of the Dauphin, who was 10 years and two months old at the time of his supposed death.

Signed Dr. G. Magitot, of the Academy of Medicine and former President of the Association of Anthropology and Dr.L. Manouvrier, Professor at the school for Anthropology.

6.We conclude that the body belonged to a person of at least 18 years old.

Signed: Prof.Oscar Amodeo, Professor at the School for Ortho-dental technique and Professor Poirier.

We now have besides the reports of the original four doctors, this report of six doctors, which include such specialists as Professors of Dentistry and Anthropology. Not one doctor finds that there is a problem with this body because there exists an extra bit of humerus bone and some small pieces are missing. Still there are people who argue with these findings.

The cemetery now had some peace and quiet until 1904 when the Commission of Old Paris decided to try some exhumations in the location suggested by Voisin. They lacked results that did not stop an eager reporter, Louis Schneider, from reporting that they did find the famous casket and that there were two doctors present who found two tibias bones that did not belong to this

body and a hipbone that belonged to a girl. This completely false report is the basis for many statements
made by so-called historians regarding the unreliability
of the other reports. Professor Francq in his book about
Louis XVII writes on page 112: "Even though the scientific conclusions of the 1846 and 1894 teams of experts
may be questioned and entirely rejected." Thereby he
rejects the findings of ten medical doctors and experts.
This is a serious work, in the introduction the professor
claims to have worked the investigation as a detective
would investigate a crime in modern police work. In the
chapter on "Solving the mystery" he speaks of the
bystanders who think this and that, the bystander's
position he considers valuable and the medical evidence
he dismisses. The following pages contain the same
poor arguments, that maybe there are different bodies
intermixed, bones that belong to other bodies etc. He
concludes that there is not a body there of a deter-
minable age after ten doctors have not found any such
discrepancy.

In 1970, the Commission of Old Paris, which does not
want to accept it's previous defeats or the results of
others, again tried an exhumation without results. I
regret very much that they did not invite a member of
our family nor they did not ask us to send an observer. I
would then be better prepared to comment on these
attempts.

In 1979 they tried again; this time they were looking
for a hole under the wall where Bertrancourt had said
he put the coffin. So they dug where the coffin was in
1846 and fully expected the hole to be still there over a
hundred years later. At least they expected to find that
there once was a hole in the wall so that a coffin could
have been there. Well they definitely located the coffin

there in 1846 I think they misinterpreted the words of Bertrancourt, when he said under but meant below or at the base of the wall. The word "under" can mean below or in front rather than underneath. The body was under the wall, not underneath it.

No matter how many more exhumations they would like to do, the results from 1846 and 1895 will stand up. *The body found and examined was that of the boy who died in the Temple on June 8th, 1795 and not that of Louis XVII.*

It must be remembered that when gravedigger Bertrancourt took the body of what he thought was his king out of the common grave, he did not bury it in the cemetery but in that very small area alongside the church that was its garden. On all the different plans that exist of the cemetery it is plain to see that where Bertrancourt buried the body was not in a designated burial area. No one else was buried in this section at this time or after and so he lay by himself. The body that they found could only have been his.

I fully agree with the historian Jean Pascal Romain that this is one of the most important aspects of the whole story. Even the current head of the Orleans family, the Count of Paris, admitted on television in 1988 that he was sure that Louis XVII had not died in the Temple. He also said that he was sure that Louis XVII was now dead, which seems likely since he would have been 203 years old in 1988.

No serious historian still insists that the body of Louis XVII lies in the cemetery of St.Marguerite, even if there is a small plaque on the wall inscribed "Louis XVII". Louis XVIII did not want this body in the Chapel Expiatoire, built as a memorial to the royal martyrs Louis XVI, Marie Antoinette, Madame Royale Elizabeth, but not Louis XVII. No ceremonies have ever been held for this body, no one pays it any attention. Those who want to honour Louis XVII go to Delft in Holland.

Chapter 9.   THE FALSE DAUPHINS

We now return to the city of Paris to see what has happened since the official death of young Louis XVII on the eighth of June 1795.

The day after the death, a police notice went out to all France to stop all boys of about ten years of age and travelling any where in France. There is an interesting story of a young man, Alexis Morin de Guérivière, born in Mauberge in 1779, and six years older than Louis XVII. He was a small boy, under sized for his age, had light colouring and bore some semblance to the young king. He lived with his father in Paris but on June the seventh he was handed over to a Mr. Ojardias for a trip to Thiers. They travelled through the forest of Fontainebleau to Thiers where Ojardias left the young man with the family Barge-Béal and he then continued on to Lyons.

Shortly there after, the police picked up the family Barge-Béal for interogation by the commissioners of the government. The young man was unable to explain himself properly although he showed his passport. The interrogators, who were not happy with the answers, prepared to take the young man to a larger city in the area. Still, after some threats from Mr. Barge-Béal they made a decree arresting young Alexis but putting him in the care of Mr. Barge-Béal. This gentleman tried to contact Ojardias to come and sort out the problem but it took some time for Ojardias to return. As a matter of fact, Mr. Ojardias played a double role and probably his trip with young Alexis was a scheme to focus attention away from the real Louis XVII who at this time was being moved elsewhere.

So it took a little while for the matter to be settled but finally Mr. Chazal, the local representative of the government, signed a decree stating that the conduct of Mr. Ojardias had been justified and that the child should be released. In Thiers, they treated Alexis with much respect and even whispered in town that he could be the young king.

Years later, on hearing about a man, who was passing himself of as Louis XVII, Alexis remembered his experiences and he knew that the police had been looking for the young king. He thus became a follower of the notorious Baron of Richemont.

On June the twelfth, 1795 the police reported:

> *"The people of the Temple quarter say quite openly that the arrangements for the funeral of the little Capet were only a blind and that he is not dead, that he has been allowed to escape and is now safely away."*

A newspaper of the day called the Courier Universal reported:

> *"Some contend that this death means nothing, that the young child is full of life, that it is a long time since he was imprisoned in the Temple. The authenticity of the secret and natural death of a child whom, notwithstanding all demagogic declarations, one cannot regard as an ordinary child,*

*since a considerable armed force guarded him day
and night, ought perhaps, I will not say for the honour of the Convention, but for public tranquillity, to
have been solemnly and publicly found out."*

There is no doubt that the author is right. At least
one person without a bias and known to the prince
should have been there. The death of Louis XVII was a
most important event that year and there should have
been no questions left unanswered about it. If it happened.

His sister was one floor up, the old servants the
Tissons were in the same building, the prison doctor,
who had cared for the young boy, Dr.Thierry was still
the prison doctor. Mrs. Simon lived less than two
blocks away. Any one them could have given that vital
piece of information that would have made that death
certificate acceptable, but they were all kept well away
from the dead boy.

If these rumours had not been rampant where did
these false dauphins come from? Beauchesne, the first
of the many biographers of Louis XVII started by deny-
ing that such rumours ever existed and many other
writers followed his lead.

On July the eleventh, 1795 the Minister of Foreign
Affairs for the Imperial Court of Austria, Mr. Thugut
asked:

*"Why should we accept Louis XVIII when Louis
XVII might still be alive. We cannot take the word
of the skeletons that reign at the Convention in
France."*

So it took only a year for the first false dauphin to
appear. He was Jean-Marie Hervagault, son of Jean-

François Hervagault, a tailor from the town of St.Lo. His mother was Nicole Bigot. According to gossip, the Prince of Monaco had seduced her and he took her to Normandie and then married her off to Jean-François Hervagault, who worked for him. The year was 1781 and the child was thus four years older than the real Louis XVII.

The young Hervagault had an adventuresome mind and ran away from home. In September 1796, at the ripe age of fifteen, he was arrested for not having any papers and for pretending to be the child of the Prince of Monaco.

They sent him home but he did not stay very long because in March 1797 he was arrested again in Alençon. In May 1798 he was in Meaux pretending to be the son of a rich farmer and refused to identify himself at the police station. He called himself Louis Antoine Joseph Frederic de Lonqueville and claimed to be an orphan. In jail he made such an impression on his jailor that he received almost all that he wanted. He became friendly with two ladies, who often visited him and they started a rumour that perhaps he was the dauphin, who was supposed to have died three years previously, but for who everyone was looking because they believed him to be alive.

Soon there was a small group of followers visiting him in jail. Although by now the police had found his real identity and his previous record, that did not stop anyone. In February 1799 the judge sent him to St.Lo for identification. His brother and his father recognized him. They now sent him back to Châlons where he received a one-month sentence for impersonation. After he came out of jail he went towards Normandie and posing as the son of a rich merchant. He managed to swindle some money out of a rich farm lady, who then caught on to him and had him arrested. This time he received a two-year sentence and left jail in 1801. In 1802 he was in Vitry and now he claimed to be Louis XVII. He had some success and soon had a fairly large following. But eventually the gig was up and in 1804 they tried him again. In 1806 he was free and on his way to St.Lo to his parents. It was the last we heard from him.

In 1927 the well-known author, Octave Aubrey, published his novel: "The Last King", which became famous and it gave a fictional account of the escape of Louis XVII. The author had followed the real story very closely and some of it was the truth and some of it was very close to the truth. The author invented a "Count of Vaisons", who never existed. He made the date the boy escaped August 25th, 1794 and Laurant helps Louis XVII under orders of Barras. In the book they send him to a former banker of Louis XVI, a Mr. Petitval, who is murdered in April 1796 with his whole family. So far, this is pretty close to the truth. They then send the child to Martinique, where Josephine de Beauharnais and Laurent originated and there he dies during an uprising of the natives.

After the publication of this book the author received an invitation to go to Rome to speak to Pope Pius XI. He spent two hours privately with the Pope and afterwards he would not discuss his visit or his book. His daughter stated later that her father burned all the papers that he had about this story, before his death.

The next important pretender to surface is Charles de Navarre, prisoner of Rouen, arrested on the ninth of

December 1815. A Lieutenant of Police of St. Malo described him in a letter, dated the fifteenth of December 1815, as having small brown eyes. Thus not the large blue eyes of the real dauphin. They discovered later that his real name was Mathurin Bruneau and that he was a real scoundrel, who ordered his jailors around, demanding all kinds of services and often getting them.

His court case is very interesting. First, Marie-Thérèse, the Duchess of Angoulème, sister of Charles, sent General Berthier to Rouen to see what he thought. He reported that the person in question did not look like Louis XVII and that he was an impostor. Why did she send the General? Obviously even twenty years after her brother's death she still had some doubts.

During the trial the government made the following rules and they show clearly what the government knew and feared:

A. The government forbids the mention of a possibili ty of an escape!

B. It refuses to give the court any papers that may establish the death of Louis XVII!

C. It refuses the prisoner the right to answer a list of questions prepared by the Duchess of Angoulème, his supposed sister.

D. It refuses to let Madame Simon, wife of the former jailor of Louis XVII to testify.

These rules of course completely prejudge the case and the truth was now not likely to come out. Charles de Navarre was sentenced and sent to jail.

There existed another fictional book about the escape of the dauphin, entitled, "The cemetery of the Madeleine" written by Regnault-Warin, and it also described the escape and the adventures that followed. Many new pretenders used this theme, which came in so handy, and which meant they did not have to use their imagination. Using these existing stories often got them into difficulties and it was easy to catch them in their lies.

Another bad error most pretenders made was in the use of the first name of the dauphin. It seems that only the real Charles knew that his name was Charles; his older brother the original dauphin was Louis, as was the custom with the de Bourbon family. Both had Louis as their first name but at home they were not both called Louis.

We now come to the most famous of the impostors, Claude Perrin, better known by his assumed name; Baron of Richemont. This character was born in Lagnien on the seventh of September 1786, the son of a butcher. He was a first class adventurer and really the one and only professional amongst the false dauphins. Examples of the many roles and titles he played were: gentleman, colonel in the cavalry, writer and diplomat. He travelled all over the countryside and resided in almost every large city in France and Italy. He moved when things got a little warm and always left some debts behind. In 1820 he assumed his best-known title and became the dauphin, Duke of Normandie. They then arrested him on demands of the French Ambassador and jailed him in Milan, Italy. In 1825 he returned to France, joined the Free Masons and in Toulon he was known as Hebert.

His next title was Baron of Richemont and now he set his eyes on Paris. He had amassed some funds and made presentations to the First and Second Chambers of the government. Left alone by the officials, he slowly gathered about him a group of followers. Then he wrote his story: "The memoirs of the Duke of Normandie, son of Louis XVI written and published by himself." He claimed to have escaped from the Temple inside a wooden horse on the twenty ninth of June 1794 with the help of Madame Simon. This is not very likely as Madame Simon was no longer in the Temple on this date and we now know so much more of what happened that really his story no longer holds water.

He had some success; he travelled all over France and enlarged his troop of followers. The police left him alone at this time. In fact many people thought and still think that the French government supported him. They hoped that his performance would take the wind out of the sails of other pretenders, especially should the real one come along. Finally they jailed him and during his trial there was an interruption when a gentleman stood up and addressed the court. This gentleman was Morel de St. Didier, who represented the real dauphin, Charles. Morel de St. Didier asked the court to hear the real dauphin and he used the name Charles when speaking of him. The Baron of Richemont cried out:

"He claims to be representing the real dauphin who does not even know his name!"

The Baron had been calling himself Louis, which seems to be correct, but the real Charles knew better. The Baron was found guilty of impersonations and sentenced to twelve years in prison. However the following year the Baron was seen walking the streets of Paris. The government and the police were then having problems with the real dauphin and the Baron was an excellent lightning rod that took all the attention off the real thing. With the help of the police he continued to pass himself off as Louis XVII in Switzerland, Italy and France. A noble lady, the Countess of Apselier took him in and he lies buried on her estate, the castle of Vaux-Renard. His tombstone did say Louis-Charles of France but the government in 1858 forced them to remove this inscription and the stone was turned over. Only the real Louis XVII lies buried under a tombstone carrying his name. It is in Delft in the Netherlands.

The Baron of Richemont was by far the most successful of the false dauphins. He was a real professional and spent his whole life under various false names. However his whole claim fails for the very simple, same reason, as the failure of the pretensions of Charles of Navarre; both had brown eyes and the real Charles had blue eyes. The Baron claimed that a fever changed the colour of his eyes, but then he claimed many things.

A new book has recently appeared, which claims that the Baron of Richemont was definitely the second son of Louis XVI and that Naundorff was the first son, who did not really die but survived in the arms of a nurse.

There were another fifty or so false dauphins, but none found any long-term acceptance. There was the Englishman Auguste Meves and even an American Negro named Eleazar Williams. Another American, called Louis Leroy, based his story on a letter, supposedly from the Count Alex Fersen, a friend of Marie Antoinette. This letter, supposedly found in Montreal, turned out to be a fake and so another false dauphin bites the dust.

The latest in this long line is the invention of Paul Bartel, who wrote an article in "The Illustration" on the twentieth of January 1934 in which he claims to have found a farmer named Joachim Capeto on an island of the Azores. There is a family legend that they are descendants of a royal prince Luigi Capeto, who settled in the Azores during the French revolution. Several historians have disproved this so-called "Dauphin of the Azores" story a long time ago but a recent book brings it alive again. The writer calls himself Xavier de Roche or known as Roche de Vercors and also H. van H., his book is entitled "Louis XVII" and in it he has completed a tremendous job of over 900 pages with every story ever printed about Louis XVII. Unfortunately it contains the good as well as the bad, the correct mixed with the silly. Some of the stories are even noted as being totally wrong, but still they are printed. About the story of the "Dauphin of the Azores" there is a great lack of information, while the rest of the book has a tremendous amount of "papers" to prove the story. He claims that the years 1798 to 1803 are missing in the history of Louis XVII and that during these years Charles supposedly married a princess of Portuguese background in the Azores lived there and had five children. After that he believes in the rest of Charles' history in Germany.

If it were true it would mean that Charles had five children in five years starting at age fourteen to age eighteen, not a bad feat. On top of that he would have used the name Louis (Luigi) which he never did. His brother was Louis. And most of all he would have had to use the name Capet (or Capeto as the writer quickly makes it), which is the hateful name that the revolutionaries gave to Louis XVI and Louis XVII that Charles would never have used.

To even hint that Charles would have abandoned his wife and children are an even greater error and shows no insight what so ever of the character of Louis XVII.

The latest book is by Jacques Hamann and Maurice Etienne and is named "Louis XVII and the 101 pretenders". Chapter one is about what they say is the real Louis XVII and thus there is no need to read any further. You just know that all others are going to be false. About Naundorff they say that a friend handed Naundorff a passport. But Naundorff never had a passport. The police chief Le coq had the passport, which was found later and described a man with black hair and black eyes. They do not hesitate to accept that that is his passport. They continue on as if he was always Naundorff, that he had old friends when he arrived for the first time in Berlin. They talk about a family VON Naundorff; none of all the hundreds of books about Naundorff have ever come up with that name. I am in constant touch with Charles Naundorff whose family immigrated to the USA. His hobby is genealogy and he has no record of any Naundorff in Berlin at that time or with the name Karl Wilhelm Naundorff.

In the end there is only Charles Wilhelm Naundorff, whose background no one was ever to find, who never tried to pass himself of as anything else, as had done so many of his imitators. Only he never had his day in court. The government prosecuted all false dauphins but managed to keep Charles from ever presenting his case in court. He is the only one who asked for a court hearing, the only one who ever tried to find his old friends and servants. He was the only one whose physical signs were so completely the same as those of the dauphin that the odds must be one in a billion. He is the only one, whose memories of his youth have stood the test of time. Finqally, he is the only one who could correctly answer the questions sent by his sister the Duchess of Angoulème to the false dauphin Charles de Navarre. He is my great- great grandfather.

Chapter 10.   SAILING TO FLORIDA

In 1982 the real estate market was bad. Just when our lot in Island Lake was registered and we had started to build our dream home the market dropped out of sight. Mortgage interest peaked at 19% and of course our mortgage became due. We put the house we had on McCowan Ave up for sale as well as the new house under construction. Our little subdivision on McCowan was finally registered and we were able to sell a lot. John Cook was a partner with me at Re/Max Markville and we both had registered retirement funds locked in for our retirement. We gave each other mortgages, which saved our bacon. So we overcame one hurdle.

We stopped building for a while but then we sold the house on McCowan and had to move, so construction went full blast. It was a beautiful home with a gorgeous view of Island Lake and Edmond and Louise moved back in with us. Michael was getting serious about Jacqueline and one of the first family gatherings was his marriage, which took place in our new home. And a few years later Louise married and we started to feel a little freedom.

Arline and I had begun to get our sea legs, we had taken sailing lessons with the Annapolis sailing school in the U.S.A. and we really liked it. Then one day I spoke to my friend Jerry Paxton and he asked if I would help him take a Trojan 47 from New York to Florida. A friend of Jerry's wanted his motor yacht in Florida for the winter and someone had taken it as far as New York. But by going full blast one engine gave up the ghost and now the boat had to be picked up in New York and $5000 dollars cheque had to be handed over for the repairs. Jerry, Mike Wade and I, with our wives, flew to New York and the following day we were underway.

The Trojan had three separate bedrooms and lots of room with a huge rear deck that was fully enclosed with clear plastic sheeting. The first day we made it as far as Atlantic City with all the glowing casinos. Since it was November the days were already short and we arrived in the dark. With all the lights from the shore it was hard to see the entrance to the channel but the buoys led us in. Arline and Mike stood in the very front of the boat and guided us as best as possible. Suddenly they yelled, we were maybe 100 feet from a huge pier and the lighthouse on top was out! We had a scare but stopped just in time and made it safely into the harbor where we tied up to the Trump Castle Casino docks.

The following morning it was time to gas up. I was very happy not to have to pay that bill; it came to around $300 U.S. We had a great view of the exit of the harbor, which we could not see at night. As we hit the ocean swells Arline went downstairs and came back with the complaint that it smelt of fuel down there. Jerry gave me the wheel and went down to have a look. He came up looking stark white and begged me to shut down the engine. Gas was spurting out of one of the fuel tanks; it had a leak at the top and with the heavy waves little spurts of gas flew above the tank. At one point a small flame ran over the top of the tank. Thank heaven the engine room was huge with lots of fresh air, on any other boat we would have blown up. Jerry bled the bad tank over to the good one as best as he could and then we ran very slowly on the bad tank until the level was down. Believe it or not we said some prayers, even I.

The rest of the trip continued uneventfully, certainly compared with those first couple of days. We did get lost one night in some fish weirs and a marina helper with a small boat came out to guide us in to his marina. Nothing much happened until we got into the Alligator canal in North Carolina. Here we were on a beautiful day passing a slow moving 2-story passenger ship and waving at the passengers when suddenly we ran aground on a sand bank. The passengers waved at us this time as we tried to get off. Mike even jumped off and tried to push us off, but then a Canadian Whitby 42 went past and turned and offered to help. We were on a motor yacht and a sailboat pulled us off. It was embarrassing.

We had bent our shaft and we could only go very slowly on one engine to the next harbour, Bellhaven, where we had to leave the boat for further repairs. But the trip had really impressed us and we started to plan to do that trip some time in the future. In 1986 we found a motor sailor that suited us to perfection. It was a Cooper 37 built in Vancouver where, due to the cold Pacific many sailing boats were steered from inside. The chap who had built it had brought it overland by truck before it had any rigging and had named it for his daughters Megan and Sarah. "Mesa" had cost him his marriage and he had lived on it in the harbor at Pickering but had never had the funds to finish outfitting it. It did have a beautiful 72 h.p. Isuzu motor and it looked inviting to us. It was ours later that summer. We installed a mast and rigging and sails and worked hard to get it ready for a long trip.

In 1986 I received a letter from Jacqueline Monsigne, a well-known French writer. She had written a novel about Louis XVII, based a little on the real story but with some poetic license. It was called "Le Roi sans Couronne", the King without a Crown and she was coming to Montreal to publicize it. Would I meet her in Montreal? It was a wonderful meeting; she was with her American husband Edward Meeks, an actor in many French movies. He also played in the famous "The Longest Day" with Robert Mitchum, who became a friend. Her story starts out that she is visiting her husband's birthplace Boston and there on a high hill she finds a grave that bears the name "Louis XVII". In Montreal the reporters that follow us around want to write about this and need photos. So we climb the famous mountain in the middle of Montreal and they take pictures of us two and a grave belonging to God only, knows whom. We laugh that the novel, which is already a figment of someone's imagination, now has a proper grave in a totally different city.

The following year the real estate market has done a complete turn around. Now the prices are going though the roof, houses that you could not sell at $200,000 in 1982 are now going for almost $400,000. It was crazy; I did not think it could last. I was the broker of the Re/Max franchise in Markham Ontario and I now had a large staff. I remember well the day that I arrived at the office and one sad looking agent was waiting for me.

I asked what the problem was and he answered that he thought that he had done something that might have been against the rules. I asked him: "What did you do?"

"I had an offer last night and my buyer was really interested in getting this property. When the owner and his agent turned down the offer I pulled out a wad of money and laid 5 hundred-dollar bills on the table and asked them if they would accept the offer now. The owner was willing but the agent got really upset and said: "I have to call my broker."

He phoned his broker and the broker said if it is O.K. with the vendor I see nothing wrong with it. And so I have now an accepted offer.

"Well" I said,"there seems to be nothing wrong with that, but I would rather not take it up with the Real Estate Board. I do not know what they would say."

"Yes, but that is not the problem, now the owner wants to buy a house and he does not want to deal with his agent, he wants me, says the agent: "He likes the way I do business and that is stealing a customer from another agency". I discussed with him the consequences that could follow, when he came out with another startling story:

"The owner asked what I would have done if he had not accepted the offer I had made and I told him that I still had quite a lot in my roll."

Now Jerry Paxton wanted to build on his lot next to ours on Island Lake and he told me he would rent our home while we could take a year off and do that trip we talked about. An offer hard to refuse. We planned to leave in August in time to be in Florida for the winter.

At the last minute however W5, the CBC news program came to see me, they wanted to do a program on the de Bourbon family. It was a great opportunity to get some publicity for our "Cause". At the same time there was an exhibition on Louis XVII in a city hall in Paris and we went there with the CBC crew in tow. The show aired in the first week of October and at the end of the show you see us sailing away leaving all our problems behind.

We were finally underway and our first stop was to be Port Hope along our side of the shore of Lake Ontario. We had been told to cross the lake only at night because if you went off course you arrived in the morning and you had all day to find your way. But small craft warnings are up the morning that we want to leave for Port Hope and we wait till later that day when we see that several boats are leaving the harbour. We are anxious and leave as well. The wind is great and by 5:30 that afternoon we tie up in Port Hope and have dinner with Cloe and Lorne Patrick from Cobourg. The trip across should take 10 to 12 hours and we leave at 7 pm. Everything goes well the first few hours but as we get to the middle of the lake the wind starts to increase. Soon it is time to reef the mainsail and up I go, tied to the boat with a harness. Arline is at the wheel and promises to keep the nose into the wind. The blasted mainsail is stuck and will not come down. I pull and haul, I try to get it up higher, nothing helps, one of the slides is stuck and nothing I do helps.

We are now really flying but thank heavens we have a self-furling jib which works and it comes in. The Loran works great, it is a little magical box that tells us where we are. We race across Lake Ontario and see only one large freighter sliding across the horizon. We arrive at the other coast at 3 in the morning. We should not have worried about finding our way, the Loran takes us across without any problem and the harbour of Rochester has a huge pier with hundreds of lights, you could not miss it if you wanted to.

We are exhausted when we reach the marina and fall sound asleep in no time. A few hours later someone knocks on the boat, when we get up and stick our heads out of the cockpit a voice asks where we are from. We tell them. They are surprised that we came across, their weather forecast had warned about the winds and their races the night before had been cancelled. We learned a lesson to determine the weather of the area where we are going, not where we have been. It was our worst adventure sailing but now we are sailors, at least in our minds.

The following day it is off to Oswego where we have to take down our mast and get ready to run through 18 locks to get to the Hudson River at Albany. We also have to deal with the customs people and obtain a one-year cruising permit for the U.S.A. We have worried about our mast but the fellow in Oswego does hundreds each year and is an expert.

In short order we do 6 locks and turn into the Erie barge canal that runs from Buffalo to Albany. The following day is the large and unruly Oneida Lake, which can be nasty. It is nice to us and we survive again. Then comes the narrow canal. We park in front of the next lock where the canal widens. We wake up in the morning and have channel 16 on to listen for other traffic and problems. Everyone uses it for emergencies

and you are required to listen to it when you are underway. Suddenly a voice asks the lockmaster:

"Where is buoy 345?"

The lockmaster answers: "I do not know, I am lock 16.
I have no ideas about buoys!"

I look at my chart and see that buoy 345 is a few hundred feet from where we are. It is very foggy out and
we are waiting for it to lift. I go out to see what is happening. Suddenly out of the fog come two guys pulling
a small sailboat, which looks like the old days when
slaves pulled barges along the canals. They are
Dwayne and Bruce, two carrot farmers from Michigan.
They are on their way south but have not brought any
charts, as they do not know how to read them and anyway you cannot get lost in a canal.

They have a boatload of potatoes, carrots and onions
and were knocked down the day we came across Lake
Ontario while they came across Lake Erie. We decide
to travel together for a while and we greatly enjoy their
company. They are underway early in the morning but
at lunchtime we usually catch them and then we tie up
around 4 pm and they arrive an hour or so later.
Usually they are frozen to the bone because they must
steer from outside while we sit in our lovely inside
cabin. We also have a stove to keep us warm and supper is ready when they arrive. They love it and we have
company. The trip is astonishing, you glide through
cities and you see not a soul, sometimes maybe a fish-
erman sitting along the canal, sometimes a couple
walking along. But most of the time it is just us, like
adventurers of old, seeing new territory for the first
time. Yet at the same time we are in the middle of civi-
lization.

A few days later we arrive at Castleton-on-the-Hudson; we tie up at the marina where we put up our mast. We celebrate and go onshore to have a meal in a restaurant. We find two restaurants but they are closed on Mondays. The fireman in the fire hall cannot help us, he knows of no open restaurant but he stands in the middle of the road and stops a policeman.

The policeman knows of one at the outskirts of town that is open and he will take us there. Arline gets in the front of the car. I am in the back behind some heavy wrought iron screen with no handles on the door. Someone yells from the sidewalk:

"Who have you got there, Joe?"

"Crim-i-nals!" yells the cop.

We are in the States all right. Everyone is friendly.

We are now in the mountains, the Catskills are next. It is fall and although we usually have frost on the deck in the morning it is beautiful. Along the Hudson are magnificent homes on both shores and high up on the embankment. We pass West Point, the American Academy for the Army. It sits high up the embankment at a narrow turn in the Hudson. Finally one day we see the high towers of New York in the distance. Dwayne and Bruce ask if we can stay with them the next day as they are frightened by the traffic in New York and they still have no charts. It is Sunday as we get close to downtown. There is no traffic whatsoever. We have the whole Hudson to ourselves. Suddenly a huge ship leaves the quay and heads straight for us. I go to starboard and Dwayne in "Sacre Blue" follows. The white passenger ship moves towards us. I get nervous and throw the wheel over to port. It does not help, the ship keeps coming and the passengers are hanging over the rail. Then we hear on a bullhorn:

"What you see now is a couple of boats from Canada on their way to sunny Florida."

We are the entertainment for this sight seeing boat.

We continue on and pass 8 or 9 million people without seeing anyone. On the left goes the Statue of Liberty and Ellis Island on the right the twin towers which are destroyed on 9/11. All the large wharves are in terrible shape; the harbor is almost not used at that time. The only traffic is the Staten Island ferry that blasts past us at great speed. Then under the last bridge and we get to Sandy Hook which guards the harbour from the Atlantic Ocean. We drop anchor and soon Dwayne and Bruce row over to discuss the next day when we must take the ocean to Cape May via Atlantic City.

We decide to leave very early because Atlantic City is a long run against the warm Gulf Stream. At 5 a.m. it is still pitch black outside but we have lifted our anchor and are on our way. Once in the channel it gets real scary, there are four lanes all heading out, but I think at least one lane is for incoming traffic. All we can see are green lights and red lights. For one channel that is fine, we know all about that but here there are the different lanes. Bruce and Dwayne are following but we are right and the numbers on the buoys are correct. Then as I look back behind Sacre Coeur there is nothing. We listen to the radio, which warns that a heavy fog is rolling out. We are about the last boats out that morning. The fog never catches up with us.

Our friends have a really bad time running against the Gulf Stream so we decide to head for Manasquan

inlet even though it is not recommended. We arrive
there late in the afternoon and have to run a gauntlet
against the current, the tide is running out. We make
it in and tie down. The currents in the harbour are
very strong; the following morning as we attempt to
leave we are pushed against another boat. It takes all
four of us to get the boat out of the slip.

We are now again on our way to Atlantic City but at
11 a.m. Dwayne and Bruce are on the radio. They cannot make any headway against the strong current. In 2
hours they make only 2 miles. We decide to go into
Barnegat inlet. Again a small fishing harbor, which we
should not enter. We have lost the air in our dink and I
find that one of the pontoons is torn off by the heavy
waves. Once safely tied up, we call the manufacturer
who promises us a new shell, which he will send to us
at Norfolk, Virginia. The next day we finally hit
Atlantic City. It is 5 days since we left New York. We
stay an extra day to rest up and do a little gambling. I
go through a whole roll of nickels and give up. When
we were there 5 years earlier it was a half abandoned
seaside resort. Now they have gambling and it has
made a great difference.

The Atlantic Ocean has decided to give us a nice quiet
ride to Cape May which we deserve. The next day we
go up the Delaware River. It is so wide that we cannot
see across. In the afternoon we reach the Delaware-
Chesapeake canal and we stop at the marina half way.
There is a very nice restaurant but our mail has not
arrived. We decide to stay and wait for the mail and
Dwayne and Bruce take us out for dinner and wave
goodbye the next morning. They are in a hurry to go
south. It is the last time we see them.

A day later we head for the beautiful Chesapeake Bay. Lots of islands, towns, and anchorages. A marvelous sailing area but we have to make tracks. We do take a day at Annapolis, the sailing capital of the East coast with a lot of marina's and stores so we fit out and buy the things we need.

On November 2 we make it to Norfolk, Virginia, just one month after leaving Pickering. We are in the little harbour just at the mouth of the Chesapeake and the following morning we want to reach the marina that has our mail and dink. It is in the middle of town and we take off in a hazy morning. Just outside the little bay the fog rolls in, thicker than any I have ever seen. We manage to go from one buoy to the next, just as we lose track of one the next one pops up. It is a bit frightening because this is the main East coast harbor for the U.S. Navy. And they are there, several aircraft carriers, tankers, frigates and submarines. All sizes and in many different shapes. The fog lifts and we can see them all. In the very large marina we meet a boat from France, two boats from England and several Canadians.

Then we begin our trip down the Intercoastal Waterway. It runs from Norfolk to Miami and starts with the Dismal swamp canal. It stays always very close to the coast but behind a long row of islands and it follows rivers, sounds and canals. Then soon we are in the Alligator canal, where we ran aground a couple of years previously. We stop again at Bellhaven and yes Mike, the pecan pie is as good as ever. The marina is famous with sailors taking this route, because it has a couple of golf carts, which you can take into town to get groceries and other supplies.

We are now heading for Beaufort, North Carolina and the wind really blows up. We first try to anchor in a small bay outside of town but the wind pushes us with the anchor so that we almost hit another boat. We decide to try the anchorage downtown. There we find almost 100 boats anchored in the space for 30. There is nothing we can do and we anchor in front of the whole gang. We may be in the way of the fishing boats but there is no other solution. Thank heavens the anchor holds. There is now a gale warning and we let out a lot of scope. We swing wide into the channel, once every minute. The fishing boats are all in and do not leave the following morning so we are O.K. A small Canadian boat behind us named Blue Jeans has a terrible time; they must have a small anchor. They reanchor at least five times. We must stay and watch the whole night; we cannot take a chance of breaking loose. It is bitter cold and the wind is howling like banshees. The stove will not stay on. No matter what we do it blows out. The cabin is ice cold and we have all the blankets tucked around us. But we survive that as well and by morning we are able to see the shore and the town.

Then it is off past Moorehead City and the new bridge. There is a welcoming party at the bridge. Five or six dolphins play with the bow wave, they are the first ones we have seen. Soon we arrive in Myrtle Beach where we wait for Arline's brother Jerry and his wife Jill. We have frost on the deck the following morning, which is unusual here, this far south. We visit "the World Famous" fishing village Calabash. It is a tourist trap with souvenir shops and fish restaurants. We also visit the beautiful Brookhaven Gardens with its show of statues spread out over the whole garden.

Then comes the beautiful city of Charleston and we feast our eyes on the beautiful homes and we see our first Xmas parade. It contains several tanks and jeeps. Yes this is the U.S.A. We are very aware of the difference between Canada and the USA, we see patrol planes every day, watching the coastline, and Army trucks pass almost daily. On December 2nd we reach Fernandina, Florida. We have arrived but Florida is a very long state and we are not home yet. A few days later we arrive in St. Augustine, the oldest town in the U.S., settled by the Spanish before Plymouth. The marina here is renovated and now we not only have water and electricity but also cable T.V. and telephone hookup. We love it and stay a few days for sight seeing. We now head for Daytona Beach where we are planning to paint the boat. The marina in Pickering had delayed us so much we never had it done. But the marina here is very expensive and they warn us that some days it is too cold to paint. We stay a week and rent a car to see Epcot Center in Orlando and several other sites in the neighborhood. We are getting tired of being on the move all the time and hope to find a spot in Fort Pierce. But the winds are strong and we run aground in one marina. The next town is Stuart and there is a new marina. We decide to stay for the Xmas holidays. This marina caters to very large motorboats and one giant lies next to us. The staff is very nice and on Xmas morning we are given a lovely basket with fruit and the paper is delivered every day. We wait for mail and visit the post office every second day. Finally we leave and give a forwarding address in Fort Lauderdale. That mail is sent back to Canada and we finally receive it in February.

We arrive in Fort Lauderdale on the 1st of January. Here on the New River there is a marina that lets you work on your own boat. The place is packed. We must tie up next to another boat and then cross two more boats before we reach the shore. But everyone is in the same predicament and friendly, so it is not too bad. We are going to be hauled out in a few days and then we work like little beavers to get the sanding and painting done. We also look for a delivery captain because we would like to take our boat to Montserrat in the Caribbean where we have a cottage. We find an experienced fellow who tells us it involves two weeks beating against the wind to a point in the Atlantic, where we can tack and get to Antigua. We need a lot more gear and he warns us it is no picnic. We decide to leave the boat and fly to Montserrat. The home we have there is our retirement home which we bought in the nineteen eighties and we spend the winter there. In the spring we make the return trip, which is not quite as eventful.

It has taken us three months for the first trip but now we manage to get to Ontario in 6 weeks. We have our first surprise when we arrive in Norfolk, Virginia. Our mail has not arrived. We phone Jerry who has been forwarding our mail. He says:

"We have it here in the car. We were just waiting for your call because we want to bring you the mail. We want to see you and talk to you. Reserve us a room and we will be there in 24 hours."

Holiday Inn is next to the marina and we wait. The following day Jerry and Janet arrive and invite us to dinner. After dinner Jerry presents us with an offer on our house. They say they love it and their plans have changed. Jerry had an architect design him a home much like ours, a bungalow with a full size walkout basement. He is on the same slope we are. In the lower level he designed an apartment for his mother on one side and the same on the other side for his mother-in-law. Both are widows and he has a driveway going down to a front door for each. A wonderful solution. Only neither his mother nor mother-in-law wants to live with their loving son. They want to stay where they are and where their friends are. So much for the best laid plans of man and beast. Jerry and Janet have decided that they would rather have our house. It will save them building a new one and ours suits them fine.

We think hard about it. We love the house we built for ourselves but the taxes alone are $5000 and difficult for us to finance we really built it for an investment. We seem to be in a neighborhood that we really cannot afford. Besides we love life on the boat, so we sell the house. Jerry and Janet are very happy and stay in this house longer than in any other. They have built at least three other homes but stay in this one for 12 years.

We continue our trip and our next adventure is when we arrive in Elizabeth City. As we near shore there is a couple ready to take our line. They help to tie us up but as Arline tries to make it to the shore she has one leg on the boat and one on land just as a gush of wind blows the boat away from the dock. We stand and stare fascinated to see her stretching and stretching and not knowing which way to jump. At the last moment she decides the shore is the best place to be and she makes it. I do not know what has come over me instead of helping her I am frozen to my spot. Anyway by the time the laughter dies down we are introduced to Bob and Marie Gartley, who have arrived shortly before us and they tell us all about this friendly town.

There is a small group of locals who have planted roses around the town dock. They try to have someone at the dock to greet newcomers and if there are more than four new boats they have a wine and cheese party at the restaurant on the docks. Fred the leader even has a golf cart and will take you for groceries. And every lady is given a rose in a small vase. It is the finest reception on the whole of the eastern seaboard.

Bob and Marie are originally from Rochester and have moved to Florida nineteen years before. They have now decided to return with their 36-foot trawler Lady G for a long visit. We decide to travel with them. We move at almost the same speed and have found friends for the rest of our lives. We have a great trip through the Great Dismal Swamp and are anchored near the last lock. In the middle of the night our anchor lets go and we are out with the dink laying a new anchor in our pajamas. A few weeks later we say goodbye as we leave Rochester for the north side of the lake. They head for a harbour near Rochester. It is June and there is a really hot spell. We are dressed in the skimpiest clothes we have. But the lake is still cold and by the time we are a mile off shore we put our sweaters on. Then half an hour later the cold drives us indoors. When we reach the other shore off come all the clothes again. Now we decide to head for Oshawa because in the harbor of Pickering we have run aground several times and Oshawa is more like a proper port.

Business is still poor. The Re/Max franchise I sold before we left has gone under. The owner thought he would do well with a second office but after a lot of expenses for new computers and office furniture he cannot hang on. He leaves with some of my money. There is no attraction to go back to work.

We have to decide what we are going to do and we have to get our furniture out of our house because Jerry and Janet want to bring their own furniture in.

Chapter 11. KARL WILHELM NAUNDORFF

Alain Decaux, Retired Minister of France in his book "Louis XVII Retrouve":

"After reading the letters of Louis XVII one finds an astonishing curious man,completely different from the one which you find if you studied his life and pronouncements, which are often not very sympathetic. Here is a man of great kindness, of an almost charming simplicity, very sensible. The advice he gives his wife over things that have nothing to do with his claims are those of a loving husband, the advise he gives his children are from an affectionate if severe father."

An undernourished young man arrived in Frankfurt, Germany, in 1808, accompagnied by a man in his forties. The older man explained that the young one had just spent four years in jail and had not seen the sun during that time. In fact, Charles had been on the run since 1795, or almost thirteen years. He had lost track of time and place, and his only goal in life was to settle down somewhere and be left in peace. Yet his troubles were still far from over. Montmorin, his companion, arranged for papers to introduce them to the Duke of Brunswick. They hoped to get protection from the Duke if only they could catch up with him, which finally they did.

When they arrived in the middle of the winter of 1808/09 in Chemnitz, the Duke welcomed them and gave them a letter to Major Schill who operated some troops further north. After some travel and yet more adventures, they met with Major Schill who had his own troubles, in that Napoleon's French troops were chasing him.

Europe was in chaos, with bands of troops roaming all over looting and stealing. Major Schill thought it safer to send his guests off with an escort because he felt that he might be caught. A Police report issued the December 21, 1809, from the region of Moselle stated that a detachment of French troops had captured Schill's troop and that they were taking thirty-seven men to Toulon. They had caught Schill himself on May 21, 1809.

Meanwhile, Charles and Montmorin fared no better, for they had run into an ambush. There was heavy fighting. The French troops killed Montmorin and the leader of their escort. Charles escaped only because he lost consciousness when his horse was killed under him and had fallen partially on his leg. Trapped, he remained unconscious until the battle was over. Again he was a prisoner and his captors took him to France. Because of his injuries, they took him to Fort Wesel near the French border where they had facilities to treat the wounded.

Here Charles soon became friendly with another prisoner and together they planned an escape from the prison. During a rainstorm they climbed out of a window while the guards, hiding from the rain, were not paying attention. After they dropped into the yard the two slowly made their way out.

They kept off the main roads, travelled only by night and thereby avoided the populated areas. When morning came, Charles could go no further and they searched for a place to hide during the day. His friend Friedrich then left to scrounge the countryside for food and drink. They lived like this for a couple of weeks, yet they were successful in returning to Germany.

It looked as though they would succeed in reaching Berlin, where Friedrich had planned for them to join the army. One day Charles woke to find that Friedrich had not returned, and that a dog was barking near by. The dog's master approached and asked who he was. Charles could not think of a fast answer and the man said,

"Do not worry, if you are who I think you are, you'll find that I am a friend."

Charles finally answered,

"I am a Prussian deserter."

"Oh la la! You mean you are a Westphalian deserter?" said the other man.

Again Charles did not know what to say.

"Do not worry, I have a son in the Westphalian army and if he is still alive, he is with Napoleon in Spain." Said the man, who was in fact a shephard.

He proposed that Charles stay with him in his cottage nearby. Charles explained that he was waiting for Friedrich and that he could not leave his friend. The newly found friend then left with his dog to look for Friedrich, but returned a short while later to tell Charles that it was no use waiting because the Police had already arrested Friedrich in town.

172

Charles gathered his belongings and noticed that Friedrich had left his rucksack behind. He went with the shepherd and stayed with him for three days hoping that his friend would somehow find him. The man advised Charles to continue his voyage. He lived not far from the capital of Saxony, just recently made a kingdom by Napoleon. The shepherd also gave Charles the rucksack that had belonged to Friedrich and, in addition to this, three coins.

Charles now travelled through a large forest. For several days he had no idea where he was and survived on berries. He continued onward and eventually found a large road that seemed to head for Berlin. While walking along the road for several hours he noticed a stone with the inscription, 'Doctor Martin Luther'. As he was resting on the stone he heard the horn of an approaching carriage so he stopped the carriage to ask the driver whether he was on the right road to Berlin. The only occupant of the carriage stuck his head out and asked several questions and then insisted that Charles come along as far as Wittenberg. Charles accepted gracefully. While the carriage rolled along the two men chatted about the strange stone along the road and many other things.

Finally, the man asked,

"What have you in the rucksack, that you carry so carefully?"

Charles answered,

"I do not know what is inside, it does not belong to me. I hope to find its owner back. He is a good friend of mine."

The other man laughed.

"You mean to say that you carry a rucksack without knowing what is inside? That seems very strange to me. Give it to me, and we will soon find out what is inside."

He took the rucksack, opened it and inspected the contents and then said,

"You would be better off to throw this away, it has nothing of any value in here. You are carrying it for nothing."

Then as he grabbed it from the side to throw it out, he had it by the seam and said,

"Hey, there is something in here."

They had another look inside and there, sewn into one seam, was a roll of coins. They amounted to 1600 francs in gold—a princely sum in those days. Charles could not believe his eyes and his companion looked at him strangely. Charles wondered how he was going to get this sum back to his friend Friedrich. He dared not tell his new friend of the adventures that he and Friedrich had experienced.

The man shouted,

"What a friend, to leave you all his money, while he gets himself arrested. He left you all this while he took the risks and got himself arrested. What a brave soul!"

Then Charles' new friend continued,

"But what are you going to do when you get to Prussia? They are very strict and you will need a passport."

"Oh, well," he said answering his own question, "we will see."

The following morning, his new friend left him for a couple of hours to find out whether he could borrow a horse and a small carriage from a friend for the ongoing journey. After he returned successfully, they left for Treinpretzen, the first town over the Prussian border. From there they travelled to Potsdam and from there in another carriage to Berlin.

Upon his arrival in Berlin, Charles 's new friend checked him into the "Black Eagle' hotel". Since the leaves were still on the trees, the time must have been about September 1810.

When Charles had stayed for several days at this hotel, the owner asked him how long he planned to stay in Berlin. They also wanted to know from where he had come and what he was doing in Berlin. The young Charles was very weary of these questions, but answered that he had come to sign up with the Prussian army as he and Friedrich had originally planned. When asked for his passport, he answered that it was in the hands of the Border Police.

A few days later, Charles presented himself at an army post to see whether he could enlist. They, however, informed him that the King of Prussia never admitted foreigners into his army. It was apparent from the accent that Charles was not a native Prussian. Disappointed, he returned to his hotel where he met a watch repairman named Pretz. They got into conversation and Charles mentioned that as a youngster he had always liked fixing watches. Pretz then introduced him to another watchmaker named Weiller, whom he joined and soon he had a small business under way.

He now began to worry that he did not have permission to stay in Berlin and no papers allowing him to operate as a watch repairman. Weiller advised him to get become registered as a citizen, and for that he needed a passport, or at least a birth certificate, or a pass of good conduct from the town mayor of the last town where he had lived. Charles did not have any of these papers, but now a new "guardian angel" appeared in the form of a Madame Sonnenfeld. He met her through the friend who had brought him to Berlin, and when the man left town, he had left with Charles a letter for his sister, Mrs. Sonnenfeld. One day a lady called at the concierge for a Mr. Naundorff. When Charles answered and said that he was Mr. Naundorff, the lady took a step back in surprise and said, "You are Mr. Naundorff?"—"Are you Mrs. Sonnenfeld?" asked Charles and when she nodded, he gave to her the letter from her brother.

Mrs. Sonnenfeld explained that she was fifty years old and that she had a son who gave her much trouble. It was this son that she was expecting to find.

Charles apologized that he was not her son, but they started a long conversation that ended with Mrs. Sonnenfeld promising to come and look after Charles, his dwelling and his workshop. This arrangement then lasted almost two years. In 1812, Mrs. Sonnenfeld spoke to Charles one day and told him that a Frenchman, a Mr. Le Coq, was the new head of the Police of Berlin. She advised him to write to Le Coq because otherwise he would some day be in trouble without papers. Charles received a summons from a Berlin magistrate to come and register himself with the city of Berlin. Charles followed her advice and wrote a letter to Le Coq stating that he was a descendant of a French Huguenot family, that he lacked papers and that he hoped that Le Coq could help him. A few days later, Le Coq came to visit Charles and brought with him the letter that Charles had written. He asked whether he was the person who had written the letter and did he have any proof that would reveal his identity?

Charles showed him the papers that he carried which had been sewn into his jacket by the faithful Montmorin several years before. The papers consisted of a letter from Marie Antoinette that described the physical signs of her son, Charles, and a letter from his father, Louis XVI, sealed with the seal of the King.

Le Coq immediately recognized the value of these documents and told Charles that he would talk to the King of Prussia about his case. In fact, Le Coq lacked direct access to the King but his superior, the Chancellor of Prussia, a Prince Hardenberg, did speak to the King regularly.

In a very clever book by the French author, André Louigot, called "The Sphinx of Potsdam", Hardenberg is portrayed as a dark force behind this whole sad story. Hardenberg was a highly initiated Freemason who would go to any length to control the French Government, and was heavily involved in hiding Charles from the rest of the world.

So now, Le Coq returned to Charles and asked him for the papers so that he could show them to the King. Charles cut his father's seal in a zigzag pattern, kept half and handed over his papers to Le Coq, who took them and promised to return them in a few days. Le Coq also gave Charles a roll of coins to help him survive in expensive Berlin.

After several days Charles received a notice to present himself in front of one of Berlin's magistrates and, once there, they wanted to know about his status as a citizen and watchmaker. Charles rushed back to Le Coq who told him not to worry and that he would take care of things. He said;

"First, I shall get your passport from the Border Police, come and see me in three days."

When Charles returned to the Chief of Police, Le Coq picked up the passport, looked it over and said:

"This will not work; it says here that you are forty-two years old and you look no more than the twenty-seven years that you are. Also it says that you have black hair and black eyes and you are blond with blue eyes. We must use something else. You cannot stay here in Berlin it is too dangerous. I will give you a letter of introduction. You may choose which town you wish to stay in. But we must keep your identity a secret from Napoleon and we will give you papers under the name of Karl Wilhelm Naundorff as it says here in this passport."

Charles never saw the passport in question except in the hands of his friend in the carriage and in the hands of Le Coq. The passport has never been found, although one of Charles' friends saw it some thirty years later when it was still in the Police of Berlin's files. This friend, the lawyer Xavier Laprade made a special trip to Prussia to check on Charles' story because even his friends did not blindly accept all that he had told them. Laprade spoke to many people who had known Charles, and for this had gone to Berlin, Spandau and to Brandenburg. He spoke to Charles' neighbours, his old friends and the local shopkeepers. The reports were friendly, everyone had liked Charles, his reputation had been good, and all that he had said had turned to be the truth. The passport was the only thing that the Police in Berlin could find in his file. It was made out to a Karl Wilhelm Naundorff born in 1775, and therefore ten years older than Charles. It was the passport that Le Coq had taken.

The other papers that Le Coq took from Charles, and that were to have been sent to Prince Hardenberg, are still missing. They were not in the Police station in Berlin, nor in the files of the Prince Hardenberg. There is a formal statement from the Duke of Saxe-Cobourg Gotha who states before a notary public that his brother-in-law, the Prince Augustus Wilhelm of Prussia and the son of William II, told him personally that he had the dossier of Naundorff in his hands just after the First World War and that from those papers the identity of Louis XVII was quite clear.

There is no doubt that a twenty-five year-old con artist would not have fooled a Chief of Police very long, nor would he have been able to get in to see the Chief, and especially so back in 1812. There can be no doubt that Le Coq and Hardenberg knew with whom they were dealing.

Charles returned to see Le Coq a few days later and when he received a letter of introduction for the town Mayor of Spandau, he then decided to go there. Le Coq had made one significant error in the letter of introduction, which was having Charles' name down as "Charles Louis" Naundorff instead of "Karl Wilhelm" and that alone shows that Le Coq knew very well with whom he was dealing. In November 1812, a new watch repairman named Karl Wilhelm Naundorff settled in the town of Spandau, complete as a registered citizen and a licensed repairman of watches.

There is no doubt that this could not have been done without Le Coq's help and as long as Le Coq remained alive Charles always had a protector. Only after Le Coq's departure did the long arm of the French Government reach into the small towns of Prussia.

In December 1812, when the French troops were retreating and marching through Spandau, they carried along with them yellow fever. Charles loved to speak French and often spoke to the passing soldiers, unfortunately this time he caught yellow fever. Mrs. Sonnenfeld saved his life by staying with him and nursing him day and night. Le Coq came to see how he was doing and even brought him some money on which to exist.

At a party held on December 31, 1812, Le Coq spoke to two former Frenchmen who now lived in Berlin. They were La Roche-Aymon and Poulain de Fays. He told them:

"Your King, and I mean, Louis XVII, was in danger here in Berlin and I hid him in Spandau as a watch repairman. I even gave him Prussian citizenship."

At this time Charles began to write to his sister, the Duchess of Angoulême, who was now living with her uncle, Louis XVIII. He received no reply. His sister had remained in the Temple after the death of the substitute Louis XVII, in June 1795, but suddenly she had received much better treatment. A week later a companion was appointed for her, and this was Madeleine Elizabeth Hilaire la Rochette. She was the wife of Bocquet de Chanterenne, a thirty year-old chief of

Confidential Matters at the Police Administration offices. Obviously, they were keeping a very close eye on the young Princess and, according to them, the sole survivor.

The Committee of Public Safety insisted that everything that happened was reported daily, and in September they even allowed the Princess to have visitors, such as the ladies de Mackan, de Tourzel and Mademoiselle de Tourzel. Madame de Tourzel was an agent of Louis XVIII, Charles' uncle, and she smuggled one of his letters into prison. They were all very curious about the death of Louis XVII, and one day Madame de Tourzel noticed the ledger of the Temple on the table. She started to read it but was discovered by Gomin, one of the old guards. He flew into a fit of rage. Madame de Chanterenne reported to the Committee of Public Safety that it would be better to stop such visits.

Meanwhile, Madame de Chanterenne had encouraged Marie-Thérèse to start writing her memoirs. It was very important for the Committee to find out how much Marie-Thérèse knew and thereby also, what her opinions were. It is obvious from the writings that the older married lady heavily influenced the young girl. She wrote about the death of her brother as if she were aware of it at the time, although she did not find out about it until much later. She had even written the wrong date. Her book was later "corrected" by Louis XVIII.

On December 6, 1796, the French Government exchanged the Princess for eight French soldiers and officers who had been captured by the Austrians. Among them was the notorious Drouet, the son of the

Postmaster who had stopped her father, Louis XVI, at Varennes.

Marie-Thérèse, upon leaving the Temple, first went to a virtually new prison in Vienna. There she was not allowed to see French people, including a representative of Louis XVIII, who desperately wanted to hear from his niece and tell her what he had in mind for her. Originally the plan had been for Marie-Thérèse to marry the Austrian Archduke Charles, but Louis XVIII insisted that her parent's last wish had been that she marry her first cousin, the son of the Count of Artois. This would mean that her inheritance, which was still substantial, would come to the Court of Louis XVIII and, because they were living on handouts, he needed it badly. The Count of Artois required a passport to leave for England, for otherwise he would have ended in debtor's prison.

After the restoration, Marie-Thérèse behaved very badly towards many people. Sometimes her behaviour was inexplicable, as it was when some officers who had fought with the Vendée for the preservation of the Monarchy, were presented to her. She turned away from them without a word. On another occasion she met some young girls who presented her with flowers. She would not hear them out, but abruptly sent them away with, "Well, what are you waiting for?"

Eventually she went to live with her uncle in exile in Austria, and later in Russia.

In France the revolution had progressed and a new type of Government was now taking over. Things had somewhat settled down and in 1799 a new constitution called for a Consulate of three Consuls to reign over France. Among the first three consuls was a protégé of

Barras, a young general who had much military success called Napoleon Bonaparte. In 1800, Napoleon became First Consul, in 1802, Lifetime First Consul; and soon after that he became the only Consul.

He married Barras' old girlfriend, the famous Josephine de Beauharnais, but he had not treated his old sponsor Barras too well. The Marquis de Broglio-Solari reported that he had lunch with Barras in the fall of 1803 in Bruxelles, and when Napoleon became the topic of the conversation, Barras said:

"I would like to see that Corsican skeleton hang for his ingratitude to me. He exiled me, who made him what he is. But he will not succeed because the son of Louis XVI lives."

Unfortunately for Barras he could not use the hostage, Louis XVII, against Napoleon, and beside that Napoleon did not need his old sponsor any more.

In May 1804, Napoleon crowned himself Emperor of France. In 1809 he divorced Josephine because she could not have any more children and he wanted to start another dynasty. The next year he married Marie Louise, the daughter of the Emperor of Austria, in Vienna. Now Napoleon felt that his new father-in-law would not attack him, yet in this he was very wrong.

Napoleon continued his fierce battles all over Europe. In May 1812, he invaded Russia and in 1813 he lost Spain to the English General Wellington. Then came the terrible retreat from Russia that cost France almost a full generation of men. Czar Alexander, having fallen further and further back, had played a waiting game with Napoleon and eventually let Napoleon take Moscow without much resistance. Now Napoleon was so far away from his supply line that his soldiers began to suffer from great shortages of food and winter clothing. It was the policy of the Russians to burn and destroy everything in front of the French and thus when the French advanced they found no shelter or food. Napoleon could not understand this way of fighting, yet it worked well for the Russians as it was also used again years later against Hitler.

On March 1, 1814, the Allies held meetings and signed the Treaty of Chaumont, which was a quadruple alliance of England, Russia, Prussia and Austria. One of its major points was that these four nations promised to come together whenever one of them was threatened. They also agreed that not one of them alone would make peace with Napoleon, unless it was along with the other three.

The discussions included terms acceptable to them for an armistice and the reign of France after Napoleon had surrendered. Everyone felt that the legitimate Government of France should be reinstated. For the Emperors of Russia and Austria and the Kings of England and Prussia, there could be no other Government but the Monarchy.

Of course, an acceptance by Napoleon of the terms of surrender might mean that Napoleon could stay, and thereby his position was still very strong and so other possibilities were also discussed. These included the Regency, during the minority of the King of Rome, Napoleon's son. Another possibility was to ask Prince Bernadotte of Sweden to reign over France. Bernadotte was a brother-in-law of Joseph Bonaparte, King of Spain. He was a General in Napoleon's army and had impressed the King of Sweden very much, who, since he lacked a son, had made him the Crown Prince of Sweden. Because he was a born Frenchman, they considered him; but he had been slow in his attack on Napoleon and therefore the Quadruple Alliance did not fully trust him.

Out of all their choices there is no doubt that the reinstatement of the de Bourbon family was the one with the most support. It was here that the King Frederick of Prussia revealed to the Czar that Louis XVII was hiding out in his country and that he was doubtful that this Prince, who had been brought up in prison, was sufficiently educated to reign over such a difficult nation as France. They then decided to support Louis XVIII, but to hold Louis XVII in the background as a sword over the new King's head.

Prince Karl von Schwarzenberg led the allied troops and had three Monarchs with whom to contend, who spent all their time visiting his headquarters. These were Czar Alexander, the King of Prussia and the Emperor of Austria. They all had their priorities and they did not make Prince Karl's command very easy.

Napoleon did not accept the terms offered at this time and he was never again given the opportunity to make a half decent deal. Of course for Napoleon there never was a compromise he wanted it all or he would fight until the end.

On March 30, 1814, the Allies reached the city of Paris and thereupon Napoleon was forced to leave so he withdrew to the Palace of Versailles. Talleyrand, the Foreign Minister of the French Government, invited the Czar Alexander to his home and that evening they discussed the future of France. Talleyrand promised the Czar that he could force the Senate to accept the de

Bourbons if the Czar promised not to make a deal with Napoleon or his family. The Czar was the major force within the Alliance and he agreed to go along with Talleyrand. The following day a Proclamation was posted in Paris announcing an interim Government headed by Talleyrand. Then the Senate voted to depose Napoleon but he was already busy planning a counter attack from Versailles. It took his Generals hours to convince him that without Government support the game was over, and Napoleon finally agreed to try one more tack.

He appointed Coulaincourt to head a delegation to go to the Czar Alexander to arrange Napoleon's abdication in favour of the young King of Rome, Napoleon's son. Alexander was much relieved that he finally had Napoleon in his hand and he therefore wanted to accept this offer. Now Talleyrand argued that they could not abandon the de Bourbons. The Senate had received assurances that Napoleon and his family were finished and that they must stick to their original plan. A further complication arose when Czar Alexander went to visit Napoleon's first wife, Josephine, in the Palace of Malmaison. She revealed the survival of Louis XVII to him. She was very bitter about Napoleon abandoning her and wanted her efforts for Louis XVII to bear fruit. Alexander told Talleyrand that Josephine was very determined to bring the survival of Louis XVII out in the open, but Talleyrand convinced the Czar that he had everything in hand.

Josephine died of poisoning four days later after having had a visit from Talleyrand. When Czar Alexander heard about this he exclaimed:

"That is a coupe de Talleyrand."

Thus they invited Louis XVIII to Paris, but only on a temporary basis. On April 10, with the Treaty of Versailles, Napoleon became sovereign of Elba with a pension of two million francs plus a further two million for his family. Two weeks later Napoleon sailed on the HMS Inconstant to the isle of Elba.

Louis XVII remained as a hostage for the good behaviour of Louis XVIII. At least he now had a normal life in Spandau, he had his work and for the first time in his life he lived like any other person.

He did not attend the Congress of Vienna which now took place and where all the Royalty of Europe met to carve up a new Europe. Even the family of Napoleon waited in the wings to see what they could rescue out of the spoils of war.

Shortly before Louis XVIII arrived at the Tuilleries, he received an ambassador from Rome who brought him an allocution from Pope Pius VI, written three days before his crowning as Pope. It showed that Louis XVII had escaped from prison and was alive and well. The historian Philippe Treberne in his story on Louis XVII wrote:

"Queen Caroline, wife of King George IV, wrote a letter concerning the great news most talked of which has her convinced in the survival of the Dauphin. Her brother, the Duke of Brunswick agreed."

It was now that Charles again wrote to his sister, who in the meantime had married her first cousin, the son of the Count of Artois. This marriage was, as we mentioned earlier, a devilish arrangement by Louis XVIII, who badly needed her inheritance. It promised Marie-Thérèse that she would be Queen of France when her uncle died, and she had to promise not to have children so that the Pope could bless the marriage of first cousins. This assured the Count of Artois that he would succeed to the Throne after Louis XVIII, and the inheritance of Marie-Thérèse therefore went to Louis XVIII. The best that Marie-Thérèse could expect from her brother was that she would be sister of the King, but now she would be Queen, after her new father-in-law's reign ended.

Charles, never, received a single word back from his sister. More than thirty letters to her went unanswered although he wrote to her about things that only brother and sister could have known. He promised to show her signs on his body that would convince her, but still she never answered.

Louis XVIII quickly began to reward the people who had helped him gain the Throne. He also gave pensions to those who had helped the Royal Family in the Temple, but never to those who had helped Louis XVII. Caron, who had been a cupbearer in the Temple, made an appeal since he had given much aid to Louis XVII. He then disappeared. If you asked about people who had disappeared, you received a severe warning.

In 1816, Madame Atkyns went to Paris to explain to Louis XVIII that she had expended all her funds to help the Royal Family. She received a good reception from all the clerks and other people in this department. They assured her that the King would appreciate what she had done, and amongst them was the Count de la Chartre. However she received nothing. She waited for several months and then received such a small amount that it was more of an insult than anything more. She wrote again, thinking that maybe they had not understood her, but by 1821, or five years later, she still had not received anything else. This was the rule for those who had helped Louis XVII. On January 9, 1816, Courtois died. He was the Member of Parliament who held all Robespierre's papers, including those from Louis XVIII, whose agent he had been. Decazes, Minister of Louis XVIII, sent twenty-five policemen to search the house to take every piece of paper. They confiscated everything. A month later, Louis XVIII even ordered a raid on the neighbours and friends of Courtois.

Four of the regicides, which had voted for the death of Louis XVI, received permission to stay in France. These were Cambacérès, Tallier, and Fouché and, believe it or not, our friend Barras. The other regicides were expelled from the country and many moved to Bruxelles and Switzerland.

The first restoration did not last very long. Napoleon announced that he was returning. When he landed in Juan les Pins on the Rivièra, many troops had already declared themselves loyal to him and a crowd awaited him. No wonder as Louis XVIII had not treated the military at all well since he took over. He had reduced their number, their titles, their pay and their pensions. Soldiers want to fight not to sit on the sidelines.

Napoleon immediately started another offensive against the Allies. They met him with the famous Wellington in command at a small town in Belgium called Waterloo. Napoleon was defeated after a tremendous battle that he had almost won. This was his last defeat, whereby he had to abdicate again and this time the Allies sent him to St. Helena, without any honours. He wrote his memoirs there and died in exile.

In ten years he had cost the French nation an untold fortune plus five million men.

There is one page in his memoirs of special interest to this story:

"There is a rumour about Louis XVII. They say he escaped, that another boy was substituted and sacrificed in his place and that everyone is trying hard to keep the truth from coming out. Josephine, while married to me, believed this strongly. She claimed she was very involved and told me who had helped, to whom he was sent and where he was now. I decided later to look into this and read the death certificate. I was very surprised to see the sentence: "They presented us a corpse that they said belonged to Louis XVII." They had nothing else that established his identity. I then had the body dug up, but all that we found was an empty coffin, Fouché and Savary were there. The box looked well preserved."

The second restoration dated from July 1815 onward. In 1817, during this restoration, Botot, the secretary of Barras, returned to France after fifteen years of exile in Switzerland. The historian, Dulance, spoke to him about the years 1793 to 1799 when Barras ran the revolution in France. Botot told him:

"The men who did the substitution of Louis XVII in the Temple were republicans and under orders from their bosses. He is not dead he should still be alive. He was our safeguard, and Louis XVIII knew it well."

On the ninth of January 1816, the famous parliamentarian, Chateaubriand, spoke in the Assembly in Paris. He asked why nothing was being done for Louis XVII. In fact, the Chapel Expiatoire did not mention Louis

XVII. This chapel built by Louis XVIII in memory of Louis XVI, Marie Antoinette and Madame Royale Elizabeth, but not the God-son from whom he had after all, inherited the Throne.

Chateaubriand proposed that a statue of Louis XVII be commissioned and that it be erected in Paris. His motion passed the Assembly, but the statue was neither completed nor erected. Louis XVIII never called for an investigation into the treatment his family had received in the Temple or why his Godson had died there of maltreatment. The last set of guards, Lasne and Gomin, received fine jobs and pensions instead of punishment, for letting the young King die. In all this Louis XVII was completely ignored, and even by his sister Marie-Thérèse who after her release from prison wrote her uncle:

"I ask you to forgive the French people, they killed my father, my mother and my aunt; but it is I who am on my knees and who begs you to forgive them and offer them peace."

Not a word about her brother. The sentiments that she expressed are those of her father who, before he went to the guillotine, talked to his children and his wife, and had told them to forgive.

Not a word about Louis XVII in the Chapel Expiatoire, no Mass said on the day of his death, and no service dedicated. A few years later there was a dance at City Hall on June 8, which Louis XVIII and his family attended. Unheard of on the day that a member of the Royal Family has died.

Meanwhile Charles was doing well in Spandau and in 1817 he befriended a French officer, Marassin, who was passing through the town. They became close friends and in an unguarded moment, Charles told him who he was. They talked about all the possibilities. Charles asked Marassin to contact his sister and to speak to her because she had never answered his letters. He gave Marassin some papers to show Marie-Thérèse and told him some secrets known only to her and her brother. Marassin left for France and Charles never heard from him again.

By now there appeared several false Dauphins in France. No doubt Marassin either played that role, or had had second thoughts and forgotten the whole matter.

On August 16, 1817, the pastry maker, Damont, who was Civil Commissioner and on duty when the supposed Louis XVII died in the Temple, went to visit the Captain of the Guards at the Royal Palace, the Duke de Gramont, to present a box made of red Moroccan leather lined inside with white velour. In the box was some reddish hair that had come from the body of the boy who died on June 8, when Damont had been on duty. Damont wanted to give this hair to the King Louis XVIII. The Duke de Gramont, who had known the young Louis XVII, looked at it and said, "It's the wrong colour hair." And he sent the box back.

Doctor Pelletan tried also to give Louis XVIII the heart of the boy that he had taken with him after the autopsy. Louis XVIII would not accept it, for despite knowing that Pelletan was the doctor who had performed the autopsy, he also knew that boy was not Louis XVII.

The following year was very eventful for Charles. He wrote to the Duke de Berry, who was the second son of the Count of Artois. He was very likely to become King of France one day because his older brother, who was married to Marie-Thérèse, did not have children. The Duke became very intrigued and sent his friend, the Count of Repentigny, to Spandau to contact this fascinating person who called himself his cousin. Simultaneously Mrs. Sonnenfeld became very ill and died in September.

Charles had become infatuated with a young lady, Jeanne Einert, who had lost her father at a young age. In November 1818, they married in a local church with the permission of the town Mayor although Charles could not produce a birth certificate. He decided that it was time to stop running. He decided to make a life where he was, with the trade that he was good at and which rewarded him well. He was so tired of running and hiding.

Meanwhile, the Count of Repentigny had been in and out of Spandau without Charles' knowledge and had made a favourable report to the Duke de Berry. The Duke now went to see his uncle, Louis XVIII, to confront him with what he had learned. There were several eyewitness accounts of this meeting because the doors were open and servants were walking in and out. It was the evening of the December 5, 1819. The Hussar J.J. Marcoux was in the hall near the door leading to the room where he heard Louis XVIII and the Duke de Berry arguing. At one point he heard Louis XVIII say:

"You are a fool, you are next in line for the Throne and you would throw all that away, for what?"

The Duke answered:

"Because he lives, my cousin Louis XVII is alive and he is the rightful King of France and I would chose justice over a crown."

The Duchess of Angoulème was also present and later told the Duke:

"This state secret could cost you your life."

At another door was the guard, d'Hozier, whose report on the same conversation varied a little, but remains basically the same:

"The King was really angry, he ordered the Duke never again to speak of his cousin. The Duke responded that he knew where he was. The Duchess of Angoulème, Marie-Thérèse, was also present and seemed to cry. It was easy to understand the conversation because everyone spoke really loudly. The Duke left by another door than the one I was guarding. A couple of minutes later the Duchess walked past me, she looked directly at me and I thought I have been caught. A few minutes later an officer came for me though my time was not yet up. He took me to the Duchess and when I entered I threw myself at her feet and asked her to have pity on my five children and me. She asked me to sit and said, "You have overheard a state secret and it could cost you your life. Do not speak of this matter as long as our dynasty reigns in France."

I did promise that, but now that they no longer reign in France I feel free to talk about it."

Six weeks later, on February 13, 1820, Louvel assassinated the Duke de Berry, as he came out of the theatre. Public opinion immediately concluded that the blame rested on Decazes, the favourite minister of Louis XVIII. Louvel claimed:

"I wanted for years to wipe out the de Bourbon race and I did not care who got it first."

Louvel believed to the last day that he would somehow get away with it. He was a liar as well as a murderer, because the Duke de Berry was definitely the chosen victim. Louis XVII was the reason.

Marie-Thérèse had also been warned that if she recognized her brother she was signing his death warrant. That was the only reason that she never answered his letters and could never meet him. Had he been a fraud, she could have exposed him in five minutes. Cardinal de Lantil gave the Duke of Berry his last rites and no doubt heard his last words.

The King did not do anything other than protect his protégé, Decazes, but when public opinion became too strong, he fired him as minister and gave him the much desired post as Ambassador to England. The death of the Duke de Berry is a very suspect affair, and current history books still do not give it the proper emphasis. Yet there is still one happy bit of an ending to this story. The Duchess found out, a few weeks after the death of her husband, that she was pregnant and the little boy, who was eventually born later, became the last member of that branch of the de Bourbon family, the Count of Chambord. He reigned for a day as Henri V and then died in 1883 without children.

The Duke de Berry had married earlier in England, when he was in exile during the revolution. His wife was Amy Brown and she had three children: George Brown, the Countess d'Issoudun and the Countess de

Vierzon. The Countess d'Issoudun married into the very illustrious French family of Faucigny-Lucinge. As the Princess Faucigny-Lucinge she left behind some memoirs and there, one can read the following:

"The Princess de Lucinge remembers well that her father, the Duke de Berry, at her mother's apartment, rue des Matharias, spoke of a violent argument that he had with Louis XVIII, about Louis XVII (Naundorff), whom he recognized and about whom he had proof."

She wrote the memoir in her own handwriting. The Naundorff name in brackets is part of the complete statement and has not been inserted by me or anyone else.

The loyalty of this family, which continues until today, will be rewarded if not by me, then by someone who stands above all this and who shall make the final judgment.

We are now in 1821 and Charles has lived in Spandau for ten years and has meanwhile become a well-known and respected citizen of the town. He had a great friend in the town Mayor, Daberkow. This year Daberkow fell into disgrace with Prince Hardenberg, who wanted him removed from his post. Charles took up his friend's fight and in the end Hardenberg relented and moved Daberkow to Brandenburg as Mayor.

Charles decided to follow his friends, because he felt uneasy to stay in Spandau where the fight had split the citizens into two camps.

There his old problem showed up again, for he did not have the right papers. However the new Mayor of Spandau sent a letter to Brandenburg, and Charles became a citizen of Brandenburg. In 1823, Goupilleau de Fontenay died. He was the friend of Barras who twice went to the Temple when there were reports that Louis XVII might have escaped. As a regicide that had voted for the death of the King, he was exiled in 1816, but allowed back into France in 1819 probably because he was in on the secret. He told his relatives:

"The child that died in the Temple on June 8, 1795, was not Louis XVII and all the pretenders are false."

By this time several pretenders had shown up in Paris, and they probably already numbered twenty. Of course, Charles was still in Germany and so Goupilleau was right.

The next year, 1824, was very eventful. On the anniversary of his father's death, Charles was overcome and wrote his uncle Louis XVIII. Thirty-one years had passed and still his uncle had not acknowledged that he was alive. He wrote that he was going to take his case to the people of France. This got a very speedy response, but not what Charles had hoped for. No doubt the French court feared the return of the legitimate King of France. And something had to be done. On March 24, 1824, the theatre next door to Charles' went up in flames. Charles had just enough time to get his family out of the house and to save one or two pieces of furniture, but otherwise he lost most of it. They charged Charles with setting the fire, which was silly since he was the only victim except for the people who owned the theatre.

The charges were dismissed but the damage done to his reputation remained. His enemies were also upset because their plan had not worked, and they needed to take Charles out of circulation. In France, Louis XVIII was deadly ill and any pressure from Charles could easily upset everything. They took the threatening letter very seriously, notified Hardenberg and told him to get Charles out of the way.

They filed a new charge on September 18th, 1824. This time it was a charge of making false money. Charles had paid an amount of money as a down payment on a new house. He had only a small amount himself, but a friend had loaned him the balance. At the time of the deposit nothing was said, but the following day when the cashier opened the receipts from the day before, he found some false coins inside, or at least that was his testimony. They accused Charles of having deposited them. They could have been his, but more likely his friend's, who had given him the larger part of the deposit or, even more likely another depositor from the bank. The Police had a witness who had seen someone throw something in the river. The cashier insisted that the deposit came from Charles, and thus they filed charges against him. At the same time the Police picked up the son of a well-known counterfeiter who had already spent time in prison once before. This felon was then prepared to testify against Charles.

They threw Charles in jail to wait for a hearing, time dragged on and there was nothing that he could do. The trial judge took his time because he was waiting for confirmation of Charles' birthplace and birth date. This caused a real problem because the judge just could not seem to find this information, and he made a very thorough investigation; yet still no records. He called Charles in and demanded an explanation. Charles told him that Naundorff was not his real name, that he came from a well-known French family and that the Chancellor Hardenberg and the Chief of Police for Berlin, Le Coq, would speak for him. The judge made new inquiries into the birthplace of Karl Wilhelm Naundorff, but he still had no responses.

Then the cashier who had testified against Charles hung himself in the room where the questioning had taken place. Now there was only the testimony of the convicted counterfeiter. Finally the trial went ahead and the judge had two existing laws under which he could find Charles guilty. Law 254 specified a jail term of four years for making counterfeit money, but Charles had only been charged with passing counterfeits. Law 256 specified eight days to six weeks for passing or possessing counterfeit money, but to find Charles guilty of that would mean he could walk out of jail, for he had already spent that much time in prison.

The judge found that Charles was not guilty of counterfeiting; however, he imposed the most extraordinary penalty that he could, that of three years in jail for misguiding the court about his name and birthplace. The judge indicated that Charles had misled the court and this meant that he could have been capable of the crime.

This sort of penalty no longer exists, of course, and it was terribly unfair since it was far more than the penalty of a guilty verdict. Still, it did the job, and it kept him out of the way.

I have yet to read a book about my forefather that finds that he was not Louis XVII which does not call him a counterfeiter, when in fact he was never convicted of this crime.

In Paris, Louis XVIII was dying in the Royal Palace and several officials gathered with the family in the hall near the death chamber. There were at least two

Ministers of the Crown and Monseigneur de Lantil, Great Chaplain of France, also Mr. Villèle, Talleyrand and the Viscount Sosthene de La Rochefoucauld. Directly after the death, they read the King's will. At the very last moment Louis XVIII decided to recognize his God-son, Louis XVII, and in his will he asked his brother, the Count of Artois, to find him and install him on the Throne of France.

There was strong consternation at the meeting. Monseigneur de Lantil stated that the country was in a time of great peril and France and its Government could easily fall if not governed correctly. He was very concerned about the position of the Church, which wanted to have its former position and possessions returned. Knowing that the Count of Artois was an arch conservative, he would then, with King Charles X, be assured of the Church's position. He argued that in this unsettled period it would be very dangerous to bring in an unknown King.

The Count of Artois was standing in the middle of the room with his brother's Will in his hand. He was stunned because his brother had always promised him the succession. Suddenly he abruptly turned, walked to the fireplace and threw the Will in the fire. The others in the room rushed to him and congratulated their new King. One of the first acts of the new King Charles X was to promote Monseigneur de Lantil to Cardinal.

The Viscount Sosthene de La Rochefoucauld wrote in his memoirs:

"I remember well the scene between the Count of Artois, Monseigneur de Lantil and several aristocrats, who found themselves in the antechamber of the room where Louis XVIII lay dying. The enigmatic conduct of

200

Monseigneur de Lantil. The sacrifice of the will that was thrown in the fire, which immediately gave him the title of Cardinal Archeveque of Rheims by him, who now became Charles X."

In 1825, Charles X told his doctor, the Baron Alibert:

"It is with hesitation that I accepted the crown and I have asked the Holy Father, through Cardinal de la Fare, if in all conscience I could accept. The Holy Father responded that in view of the circumstances and in view of the troubled state of France, and to create the least problems, that I could for the moment accept."

Yet for his cousin Charles in Germany, it did create some great problems, because as father and main provider of his family, he had to spend three years in jail for a crime that he did not commit. They crowned Charles X in Rheims, something Louis XVIII had never dared, and the Church now again became so strong in France that it reigned over the King. The old families flooded back to France and started to demand back their properties and titles. These moves would soon bring France back to a nation before the revolution, and to all its former abuses. So, when an election was held in 1827, only 50% of the electorate voted for the Monarchy. The country lacked a leader, and there was no real direction.

In 1830, there was another election but it too resolved nothing and in July, Charles X was forced to abdicate in favour of his grandson. The Government then decided to call on his cousin instead. He was the Duke of Orléans—Louis Philippe.

The Orléans family had been scheming for the Throne since well before the revolution, they had voted for the death of their cousin Louis XVI; but this had lost them much popular support.

Now came their opportunity, but not as King of France, for Louis Philippe became "King of the French".

Chapter 12.   THE CROSSEN MEMOIRS

When Charles was released from jail in 1828, he had served his full three-year term. He had to leave the city of Brandenberg and went to the town of Crossen, where he applied for citizenship. Although he could not satisfy the laws regarding papers from the previous place of residence, nor those laws that stated that citizenship could be refused someone with a criminal record, again Charles had no problem and was accepted without delay. The town council found that.

"...there is no good reason why the watchmaker, Charles Naundorff, should not be given citizenship."

Once settled in Crossen, Charles soon met a Colonel Netter who had twice been in the Palace of Versailles. He had been part of the occupancy forces in 1815 and knew the Royal Palace very well. Charles told Netter that the French revolution had wiped out his family, but did not tell him which family that was. They talked about the layout and about the furniture in the Palace. Charles amazed the Colonel with his knowledge, and the Colonel later stated that Charles had convinced him that he had been there, before.

The Colonel's wife became Godmother to one of Charles' children and, two years later, Colonel Netter himself became a Godfather to another child. Charles had also made friends with Mr. Pezold, the local Commissioner of Justice for Crossen, who became his first really serious follower.

It was Pezold's duty to check on new citizens for the town of Crossen, and he was soon intrigued by the newcomer from Brandenburg. They became close and Pezold started to write on behalf of his new friend. He wrote to Charles X, to the King of Prussia and to the Duchess of Angoulème—Charles' sister. This time she did write back, but only to say that.

"...she did not want to mix into this affair."

As the last three years had really put him behind, Charles worked very hard to keep his family fed and sheltered. Slowly he worked his way out of his debts and was soon again the good provider of before. Pezold however, had little success with his letters. He asked his friend to write down his adventures so that they could be published in order to divulge the story that way. Charles, with much help from Pezold, then wrote his 'Crossen Memoirs', but he could not get them published because the King of Prussia forbade it for "diplomatic reasons". These memoirs, written in the romantic style of the day, today might sound a little exaggerated to us, however, we must remember that his lonely travels started when he was only ten years old. He was without friends or family, and lacked relatives who could remind him from time to time of things that had happened. He was always under constant supervision or in jail. Never free for even ten minutes to play outside as other children did. Not knowing where he was or what day it was he only knew day and night by the sun. For one horrible stretch, from 1804 until 1808, he did not even see the sun even once. Names given to him by strangers were most often false, and he never located any of them afterward. He tried to locate "Lebas" in Switzerland, but the real name was Leschot. Many people who had looked after him died under strange circumstances.

The full text of these memoirs had never been published in book-form until 1992. Charles did publish another memoir years later, but that book called, AN ABRIDGED ACCOUNT OF THE MISFORTUNES OF THE DAUPHIN was written for the most part by Charles' lawyer who sometimes changed things to fit with history the way we know it; but it was not always as Charles had remembered it. In a few instances, Charles' memories were better than the guesses made by his lawyer. Because Charles and Pezold wrote theirs earlier, and outside information affected them less than the later version, the Crossen memoirs are therefore probably closer to the truth.

As Charles spent so much time in jails or in hiding places, he had a great amount of time to think about his past. He had very few current experiences that were of any interest, and so his mind kept going back to the days in Versailles, the Tuilleries, and the Temple, to his parents and to his sister. It is therefore those days and scenes that he remembered so well, having a remarkable memory for those events. From 1795, when he escaped from the Temple, to 1808, when he finally got out of the prison of Vincennes little is known.

He begins his story during the time that he spent in the Temple prison—first with his father and the manservant Cléry, then with his father teaching him, and then with the visit of the gentleman who left his father with a roll of gold coins, which meant they could buy a few extras while in jail. Only the Dauphin, his father and this gentleman know this story!

He remembers very well the day that they took his father away. He remembers very well the moment that he was with his mother, and the terrible pain he felt when they tore him away from her and put him with the Simons. The shock for a boy of nine years old to be torn away from his family, must have been grave and he dwells on it throughout his story. He tells of being sick with pain and of the terrible things they made him say and do. He remembers the period when his bedding became infested and when he had sores on his body from insect bites.

He describes how Laurent came to see him one night to take him out of his cell, and put him in the furniture storage area. He remembers how he promised to keep quiet and how cold it was, but that he was still happy to tolerate these inconveniences. This is followed by the escape and the meeting with his new "stepmother". He does not want to give names, wishing to keep some information for his day in court when he will reveal everything His "stepmother" tells him that she will only speak German to him, that he must only use that language to speak to anyone, and that he must act as though he was her son for it is the only way they are going to succeed with the escape. He is finally treated humanely and recuperates from his terrible experiences in the Temple. He stays with her for some time when suddenly one night some men come, grab him, take him away, and put him in a dark cell. Later they take him away again, to another cell where an old woman takes care of him, and there he stays for a long time. He is eventually rescued from this prison and recuperates again with a father and daughter who are very tender with him. The girl's name is Marie and they become good friends, telling each other their problems.

One day they introduce him to a young hunter, Jean Montmorin, who then guides him for the next few years. He thinks this is happening in Italy and that he has travelled there through Switzerland. They tell him that they are in Milan and then in Venice, but he never really sees anything and must simply take their word for it. They then come to a port and leave on a boat, he goes with them willingly because they keep telling him that they are taking him to his mother. The father, his daughter and Charles settle into a small country house and from time to time Montmorin comes to visit. He may be in England or perhaps America, and even the Caribbean seems a possibility. He falls very ill again and once more Marie nurses him well. Then one day she tells him that his mother has died several years before, and this news breaks his heart.

Then he meets his "stepmother" again. She has since remarried and her new husband is a watch repairer. Now for a while at least he lives an almost normal way of life. He is being taught the watch-repair trade and enjoys almost complete freedom, spending his free time with Marie. He believes that he is in the "land of freedom", and therefore could this mean America? But most likely it is Switzerland and he is with the Himely family. Then suddenly his "stepmother" and her husband are poisoned, and die. Who is behind this? It is time again to move, and the house blows up just after they have left it. They arrange to leave by boat. Charles recognizes the captain as someone who has been spying on him. The following morning he finds

Marie and her father dead from what seems to be poison. The boat takes them to the coast of France instead of England, as had been arranged. There they lock him up again, and by now he is beginning to doubt whether even his friend Montmorin is a true friend.

Because there are just too many strange circumstances, he confronts his friend who explains that indeed the captain of the boat had sold their secrets. He confirms that Marie's father was poisoned, but he does not know why Marie also died. Did she possibly drink out of the same glass? Montmorin explains that several people have now lost their lives because of Charles, and that he is still in constant danger and therefore sometimes he must be locked away where no one can reach him. Montmorin explains that they are on their way to the Duke of Enghien who is at Ettenheim. Charles is so tired of all the running and Montmorin promises to go and fetch a carriage. While waiting for Montmorin, their pursuers find Charles, catch him, travel for several days in a carriage, and once again he finds himself back in jail—this time for several years.

His jailor has a slash mark on his face and is later identified as the jailor of the castle of Vincennes. The story then continues with an escape arranged from this prison by Montmorin. They then travel to the Duke of Brunswick, who sends them to Major Schill. This is followed by the death of Montmorin and Charles travels to Berlin.

This, therefore, is the story of Charles from his escape from the Temple to his arrival in Berlin. There is almost nothing here that can be checked, for there are neither dates nor definite places by which to go. They only told him what they wanted him to know, and he was under constant supervision or in jail. Never once did they let him out of their sight.

I doubt very much that these people were all his friends. It would have been very easy for them to travel to England where King George had promised to look after the children of Louis XVI and where the Duke de Berry lived along with several other members of the family. Or they could have easily taken Charles to Austria where the family of Marie Antoinette still reigned and where they would have welcomed him with open arms. Or they could have taken him to Spain where the Spanish de Bourbons were after all waiting to take him from the revolutionaries. No, he was NOT in friendly hands!

Over the last one hundred and fifty years, parts of this story have been confirmed. The period of 1804 to 1809 that he described as an internment in a building with a dark, long hall and by a man with a long scar on his face was definitely the dungeon in the Chateau de Vincennes – used as a prison. The writer, Robert Ambelain, in his book, LE SECRET DE BONAPARTE, reveals the warden as a man with the nickname "Le Balafre" or "The Scar", and whose real name was Jacques Harel. Ambelain rediscovered the letter that Mrs. Louise Ducrey, the daughter of Mr. Bremond, and secretary to a minister of Louis XVI, had addressed to my great aunt Amelie. In it Mrs. Ducrey writes:

In about 1834 or 1835, I do not remember exactly the year, my father met a German political refugee named Strohmeyer. He told my father that during his years as a political agitator he knew a man called "Le Balafre" or "The Scar", because of a large scar he had on his left cheek. This man was the jailor of Louis XVII and had him in his prison for four years from 1804 to 1808, I think. The same Strohmeyer told my father that not only could he verify the story of that imprisonment, but that he later knew the same Louis XVII when he lived ignored and hidden under the name Naundorff.

The jailor's real name was Jacques Harel, Captain in the 45th Brigade, and he was the jailer of Vincennes until 1808 —when Doumesnil replaced him. In 1813, Harel became Governor of the Fort Morland in Holland, where he died the following year. His portrait is in the book by Colonel de Fossat about the Castle of Vincennes—complete with the scar on his cheek.

Books written on his life in Switzerland with the families Himely and Leschot have substantiated a much earlier segment of Charles' travels.

Charles did not want to give away all his secrets either, because he kept hoping for his day in court. Unfortunately he never had that day because, being persecuted to the day that he died, he has found justice only with God.

Yet his friend Pezold in Crossen remained convinced and continued his letter-writing campaign. He wrote to every Head of State, including the Ambassadors of Denmark, Sweden, Russia, Naples and France and to many members of Charles' family. Not one of them answered.

Then Pezold put an advertisement in the Gazette of Leipzig on August 1, 1831:

"In Crossen, close to Frankfurt on the Oder, there lives the supposed son of Louis XVI, under an assumed name. He is Charles Louis, Duke of Normandie, and since the death of his older brother, Dauphin of France. He has written his memoirs, the history of his life and sufferance. Forced by circumstances to have them printed, he seeks an editor. Please send all inquiries to Justice of the Peace Pezold in Crossen."

Even publication of this advertisement was suppressed. Pezold received a letter from Hamburg that the advertisement could not run there. The Ambassador of France had objected strongly to its content. However a retired lawyer, Albouys, of Cahors, France read the appeal and an active correspondence now began between Pezold and Albouys.

In early 1832, Pezold received a visit from the Prince of Carolath and his secretary, the Baron of Sender. They had come to warn Pezold about his association with the supposed Louis XVII. They were very upset; but still they could not sway Pezold and neither could Pezold convince them of the sincerity of Naundorff. They left and the following day Pezold became violently ill. He died a few days later and his doctor wrote later in a letter that he was convinced that Pezold had been poisoned. The Government confiscated all the papers in Pezold's possession. Unfortunately he had held some papers for Charles and these too were taken away. Even after several requests, nothing was ever returned. Pezold's friend, Lauriscus, now took over the position left open by Pezold's death, and he promised to continue the support that Pezold had given to Charles. Four weeks later Lauriscus also died.

Then Charles heard that the King of Prussia had decided to put an end to these efforts initiated in Crossen and had planned to put him back in jail; but this time for good. Charles knew that they could carry out their threat as they had done so often before. He decided that he had but one option, and thus he said good-bye to his family and with three shillings in his pocket set off to Paris to reclaim his rightful name.

Chapter 13   RETURN TO PARIS

France's General Doucot in 1870 :

"I believe I also speak as a political man when I say that a great nation such as ours has always risen from her material ruins, but it will never rise from her moral ruins."

Charles leaves Crossen with three shillings in his pocket and a passport that allows him to travel only to Berlin. There he must apply for a passport to go to Paris. He had tried to obtain one for France, but it had been refused. He is afraid that they will use that opportunity to detain him and thus decides to leave the Kingdom of Prussia as soon as possible. If you think back to those days you rode a carriage if you were well off or you walked.

He heads for Dresden in the hope of seeing the Royal Family of Saxony, whom he knew from before. When he tries to see them, the Police threaten to throw him out of the country because he lacks a valid passport. He goes to see the French ambassador and after some difficulties manages to obtain a letter that allows him to travel to France, but because some of the ambassadors' objections seem a little far-fetched, Charles becomes weary of the way that he treats him.

By now he has spent his three schillings, but he meets a Priest in Freiberg who loans him twenty-five crowns. He can pay for his hotel bill and continues toward the border of Bavaria. He travels on foot to save money and when he gets there he has a chat with the border guard. The guard tells him that the ambassador of France has passed through a little while ago and had asked many questions about Charles who had not yet reached there. Charles now decides to head for Switzerland because he is afraid of what might be waiting for him if he tries to cross the French border here. He remembers both his friend 'Lebas' who helped him and his "step mother" when they first escaped from the Temple, and he hopes that he can find the former in Geneva. Yet again he runs into trouble because he does not have the right passport, and they expel him.

On May 26, 1833, almost a year after leaving Crossen, he finally arrives in Paris. He is broke and lacks a clear idea of what he wants to do. His French is poor and his only contact in all of France is the old lawyer Albouys, in far away Cahors. Albouys had been corresponding with Pezold and had accepted the job as representative of Charles in France.

So Charles writes him for money and meanwhile lives in Paris eating unripe apples that he picks in the park, and at night sleeps under the stars. During the day he visits the old places that he remembers from his youth. The Temple has been destroyed and it costs money to visit the Tuileries, so he sees only its park. He travels to his dear Versailles that is almost two days on foot and again all he is able to see is its gardens.

One day, very disillusioned, he sits in a park and a young boy asks him if he has a place to stay. When

Charles tells him that he lacks the money for that, the boy replies that he knows some good people who will give him a room while waiting for the rent. Charles follows the boy and meets the family Jeannot at 19 rue de Menilmontant. The room is about the size of a broom closet, but still it is much better than the outdoors. Albouys finally writes him a very cool letter to a hotel that they use as a mail drop. In it he tells him that he should see his brother who lives in Paris and who will put him up So after a month of utter poverty, Charles moves in with the family Albouys at the rue de Buci.

At last in August, Albouys himself comes to Paris and meets Charles for the first time He wants proof of his Royal birth, but all Charles can show is his body. Together they check the marks that Louis XVII carried and now Albouys sees the same ones on Charles. Albouys is finally convinced and starts a letter-writing campaign, yet, because there is very little money, they live a very frugal life.

One day a friend of the family named Ferdinand Geoffrey, former official of the Court of Charles X, comes to Paris and here we let him tell his story:

"The day of my arrival in Paris, August 8, I met on the Circle Buci one of my old friends, Mr. Bricon, who is a librarian. "Nice to see you in Paris," he said. "Let me tell you a bit of news. You have often talked to me about your belief that the son of Louis XVI is alive. Well he is here, or at least there is. Listen all pleasantries aside, there is a Mr. Albouys, a former magistrate, a very honourable man who has introduced me to this person. I have read some really amazing letters from Germany and Mr. Albouys has asked me to publish the man's memoirs. But it is necessary to add to the proofs the testimonies of several old servants of the Court. Do you know any? After all you were at the court of Charles X. Come and see me tonight, Mr. Albouys will be there and we will talk about it.

I made it to our meeting on time and they showed me those important letters of Mr. Pezold, the Justice of the Peace for Crossen, in Prussia, whose death is subject to so much inquiry. Still he had managed to send enough information and his convictions to the French magistrate that I see in front of me.

I accept an invitation to go with them that same evening to the rue Buci and to meet "Mister Charles", as they now call him. His speech has an accent and sometimes he has to search for a word, but it is well worth meeting him. Our interview was wonderful and he resembled very much the former Royal Family.

After I returned to my room I really needed my sleep after such a hectic day and sunrise takes me by surprise. Have I just dreamed it? The hand that has pressed mine, whose is it, that emotions have so overtaken me?

Five days after this strange meeting I am busy with plans to continue my trip. Then in the evening of the 14th I am in Versailles to see Madame de Saint-Hilaire, a very distinguished lady, formerly from the household of Madame Victoire, aunt of Louis XVI and later attached to the household of Empress Josephine. The lady listens with much interest and with astonishment when I tell her about the Prussian watchmaker and about his friend Mr. Albouys.

Mr. Marco de Saint-Hilaire, her husband, is a former Hussar of the household of King Louis XVI, and he also listens and is very surprised. "Will you spend tomorrow with us, Mr. Geoffrey?" asked Mrs. de Saint-Hilaire very graciously. "It will be a beautiful day to contemplate all that you have told us."

The following day, August 15, as we are leaving for church, Mrs. de Saint-Hilaire says to me:

"I have an excellent idea, I know in Paris Madame de Rambaud, formerly chambermaid to the Dauphin. I know her well enough to write to her and, if she believes at all, in the survival of the Dauphin, then I am sure she will follow where you will guide her. I will give you the letter to deliver. If it is him! Oh, how we will want to know about that interview, and if not she will expose him and will surely embarrass the good gentleman from Cahors."

Thus on August 17, at 8:00 a.m. I present myself at Madame de Rambaud, who lives in the Bonne Nouvelle area of Paris. She is very surprised when she reads the letter of Madame de Saint-Hilaire and she listens very attentively to my short story. "Very good, Sir," she says. "Let us take a coach. But just a minute, I have here somewhere a costume that the Dauphin wore when he was five or six years old."

Madame de Rambaud brings it along and also a bust of Marie Antoinette, dressed in a veil, and we depart. When we arrive at the house on the rue Buci, they let us in and we entered the living room. After a few minutes Mr. Charles enters. Madame de Rambaud sat in a chair; she rose and sat down again, without any emotion. She did not give him her name, only that when she was young she worked for the Queen and was attached to the Dauphin.

"You must have been very young, you are Madame de Rambaud? Oh, I am so glad!" Charles said.

That he knows the name does not mean very much, because anyone could have learned the names of the Royal household. Now Madame de Rambaud, still with a reserve, starts to ask several questions about Madame de Tourzel. Then she asks about the Abbey Davaux, the teacher of the Dauphin. To all she received satisfactory answers or sometimes he would say he had forgotten, but never half an answer or a guess. About the Abbey Davaux he remembered very well tripping over his coat and falling down a staircase.

Then Madame de Rambaud gave him a statue and tears came into his eyes. He gave me the statue while he searched for his handkerchief that he had left it in another room, and so I got up to get it. When I returned he said while he pressed my hand, "You have brought me a mother."

The conversation continued Madame de Rambaud kept her emotions well in control, she said, "I have here a costume that I have saved as a remembrance of my little Prince. They would not let me enter the Temple with Madame de Tourzel. Maybe you remember when and how you wore it in the Palace of the Tuileries?"

The minute he saw the little light blue costume he spoke up, "Oh, I remember it well, it was not in the Tuileries but in Versailles that I wore it for a holiday, but I think I wore it only that once because it did not fit me very well."

Then Madame de Rambaud could no longer hold her emotions and she approached him and fell to one knee and said, "Only my Prince could have told me that."

And she took his hands and pressed them while tears came to her eyes.

I had listened to all this and I was sure that Madame de Rambaud had laid a trap for a possible impostor. Afterward Madame de Rambaud again got a chance to look after the Dauphin because he became ill and she got an opportunity to see on his body the signs that really identified him—the scar of the rabbit bite on his lip, the scars of the inoculations and especially the birthmark on his thigh. The mark that looked like a bird with its wings extended.

Madame de Rambaud later left a notarised statement about these signs and, in part, she said, "The signs, which I noticed when he (Charles) was young, I noticed now again and together they took away any doubts that I may have had. The Prince had, even as a child, a short heavy neck with strongly wrinkled skin. I have always said that that was a sign for me that I would always recognize. Now that he is older, of course, and his neck has become much thicker but it has basically remained the same. He had a large head, a broad and high forehead, blue eyes, wavy eyebrows and blond hair, which was naturally wavy. His mouth was that of the Queen and he had a dimple in his chin. On his wide chest, I knew of several markings especially a sign on his right breast. His walk was always strange. Except for his age, this is the same person that I knew before."

Madame de Rambaud was a very astute lady, and even if some writers have described her as a dithering old lady who did not live for anything but to see her Prince again, she was not someone who would easily be swayed. Theirs is an entirely wrong picture, for she was well in control until she received overwhelming evidence of mental as well as physical nature.

Madame de Rambaud immediately wrote to Charles' sister, the Duchess of Angoulème, saying:

"I have seen him, he is alive."

The Duchess does not answer.

Two days later the family de Saint-Hilaire dropped by and they also recognized the 48 year-old Prince, who has not been in France for almost forty years, who speaks a terrible French full of German words; but who nevertheless, by his stature, his gentleness and his knowledge of his youth, convinces everyone whom he sees.

A recent book written in France claims that Charles could read minds and that is how he could read the correct answers in people's minds as they asked questions. That then would explain how he managed to get these right answers. If this were true, he would have been a lot more successful and he would not have needed his illustrious background. It would have also warned him about all those who were good to his face, and who had turned against him once out of sight.

There can be no doubt that Karl Wilhelm Naundorff knew intimately personal details about Louis XVII, his family and his friends and many details about the court that never had been disclosed before. Of course, some of it he could have learned from books and articles, although not that much was available in Germany about the last days of the Royal Family of France. Many memories first revealed by Charles were later confirmed by other sources.

Besides the nonsensical theory of mind reading, several historians have come up with even stranger theories, such as the tale in which Naundorff met somewhere with the real Louis XVII and learned all his secrets and then used them to impersonate him. Why are these strange theories necessary to set aside a very simple explanation, unless you need to hide something with imaginative words?

Several days later the family de Saint-Hilaire gave a dinner for the Prince and invited about twenty guests. The number of converts climbed almost daily and while most were simple people, several had held important posts at the Court.

Among the fifty-three former members of the Court who recognized Louis XVII were Bulot, the lamp watchman of the Temple, the English Admiral Sidney Smith, who had been a prisoner of the Temple, Jacques Cazotte, page to the King, and also Madame de Saint Brice, the Dauphin's chambermaid.

Yet another letter from Mrs. de Rambaud to Charles's sister had by now also remained unanswered. Then Madame de Saint-Hilaire tries with:

"God, my conscience and my soul impose on me the obligation to write to you that your poor brother is alive and he is living with us. I can assure you that I am as sure of his identity as I am sure there is a God."

The Duchess of Angoulème again does not answer, but this time she does at least send the Viscount of Sosthene de La Rochefoucauld to her brother, to observe him and to speak to him. He sends her a written report:

"His attitude is simple, he does not seem calculating or put on. He speaks well and full of feeling, he understands French perfectly but speaks it less easily. It must be difficult for Madame to understand my strange feelings when I hear a man like him speak so normally about his family, his sister, who you are, Madame, of his highness the Duke of Berry, who died because of him, of Henri V whom he wants to recognize, and whom he wants to crown and see blessed simultaneously as himself. My heart and my head are turning. Still he has in his manners and in his tone and in his stories about himself nothing that resembles audacity or pride, and he does not come across as a rogue."

In January 1834, Charles sends one of his dear friends, Morel de St. Didier, to Prague where the Duchess is in exile. There he asks for an audience, which she then grants. The Duchess listens with great care, but she continues to comment negatively about everything that St. Didier says. She ends the interview with:

"It is absolutely necessary that I speak to the King and to the Dauphin (her husband) about this, because I can do nothing without letting them know and without their consent."

She remembers well the arguments she overheard between the Duke of Berry and Louis XVIII, and she knows well what happened to the Duke when he decided to recognize Charles. Besides they have told her that if she makes any moves to recognize her brother, she signs his death warrant at the same time.

Thus nothing ever comes of all the interviews, letters and pleas to her, and it is the rejection of his sister that hurts Charles the most. Having lost both his parents at such a young age and under such horrible circumstances has been a very traumatic experience for him, and now the only living member of his immediate family does not even want to see him! It is this rejection, with that of his Church, that finally affect Charles so much that he starts having visions and becomes mentally unbalanced.

Still the group around him grows and thereby becomes ever more influential. Among the young men who follow Charles is a Mr. Thomas who now proposes that the group sponsor a daily newspaper that he will write and publish. Everyone likes the idea and for it they start a fund. Once it reaches 20,000 francs they give it to Thomas, and he starts 'La Justice' which informs the public of Charles' story and about his efforts to get his name back. Unfortunately young Thomas had some heavy debts from previous bad investments and his creditors, who see that he is again gainfully employed, begin to chase him for their money. It takes only a little while and the money is all spent. Now Thomas gets an offer of funds from the opposition to work against Charles, and he turns against his benefactor.

With these funds Thomas instigates a suit against Charles for misrepresentation and fraud. Charles has no option but to start a counter-suit for the 20,000 francs. The case finally comes to court but twice Thomas claims that he is not ready to proceed. He is also to deposit with the Court the papers that prove his claim, but these nobody ever sees.

Finally the judge sets a new Court date and Charles is ready, but again Thomas asks for a postponement. This time the judge refuses to grant the postponement and finds the case in favour of Charles. Charles is very disappointed to win by default, because he thereby loses his chance to present his own case in Court. He will never get that opportunity.

Due to the publicity, Charles now gets a chance to meet two very important people whom he has not seen since the revolution.

The first one is Étienne-Louis-Hector de Joly, born in Montpelier in 1756, who was secretary of Louis XVI's Council and a confidant of the King. On July 3, 1792, he became Minister of Justice, which already then was one of the highest positions in the Government. During and after the revolution he made his living as an independent lawyer. I am going to let Mr. Marcoux, whose testimony on the fight between the Duke of Berry and Louis XVIII we have already seen, tell us the story:

I, the undersigned, declare that the facts from now on are the complete truth.

I know Mademoiselle the Countess of Mouvoir, who, if I am not mistaken, lives on the rue des Augustines in Paris. One day, I do not remember the exact day; I met her and spoke to her about my meeting the Duke of Normandie (Charles) and about how he had convinced me. What I said surprised her and she did not agree with me. We went over it, several times. I gave her all the information that I had. These details did get her interest and she asked me, "Does the Prince really exist?" I told her, "Madame, I assure you, the son of Louis XVI is alive. "Then she said, "I know Mr. Joly, the last Minister of Justice under Louis XVI, and maybe he could verify the claims of the Prince and help him be recognized. I will talk to him."

Sometime later Madame de Mauvoir told me that she had seen Mr. Joly, that she had spoken to him about the Duke of Normandie, that the conversation was very lively and that the Minister had said, "Ah, not you too Madame, how can you say a thing like that and divide the Legitimist Party when the whole world knows that the son of Louis XVI is dead! Send me the man who told you the opposite and I will soon straighten him out."

I was very surprised when Madame told me that. I live in Versailles and, before I went home, I presented myself at the home of Mr. Joly. He answered the door himself. I did not know him. I asked if I could speak to Mr. Joly, he answered that he was Mr. Joly and what did I want. I told him that Madame de Mauvoir had sent me and he asked me into his study and sent his secretary away. When we were alone he said, "Madame de Mauvoir told me that you are convinced of the existence of the son of Louis XVI."—"That is true," I replied,

"But you would have to be insane to think that. No one doubts the death of the Dauphin. I have many books on the revolution. Every author writes about the death of the Dauphin."

I do not remember everything that happened during this interview, I told him all I knew. He insisted that he was going to show me that I was the dupe of some impostor, who wanted to upset the Legitimist Party.

I told him that if I were wrong, it was with the best intentions, that if he could convince me I would not object to his proofs. The discussion became quite heated, but we both stayed with our own opinions, our discussion broke up without any results and with a somewhat bitter feeling, and I did not think I would see him again.

I was therefore surprised when, on another trip to Paris, I again met Madame de Mauvoir and she told me that Mr. Joly wanted to speak to me again, to prove to me again that the son of Louis XVI was dead. I told her that I would certainly like to be better informed and I promised her that I would go to see him.

When he saw me he said, "I have asked you to come because I believe that you are sincere. Can I meet your so-called Prince?" On my affirmative reply and my assurance that the Prince willingly could meet with everyone, he asked if we could see him today. When I went to see the Prince, he was very happy that he was going to see a former Minister of his father's Court, and he begged me to bring him at four in the afternoon and for me to be there as well to see what would happen.

Later the Prince came in accompanied with several other people, and I got up and introduced Mr. Joly. The Prince looked carefully at the man and said to him, "I hear you have served my father, my friend." The Prince greeted everyone as a friend. Mr. Joly replied: "That is possible, Sir."

The Prince asked him to sit and sat across from him. Soon the conversation was about the survival of the Dauphin. To make sure of his memory Mr. Joly started to ask him questions about his youth. The Prince soon corrected the errors that the minister made on purpose. I do not remember all the details, but the conversation was very interesting and all went well for the Prince. It seemed as though his memories were correct as Mr. Joly listened attentively and made no comment.

226

It particularly concerned the trip from the Tuileries to the national Assembly. I remember clearly how Mr. Joly on purpose made an error and the Prince told him right away, "You are wrong, I remember that there were large windows." I think even, but I may be wrong, that he added that these windows had iron bars. I do remember still that Mr. Joly said, "You walked most of the day." The Prince said, "No, my friend, I was on my mother's knee, I even slept." I am almost certain that Mr. Joly said, "You asked me for a piece of bread." The Prince said, "I do not remember that, but I remember complaining about being hungry and I remember eating soup." Then Mr. Joly decided to leave and said, "I do not know who you are, but you do remind me of someone I knew."—"Maybe I am the truth." said the Prince. "That is not always the case," said Mr. Joly, "I have three children and two resemble me but the third one does not at all, I still consider myself as his father."

This all happened on a Monday in 1835. The conversation had been long and involved and we made an appointment to meet again on the following Wednesday. I was not at this meeting. Having brought Mr. Joly back home, I asked him, "Frankly, what do you think about the person to whom I introduced you?"—"I am not convinced," he said, "but I can tell you that he has the words, the gestures and the way of walking of Louis XVI and those things are hard to imitate."—"Well," I said, "you make me happy saying that."

We said good-bye and promised to see each other sometime in the future. I saw Mr. Joly a few days later when I again visited Paris. It surprised me that he had again seen the Prince and he said, "Yes, he is the son of Louis XVI." I said with sarcasm, "Well, Mr. Joly, now you are also dividing the Legitimist Party."—"Yes," he said, "you have the right to laugh at me. If I had not heard it with my own ears and had not seen it with my own eyes, I would never have believed it. Now nothing in the world can change my opinion that he is the son of Louis XVI, because all that he told me I know about and cannot be known to anyone other than the Dauphin and me.

I have read this testimony, dictated by me and it contains the whole truth.

Signed: Marcoux

Retired Hussar of the Chapel of the Palace and Member of the Household of the King.

The recognition by Mr. Joly is very important in the list of fifty-two servants and members of the old Royal Court, all of whom acknowledged Charles. Mr. Joly held a very high position and was very close to Louis XVI. He was an excellent lawyer, well aware of how people could be fooled and taken in, but he also knew that Charles' memories were of a very personal nature and just could not have been known except by people who had personally gone through these events.

Mr. Joly was one of the very few people who accompanied the Royal Family during that last day of their freedom, when they went from the Tuileries to the National Assembly. He was thus in a very good position to ask questions about that day, but he did make an error about the iron bars on the windows. The Prince had corrected him, but Mr. Joly had not been sure. On the next meeting he had confirmed that the Prince was right and it was this that so impressed Mr. Joly. It convinced him that this man must have been there and observed things that he himself had not noticed.

Mr. Joly wanted to make sure that his testimony would remain after his death and a notarised original of this still exists.

The reluctance of Mr. Joly is rather typical of all the old friends and acquaintances of the Royal Family whom Charles encountered. On first hearing of yet another Dauphin the common reaction was:

"I want nothing to do with this phoney, take me to him and in five minutes I will show you another false Dauphin."

So Charles had an uphill battle with almost all of them, because every one of them wanted to prove him a fraud, and therefore all the false Dauphins stayed far away from these old servants.

At this time one man was still alive who was even closer to Louis XVI than was Mr. Joly. His name was Jean Baptist Jerome Bremond, born at Brindles on February 8, 1760. He was Deputy of the State of Provence at the Assembly of Notables, and he did his work so well that Louis XVI soon noticed him. He made him his Personal Secretary and Knight of the Order of St. Louis. In 1792, he became Secretary General of the Ministry of the Interior under his friend Antoine-Marie-René Terrier—the Marquis of Monciel.

In July 1792, he and the Marquis of Monciel left France and fled to Switzerland. The United States Ambassador, Governor Morris, who was in Paris reporting on the revolution, often mentioned him in his dispatches. Both Bremond and de Monciel were in his complete confidence, and acted as intermediaries between Louis XVI, the political parties of the time and the American Ambassador. Bremond received from Louis XVI a sum of 60,000 gold francs for safe keeping for the Dauphin, should anything happen.

In March 1835, Charles wrote to the then King Louis Philippe and told him that to prove his claims he needed to get a box that his father, Louis XVI, had made and had hidden in the palace of the Tuileries. Charles wanted permission to look for it. There were also precious stones and gold coins in the box. Louis Philippe gave the Duke de la Borde, his personal assistant, the job to look into this matter. He was to give permission for the search, but, if he found any papers, he would have to give them to Louis Philippe. That, of course, was not in the interest of Charles and therefore he dropped the matter.

Still, six months later the story became public knowledge and was published. Mr. Bremond read it and knew immediately that here was the real Dauphin, and he contacted and invited Charles to come to Switzerland.

Mr. Bremond had heard officially in 1796 that the Dauphin had escaped and therefore he had watched and listened to all the false Dauphins. This because he had promised his former master, Louis XVI, that he would look after his son. But repeatedly he had been disappointed because they were all impostors. Now it was almost forty years after the revolution and Bremond had practically given up finding the Dauphin.

For Charles it was also a wonderful encounter, because he continued to live a precarious existence with no income except the help that his friends had given him. Now, with the acceptance of Bremond, he finally had some funds. He could send for his wife and children who could then stay with Mr. Bremond in Switzerland. He could buy them a few presents and new clothes. The mother and the oldest daughter, Amelie, had been holding the family together for two years without any income except what they themselves could earn. Life had been very hard for them because their husband and father was on his way to Paris. Without work and funds, he had been able to send only small amounts from the meagre donations that he had received. Now, for a while, everything went well.

A few years later, when the French Government sent Judge Zangiacomi from France to Switzerland in an attempt to get information on Charles in order to prepare a case against him, Mr. Bremond had testified. Not being able to build a case the Government dropped the matter, but the testimony still exists and it shows very well how much Mr. Bremond trusted and accepted Charles. His statement reads as follows:

Bremond: "I am ready to testify to the truth, as far as my conscience allows me to say, without divulging secrets that I must guard for his excellency Prince Charles Louis de Bourbon, Duke of Normandie, until he will divulge them in front of a court in Paris or an assembly of Kings of Europe."

The Judge: "Do you know a person who calls himself Charles Wilhelm Naundorff and also calls himself Charles Louis de Bourbon, Duke of Normandie and the son of Louis XVI?"

Bremond: "Yes, I know him and I will tell you all about him."

Judge: "Were you in Paris in 1792?"

Bremond: "I lived in Paris since 1786 as a Deputy to the Administration of States for the State of Provence, and I remained in Paris until about four days after August 10, 1792. Since then I did not return to Paris until November 1819."

Judge: "Were you the Private Secretary of Louis XVI?"

Bremond: Yes, I was his Personal Secretary and honoured to be in his confidence, and I filled that position from the beginning of 1788 until August 10, 1792."

Judge: "During that period of 1788 to 1792, did you know the son of Louis XVI?"

Bremond: "I saw him up close several times between 1788 and August 10, 1792, but I do not remember speaking to him during that period. I saw him years later and I will explain myself when I am asked a specific question about that."

Judge: "Have you reason to believe that this Prince, son of Louis XVI, escaped from the Temple prison in Paris?"

Bremond: "I am convinced of it before God and before my fellow men. I would like to add that certain proofs on which I base my conviction I couldn't divulge because the Prince wants to speak about them himself."

Judge: "Do you believe this person is still alive?"

Bremond: "I do so believe and he honoured me by coming to visit me in Semsales in 1836, that is last year. That is when he came to consult me about whether he should take his sister, the Duchess of Angoulème, to Court or not, to reclaim his rights. He returned to Paris and on his arrival at that city he did seek an appointment at Court, but instead he got thrown out of the country over the legal objections made by his friends."

Judge: "What makes you think that he is still alive?"

Bremond: "Because I saw him last year at Semsales and even today I am in contact with him by mail. He is in London under the protection of the 'Habeas Corpus' law and the custom of the English which protects the safety of its citizens."

Judge: "What proof did the Prince give you?"

Bremond: "In particular because he knew about the box his father had made at the Tuileries, the box that he alone knew about, since he was the only witness when his father closed it. Also the Prince told me other details and those he wishes to keep secret until he tells them himself. The details he gave me about the box at the Tuileries are for me positive proof."

Judge: "How did you know about the box at the Tuileries?"

Bremond: "From his majesty King Louis XVI, through the Count of Monciel, then Minister of the Interior. He asked about the safe that held the secret papers that could be uncovered in bad times and when it was necessary to take some papers out. The King mentioned that that had already been done and that if he died he had deposited in a secret box, with his son, the authentic documents that his son would need one day to establish his identity. The Count of Monciel told me about the King's answer."

Judge: "What was the name of the lady, born in Switzerland, widow of a Swiss guard who was killed on August 10, 1792, who was disguised as a man in the Temple who looked after the Dauphin after his so-called evasion from the Temple?"

Bremond: "I do not know her name."

Judge: "Do you know if Charles Wilhelm Naundorff still has the papers that without doubt establish his identity, papers that supposedly were sewn into his jacket by Montmorin and later presented to Mr. Le Coq, President of the General Police of Prussia?"

Bremond: "I know that the papers given to Mr. Le Coq and by him to the Prince of Hardenberg have been lost, because the search made by Mr. Laprade in Berlin lacked results. But these are not the only papers the Prince had in order to show his identity. He told me that he still has in his possession a paper, in Latin, signed by Pope Pius VI and there also exists in his Holiness' archives in Rome a letter that confirms his escape from the Temple. I also know that the Prince has a key that opens the box that his father made. His father was an expert in locks, he is the only one that knows how to open it, and that means no-one else can open this box even with the key."

Judge: "From whom do you know that there is a letter in Rome that proves that the Dauphin escaped from the Temple?"

Bremond: "Mr. Laprade told me this, he said that in his researches in Rome they made him aware of its existence."

Judge: "You speak of a key belonging to a box. Where is this box?"

Bremond: "This is the box that Louis XVI made in the Palace of the Tuileries. It is the box that I spoke about a minute ago."

After the interrogation Mr. Bremond made a statement and the following sentences out of that statement are of particular importance:

"I regret the way that the French Government has chosen to bring justice to this case. I regret very much that the French magistrate is here to make inquiries to try to prove a case of swindle against Mr. Naundorff, the son of Louis XVI. Nevertheless, Naundorff will speak the truth before God and my fellow men.

I also wish to say that King Louis XVI knew that the conspirators wanted to proclaim a republic and to lock up the Royal Family in the Temple. I know this as his Private Secretary and I was honoured to be in his confidence. The King then also sent some observers to the Temple to see if anything could be done to make their future stay there easier.

I personally know an observer, the late Mr. Thor also called de la Sonde, and I wish to say that while I was in Paris in 1820 I ran across a nephew of this man. When I asked how his uncle was he replied that he had stayed at his uncle's home in 1797 and that his uncle was accompanied by a blond boy of about eleven or twelve years whom he did not let out of his sight. He called him Mr. Auguste and after staying there several weeks, he left one night with the child and returned several days later alone and he told me, "You have had the pleasure of meeting the Dauphin, who escaped from the Temple. Do not say anything about this."

I confirm with this that I know, from what he has revealed to me, that Mr. Naundorff is this Dauphin, the true son of Louis XVI. I swear before God that nobody but the real son of Louis XVI knew about the box that I mentioned since he was alone with his father, when he hid it. I add for the benefit of Madame the Duchess of Angoulème that this may turn her away from all the misinformation that she has heard. The box held souvenirs from her dear parents and was made by the Kings' own hands, it was hidden in the presence only of her brother and this alone shows her who her brother is. He is the only one who knows where it is, because she knows that everyone was looking for this box while the Royal Family made their first visit to the Palace at St. Cloud. (The revolutionaries in fact tore the walls apart to find evidence for the trial of Louis XVI.)

I also want to say that the King wanted to reconcile with the King of England, George III. Count Mercy d'Argenteau, Ambassador to Austria, was charged with that delicate task. He went to England, obtained an appointment to see the King, and brought him a hand-written letter from Louis XVI, asking for his friendship.

They made a secret treaty by which the King of England would undertake to do his best to help the Royal Family of France escape from the Temple, and to help the Dauphin, should he become an orphan, against the conspiracies that would surround him. In England the King does not always gets his way, for the ministers of his Government often prevail.

Further I wish to say that Louis XVIII, after the assassination of the Duke of Berry, came to his senses and wrote a note in his own hand in which he wrote that his nephew, the Duke of Normandie, was alive. He urged his brother, the Count of Artois, to recognize their nephew, to place him on the Throne and to declare him King of France. This extraordinary paper was locked up in a special safe with a double lock and put in his room.

I finish my testimony by again stating that the son of Louis XVI is alive and this is now a historic fact.

Signed: Bremond

We have seen what happened to the will of Louis XVIII.

Bremond was a very active writer and wrote to everyone whom he thought might help. After the abdication of Charles X, the French finally turned to the Orléans branch of the de Bourbon family. Louis-Philippe became King of the French, not King of France, and the last thing that he wanted to see was to have his cousin recognized.

Miss Bremond, daughter of Mr. Bremond, has left us a statement about her father. In it she speaks of the requests that her father received from time to time to surrender the funds that Louis XVI had left with him for his son. The first invitation came from Napoleon, then Louis XVIII and later Charles X. All promised Bremond a brilliant career if he would return it and if he would accept them as the legal heirs of Louis XVI, but Bremond stayed loyal to his promise to Louis XVI to the end, and he kept the funds for Louis XVII. Louis XVIII and Charles X both treated Bremond equally; both gave him twenty-four hours after his refusal to leave the country. In fact, Charles X had him picked up and escorted out. That is why, although the revolution had long been over, Bremond still lived in Switzerland.

Meanwhile, Charles was attacked while walking in Paris, and de La Rochefoucauld wrote to the Duchess of Angoulème:

"Madame,

There has been a noteworthy occurrence. On January 29, a man came to see me in great haste to inform me that on the previous evening at about eight o'clock the personage (Charles) had been stabbed several times with a dagger. That one wound was deep, but that his life did not seem to be in danger.

I went to see him the next day and I inquired with great detail in all that had happened. I asked to see the wound and they showed it as well as his clothes, which were cut by several thrusts, and all his clothes were soaked in blood. The wounds are close to the heart, and over the heart there is a large bruise from a silver medallion which has a hole right through it and seems to have stopped the knife, which otherwise would have been fatal.

I realize how important it is that you are fully informed of everything, so I have sent a clever and discreet surgeon to see him (?), he knows nothing about his identity. The facts have been checked with scrupulous precision. He has been bled (!) and a diet prescribed for him. The patient is in good spirits, but the festering of the wound shows that it must be very deep and must have been nearly fatal."

Two men had attacked Charles in the Place de Carrousel. They had not robbed him of anything, and a motive for the assault was never established. Writers who disbelieved the survival of the Dauphin caused rumours that the wounds had been self-inflicted.

I personally saw the scratch on the shoulder blade as I stood next to Doctor Hulst in Delft in 1950. As the forensic specialist back then also confirmed, it is impossible to stab yourself in the back on the shoulder blade with any force.

Many more of the old servants and friends joined Mr. Joly and Mr. Bremond. Among them was the Marquis de la Ferrière who had also been locked up in the Temple, and who was convinced by the things that Charles knew about the interior of it. Then there was Madame de Forbin-Fanson, mother of the Bishop of Nantes, the General, Marquis de la Roche-Aymon, who knew Le Coq and who had heard from him about Naundorff, the Count de Brean, the Abbot Jouy and, very importantly, Pauline de Tourzel—one of the first visitors to the Duchess of Angoulème in the Temple and an old friend and daughter of the Governess for the Royal Children.

Charles had gathered all his papers and the testimonies of his friends and old servants who had recognized him. His case was complete, he had his lawyers prepared, and his funds were in place. He finally found himself strong enough to take his case to the Courts.

Chapter 14.   EXILE AND DEATH

On June 13, 1836, the Hussar, Louis Jules Garnier, brought a petition from Charles Louis, Duke of Normandy, to the Court in Paris. It demanded to have his death certificate set aside because it was in error, and he was very much alive. The petition also mentioned Charles X and the Duchess of Angoulème, both of whom were now living in exile in Prague.

Two days later the Police picked Charles up at the home of Madame de Rambaud and confiscated 202 papers that he had ready for the trial. They used a law permitting the Police to pick up any tourist in France, although by now he had been in France for over two years and was thereby a resident. They held him for twenty-six days without charges. His lawyers and his friends made appeals but they were all rejected. Even the Courts ruled that, since the order came from the Cabinet, there could be no appeal.

The lawyers for Charles filed the following appeal to the King:

"Sire,

We appeal to the justice of the Throne against an illegal action of your Government, which the Government took a fortnight ago, against the illustrious Duke of Normandy, the real son of Louis XVI. He has been unlawfully arrested, his papers have been confiscated, and orders have been made to have him expelled from France with the intention of preventing him from prosecuting his suit before the proper judges.

An appeal to Your Majesty to prevent an unconstitutional act will no doubt suffice to obtain the immediate liberation of the Prince, in whose name we make this protest.

We are, Sire, most respectfully Your Majesty's most humble and obedient servants.

Gruau, Barrister at Law, Formerly State Attorney.

Bourbon-Leblanc, Barrister at Law,

Xavier Laprade, Barrister at Law,

Briquet, Barrister at Law.

Paris, June 28, 1836

Gruau is the latest of Charles' converts and he has given up his job, his home and his practice to devote all his time to help Charles. He stays as an adviser to the family, and eventually as foster father to all the children until he dies some fifty years later. Charles also gets help from an unexpected source, Cremieux, later Minister of Justice, who took Charles' side and told the Cabinet:

"Before the Minister gave the order for the arrest and expulsion of the man whom he calls Naundorff, the latter, under the name of Charles Louis, Duke of Normandy, son of Louis XVI, brought an action in this matter before the French Courts, which, since it is a matter that concerns the State, are the only competent tribunal. He had appealed to the Kings' Courts and a

Minister of the King has had him imprisoned without a warrant. Gentlemen, the revolution of 1789 abolished 'lettres de cachet' once and for all. Is it possible for a Minister or a Prefect of Police to keep a man in prison for twenty-six days without a warrant? Really, gentlemen, one must not be able to say that we live in a land of barbarians, we, whose hospitality has almost become proverbial. I declare plainly, gentlemen, I am not afraid of the answer to that question, the arrest is contrary to justice, and the expulsion is illegal."

The Cabinet still rejected this appeal on the pretext that the matter concerned the Secret Police. The fear of having this man bring a case to Court was too great for France! It had to resort to illegal manoeuvring to have this case from coming into the open.

The papers that were taken from Charles have not yet been returned, and without them a Court case has been a farce. The excuse is that the papers are missing.

A police escort accompanied Charles to the coast where they put him on a boat for England, rather than expel him to Germany from where he had come. It is the last time that he sees his homeland, and it is the end of his day in the Courts of France.

This alone really sets Charles apart from all the false Dauphins. All others got their day in Court, and many received long sentences; but such a chance could not be taken with the real Dauphin.

The Court cases in 1874 and 1954 came too late, for by then death had caught up with the principal witnesses such as Madame de Rambaud, Minister Joly and Mr. Bremond. And of course the papers were still missing.

It is only through the persistence of the lawyer Gruau that the family could finally obtain a receipt for the 202 lost papers from the Police Commissioner Barbes. From England, Charles continued his fight by dictating his memoirs to his lawyer Gruau de la Barre.

Unfortunately Gruau made changes where he thought Charles was making mistakes in dates and places. Gruau made them fit with history as he knew it, and the results later backfired because it turned out that Charles was right—his memory being better than Gruau had expected and the changes that Gruau had made turned out to be errors. They published the memoirs in England and sent them over to France.

Customs promptly confiscated them all in Calais so that the original French version is not to be found. The French Police did not treat this as a simple case of impersonation, but as an Affair of State.

In Vienna, the police arrested a bookseller who had sold the memoirs. He was fined and all his copies impounded. In France the police invaded the home of the family de Saint-Hilaire and seized all the papers that they can find.

In England the Reverend George Percival translated the memoirs. He is the second son of Lord Arden and a nephew of Spencer Percival, the Prime Minister of England, who was assassinated. The Percival family helped the de Bourbon family a great deal and later after the death of Charles, paid the widow Jeanne de Bourbon-Einert a pension until her death in 1888.

The English Royal Family could not help because they had a problem in that the cousin of the Queen, Helene de Mechlembourg, had married the Duke of Orléans, son of Louis-Philippe—King of the French. Another problem was that the Duke was a Catholic and Helene an Anglican. Also, the English Parliament was a partner in the decision made to back Louis XVIII rather than Louis XVII.

The funds from Bremond kept the family going for several years and some of it was spent on paintings of the Royal Family of France and on good furniture. Much had also gone into experiments that Charles was conducting, for he had a great interest in explosives. Unfortunately almost nothing was coming in and Charles again gets into trouble with his creditors.

The circumstances did spur him on to work hard on his inventions and to finish his book on religion. When the book was finally ready and published, its only result was that he loses many of his adherents. His gains are nil, but he has done it because he believes in it and Gruau de la Barre supports him in this Where Gruau should have warned him and kept him in line, he instead encourages Charles. Gruau himself publishes two books on religion under the pseudonym of Eliakim and his influence over Charles was great.

In 1836 Charles' family is living in Dresden. The famous doctor Jean Carro treats the mother and becomes so convinced that he is dealing with the French Royal Family that he writes that he would sooner believe his own son is not his than that Charles is not Louis XVII. In 1838 the family joins Charles in exile in England and for the first time in five years they live an almost normal family life. Charles continues to work on his inventions and his followers continue to try to further his claims.

Fate eventually catches up once more and on November 16, 1838, he is again attacked. This time he is shot twice while walking through a park near his home. His assailant is Désiré Roussel, a Frenchman who has visited Charles in Clarence Park and asked him for help. He claims to have left France because of his political views. Charles decides not to press charges and again his detractors claim that he has shot himself. For what reason is not clear, because he gains nothing from it, just as he had not gained anything after the first attack.

Then in 1841 there is a fire, and the explosive materials, which he was working on, do much damage. He loses much and he lacks insurance. The creditors are after him and again life becomes difficult. They move to a smaller house and in 1842 there is another explosion and fire. This time he is thrown into debtor's prison for nine months, while the furniture and the paintings are seized and sold.

However, the inventions are finally starting to pay off, and the most important item is almost ready. It is a bomb, actually a grenade that explodes on impact. The reporters call it "the final weapon", with which the whole world can be destroyed. They write that this "Bourbon bomb", is so powerful that nobody would dare again to start a war, as it could destroy the whole world.

Charles first offers his weapon to France, which is his country, but it declines and wants no part of the man who claims to be the son of its former King. Perhaps they feel that he is trying to further his claims with his invention.

He then offers it to England, but the engineers who are investigating his product continue to come back for more and more information, and Charles suspects that they are trying to duplicate his work and thereby copy his invention.

There is interest from the continent, especially from Austria, and Charles decides to travel to Europe; but he must go via Holland because he cannot travel through France. He obtains a passport from the embassy in London, and it reads Charles Louis de Bourbon, born in France, naturalized in England. He travels with an English artillery officer, Colonel William Butts, and since Charles has had so much trouble in the past with passports, the colonel also has, just in case, a pass for himself and one for a servant. Even before they leave, the ambassador tries to make Charles come back with his passport, for he has the intention to tear it up and now claims that he issued it in error. Meanwhile he has notified the Dutch officials in Holland that Charles is coming, and several letters exist in the Dutch archives that show the great interest that everyone has in the Duke of Normandy. The Police Chiefs of Amsterdam, Rotterdam and The Hague have been notified to keep a sharp lookout for him. The description given is: grey hair, balding with grey temples, a light coloured moustache, a rough exterior and a somewhat heavy build.

The boat arrives in Rotterdam, the passports of Charles and the Colonel are sent to the Minister of Justice, and they receive permission to land. The same day the Police notifies the King of Holland, and he has no objections except that he hopes that the man will not stay in the country for a long time. They move into the Hotel St. Lucas where the Police keep them under daily observation. The former archivist of Delft, the excellent Dr. Oosterbaan, even discovered a policeman's daily report on their surveillance. It is dull reading.

After a few days Charles tries to get his passport back but is refused, and so he then attempts to make an appointment to see the King. He wants to show the King his inventions. He writes that he is not here to further his claims to the French Throne, that he has given up trying to do that and he now only wants his inventions to be recognized. The King orders his Minister of Foreign Affairs to see him and there is a conference; but the results are again negative. They do not want to become involved with him, and they would like him to leave the country.

Meanwhile Charles is trying to see everyone he can think of, including the Minister for the Navy. The Minister lacks funds for new weapons or for demonstrations. Charles keeps on trying, and the Minister for Defence is next; but since the King has said no, the Minister can do nothing. Charles decides that he must hire a lawyer to help him and he chooses a man known for his monarchist feelings His name is van Buren and Charles makes an appointment to see him. They get along very well right away, which is unusual because van Buren, being very bright, is not easily convinced by fancy stories. At school he was first in class and he is a very shrewd lawyer.

Van Buren goes to work immediately, demanding that the Minister of Justice return Charles' passport and gets Charles an appointment to see his friend, the Governor of the Dutch Military Academy—a Mr. Seelig.

The Academy is in Breda so Charles and van Buren travel there.

After a long conversation Seelig becomes convinced that Charles does know what he is talking about, and decides to call his staff together to have a look at a demonstration of his inventions. Among those who attend is Lt. Colonel Delprat, still today considered a top Dutch artillery officer. Charles throws one of his grenades on the frozen river and causes a six foot hole and ice flies all over the place. He then makes a miniature cannon with a percussion starter instead of a common wick. This new method results in the cannon to have almost no recoil and thus it is far more accurate at an even greater distance. Charles also claims that with the same discovery he can take most of the recoil out of a rifle. The Dutch officers are most impressed, but they want to see more and would like to have further proof of all that Charles tells them. Charles, on the other hand, is reluctant to show too much since in England they have held him back for months while trying to copy his inventions.

He has a solid backer in van Buren whom he trusts, and he prepares to show his experiments on a larger scale. Seelig writes the Ministers of Defence and of the Navy, and, because he feels that he can learn a lot from this man, asks that he be allowed to continue to deal with Mr. de Bourbon.

The ministers confer with the King who decides to give his permission, but the dealings, because they cannot become common knowledge, must remain strictly between Mr. Seelig and Mr. de Bourbon.

Meanwhile the King will make further inquiries about Charles through his Minister of Foreign Affairs, who contacts his people in Germany, Prussia and in France. Charles now gives a much larger exhibit of his inventions. He shows them some of his rockets with which he has trouble since he cannot control their directions. He shows more of his exploding grenades, which are very impressive. His greatest successes were the rifle that had almost no recoil and a small marine mine that exploded with great noise and a huge fountain of water. The whole academy turned out to see the demonstration and everyone was most impressed.

Then the Dutch Government starts to get back some reports from their embassies. From France, of course, it is bad news. The King Louis-Philippe could hardly say anything good about someone who was after his job and whom he himself had thrown out of the country. Yet the report from Prussia has an interesting line in it:

"The Prussian Government can neither come up with the town where this man was born nor with his parents. We made all kinds of efforts but we could not find any records of this man before 1810, we do not know where he was and who he was."

The report from England states that this man may very well be an impostor and con artist and to treat him carefully. A further report is ordered from Prussia and Dr. Oosterbaan has found it in the Dutch archives. Dr. Oosterbaan is in charge of the municipal museum in Delft, where there is a substantial deposit of items about the de Bourbon family. It gives in great detail the story as told in this book from 1810 onward, but it claims that Le Coq's papers cannot be located, and it gives no indication of what happened with the papers confiscated to the estate of Pezold.

250

Dr. Oosterbaan argues that it seems clear from these reports that Holland is dealing with a type of impostor, and that makes the Dutch Government's ultimate decision so very important. After the second demonstration the Government decides to appoint Lt. Colonel de Bruyn, another artillery officer, to investigate fully the discoveries presented by Charles. Charles has decided that the price for his discoveries is 1,000,000 Dutch guilders. The oldest son, Charles Edouard, who has helped his father from time to time, now also arrives from London and he registers into the same hotel in Rotterdam under the name of Charles Edouard de Bourbon. This makes the Chief of Police for Rotterdam upset and he writes to his superior at the Provincial Government. They tell him to leave Charles Edouard alone and in peace.

The Government decides to make a deal with Charles over the objections of the Ministers of Justice and Foreign Affairs. The King has undoubtedly received information from somewhere that convinces him that what he is doing is right, yet unfortunately the archives have been searched and that what influenced the King cannot be found. The decision is made to offer Charles a contract and the terms are spelled out. The Government decides that all must be kept secret and the King signs a secret Royal Decree on June 24 1845.

The terms of the contract are certainly unusual for that time. Charles has promised to bring the Dutch Government an explosive that is greater than anything yet existing. From now on rifles will be designed so there will be almost no recoil, new grenades will be made that will explode on impact and new sea mines will have a power greater than ever before imagined.

Charles will become the Director of a new Ammunition Factory, and he will live in Delft. They will pay him 80,000 Dutch guilders the first year, 20,000 the second and 16,000 the third. Should the inventor die, then his son, who knows most of his father's inventions, will be paid 12,000 per year. If the inventor can stop the recoil of rifles, then he will immediately receive 60,000 guilders. If he fulfils all the conditions of the contract within one year, then he will be paid 1,000,000 guilders. In 1845 this amounts to a real fortune!

Charles signed this contract and the Minister of Defence, the Minister of Colonies and the Minister of the Marine all countersigned it. This then is finally a victory for Charles. It was Louis XVI who had installed in his son a passion for mechanics. He finally receives the recognition that he deserves not so much for his noble birth, but rather for his personal endeavours.

Yet now a new enemy arrives. During a walk on the beach in Scheveningen, a mile or two from my old high school, Charles fell ill with heavy stomach cramps. He stayed ill for two days in The Hague where he was attended to by one of the best doctors in town. Then he felt better and most anxious to start on the design of the recoil-less rifle that would have immediately given him sufficient funds to pay back Mr. van Buren and to allow him to send for his family, which was still in England. After a few days, however, the pains returned. Meanwhile the loyal Gruau was busy making arrangements through the Government to bring the family over. The King himself took great interest and wanted to be informed daily about Charles' health. The Minister of Defence sent the Army's Inspector General of Health, Dr. Snabilié, over to Delft to see if he could help.

The final fight for life had started. When the family at last arrived from England on August 4, only his wife and daughter were allowed to visit him, yet by this time Charles could barely recognize them. Although he lived six more days, from then onward he seemed unaware of what was happening around him, and every day he was in agony.

During these last six days he often cried out. He spoke of going to see his Holy God, the Father, who will give him back his name. He said to his children:

"Poor children, you no longer have a name."

He cried out:

"Since my father's head was cut off, I have lived in darkness."

On seeing his daughter, Amelie, he thought that he was seeing his sister and blamed her for not leading him out of his misery, but rather abandoning him. The day before he died he cried out:

"Children, tomorrow I shall climb to heaven and there I will be given a heavenly name that nobody can steal from me."

On August 10, 1845, exactly fifty-three years to the day after the attack on the Palace of the Tuileries, which was the first day of prison for the Royal Family, the son of Louis XVI died

Two of the doctors who attended Charles wrote and signed a statement about the last days that they spent with him, and in part it reads:

"We have treated him who was called Charles Wilhelm Naundorff, but who later evidently was Charles Louis de Bourbon, Duke of Normandy.

There was much interest in his health and we made daily bulletins to the Minister of Defence. The illness (Typhus ecteroides) was psychologically very interesting. The patients' thoughts were mostly about his father, the poor Louis XVI, about the horrible spectacle of the guillotine, and he joined his hands in prayer and asked to join his royal father in Heaven quickly."

The Lieutenant General van Meurs, who was vice-director of the munitions factory in Delft, declared:

"I was constantly present at the death-bed of the Prince, and I could observe all his actions and all his words. All that I heard during the long sleepless nights, all that he said while he was delirious and all that he said just before his death, have convinced me that he was the Duke of Normandy, the real Dauphin, son of Louis XVI, martyr of the politics and the hate of his closest relatives.

I hereby sign this declaration,

Van Meurs, Lt. General

Deathbed confessions are a very important matter, seldom does a person lie in the face of God, and seldom has anyone kept up the pretence of an impersonation on his deathbed. The death certificate is most important because now finally Charles again officially becomes Charles Louis de Bourbon. The declaration, which is the most popular document in the archives of the town of Delft, is numbered 338:

"In the year one thousand eight hundred and forty five on August 10, at six o'clock in the afternoon there appeared before us, Daniel van Koetsveld, Clerk of the registry office for the town of Delft; Charles Eduard de Bourbon, aged twenty four, citizen; and Modeste Gruau, Count de la Barre, fifty years old, formerly King's Councilor at the first Court of Mayenne in France, both living here, the first the son of and the second one a good friend of the deceased.

They have declared to us that on August 10, in this year at 3 o'clock in the afternoon in the house of neighbourhood two, number sixty two of Old Delft street, Charles Louis de Bourbon, Duke of Normandy (Louis XVII) has died, also known as Charles Wilhelm Naundorff, born in the Palace of Versailles in France, March 27, seventeen hundred and eighty five and thus sixty years old, who lived in this town; son of the former Royal Highness Louis XVI, King of France and of her Imperial Highness and Royal Highness Marie Antoinette, Archduchess of Austria and Queen of France, both died in Paris, Husband of Madame the Duchess of Normandy, born Johanna Einert, who lives here.

The declarants have hereby signed this act,

M. Gruau, Count de la Barre, Charles Edouard de Bourbon, D. van Koetsveld.

The Mayor of Delft personally took this act to the Minister of Justice because he did not want to take the responsibility for writing this act into the registry for Delft without specific permission. The King of Holland accepted the act as written and so it stands until today.

This is therefore the first and last official acceptance of the Charles' claim.

Much later at a trial in the courts of France, the lawyer for the opposition, Maurice Garçon, said:

"Who were they, these people that declared at the City Hall that this was Louis XVII? A lawyer who had only known the man for three years and a son who was not born until years after the event. How could they certify that this was Louis XVII?"

First this question should be asked about the first death certificate on June 1795, when the young boy died in the Temple. Not one reliable witness signed that document, and no one who had known the boy for more than three months.

Secondly, the lawyer had spent that whole three years, day in and day out, trying to prove that this was really Louis XVII. He had lived with Charles daily every day during those three years, and therefore was hardly a stranger.

Thirdly, a son who had known his father for twenty-four years is not exactly a witness who has just walked in from the street.

A short while later the King of Holland made a secret act which received the number 317, dated January 7, 1846, King's Council, by which he appointed Charles Edouard de Bourbon as the new director of the Pyrotechnical section of the Artillery and Construction factory in Delft. This act survives until today and clearly the King fully intended that the family be accepted as the Royal Family of France, which is remarkable when one sees the reports that exist about Charles.

The King of Holland learned the story of Charles and knew it as well as several other Royal Houses of Europe. Thus Charles received the recognition in death that had eluded him in life. The French Government tried several times to have this death certificate cancelled on the books of Holland, but could never prove to Holland that Louis XVII had died in France. The Duchess of Angoulème never tried this, never attempted to have this act changed and never claimed that her brother's name was falsely used.

From this relatively short stay in Holland do come some interesting points about Charles. First, Charles could convince several very important people in Holland of his claims, and that was not easy, as the Dutch, not given to easy acceptance, tend to be a very suspicious people. They are known for their cold, well thought-out opinions; and I dare anyone to try to trick three Ministers of the Crown, the lawyer van Buren, the Lt. General de Bruyn, the Mayor van Meurs, the future Minister of Defence, and the military men—men who knew men—technical men who worked with precision every day. Then also the doctors who saw the man, naked, vulnerable, through six long days of agony, in his last dying moments. Amongst them military medical men who had seen men die before and all of whom saw something in Charles that convinced them of his sincerity.

The funeral was a grand affair. The Government, the Army and the Navy all sent representatives, and there were many friends, family and followers. The grave in the small town of Delft lies somewhat hidden in the corner of a park in the middle of town. Some magnificent trees and a heavy iron railing topped by gold painted lilies surround it. It is visited every so often by a few of the locals, and even now once a month by someone from France who has come to see this extraordinary grave, that is marked:

ICI REPOSE

Louis XVII

CHARLES LOUIS, DUC DE NORMANDIE

ROI DE FRANCE ET DE NAVARRE

Né ‡ Versailles le 27 Mars 1785

Décéde ‡ Delft le 10 Août 1845

Chapter 15.   THE STORY CONTINUES

The oldest son, Charles Edouard, continued his father's work and successfully finished with the percussion grenade. The Dutch army used it for over sixty years, when, of course, even more powerful discoveries were made. The King signed a new contract with the young man as we have seen. It was a secret act and it gave Charles Edouard the name de Bourbon, yet unfortunately it lasted only for another year. Then Holland also went through a revolution and became a constitutional instead of an absolute Monarchy. Charles Edouard was only twenty-five and, although he had worked with his father, he was not fully aware of all his father's formulae; and the papers left behind were not entirely clear and so the Government closed the laboratory.

The mother survived on a small pension given to her by the loyal Percivals in England. The eldest daughter, Amelie, finally consented to marry one of her father's first and strongest converts, the lawyer Abel Xavier Laprade. She moved to France and, through marriage, became a French citizen. She remained the head of the family for a long time and had always been the strong one in the family. Always helping her mother when there was no income at all, and writing her father constantly, thus keeping him informed. She had been the father's favourite and until her death, continued the fight for recognition along with the lawyer Gruau de la Barre.

The second son, Louis Charles, on the death of his brother, in 1866 who left no children, was now the head of the family. Louis Charles unfortunately did not like his role as pretender to the French Throne, for he lacked interest and did not really want to continue. The next brother, Charles Edmond then decided to marry his mother's maid without permission from the head of the family. In order to regulate who would inherit, the family made an agreement amongst themselves, so that Charles Edmond abdicated in 1877. Louis Charles, who was next in line had no children and for the good of the family also decided to abdicate formally in favour of his younger brother, Adelberth.

This now brought the whole family together and now all would support Adelberth. The ceremony took place on November 14, 1883, and was duly witnessed and notarized. Adelberth thus became head of the family and his branch, from which I descend, is now known as the "Dutch and lately Canadian branch". Charles Edmond followed the sister Amelié and settled in France, and his branch then became the "French branch" of the family.

Adelberth had decided on a military career, but to be accepted in the Dutch Army he needed to be naturalized, and so he made the necessary applications to the Dutch Government. The application presented a problem to the Government because Adelberth was born while the family was in England, and the Dutch had a law on the books that prohibited any Britons from becoming Dutch citizens. But a French Prince is still French, no matter where he is born, and this was how

Adelberth then pleaded. The Lower house of Parliament took up the case and the arguments raged for three full days. The deputy Heemskerck welcomed a French Prince to the Dutch Army but made it clear to Parliament that if Parliament voted in favor of this application, they would automatically, by implication, be confirming that Adelberth was a French Prince and that his father had indeed been Louis XVII. When the application finally came to a vote, the son of Louis XVII became Dutch by a margin of 49 to 3.

He was my great-grandfather.

The French Government has since, more than once, tried to get this naturalization removed from the Dutch records, but to no avail.

There are monarchists who claim that the abdications are not possible under the rules of the French Monarchy, but four precedents had already been established. Louis XVIII had bypassed his nephew Louis XVII and had become King while young Charles roamed all over Europe—a fact Louis XVIII knew all too well. A second abdication of Louis XVII occurred when Charles X overruled Louis XVIII's last will and the third was by Charles X, who could not hold his position and had abdicated in favor of his grandson, the Count of Chambord. This Count of Chambord later also abdicated and refused to accept the responsibility that was his. It has often been implied that he did so because he knew he was not next in line and aware of the Dutch de Bourbons.

Years later Charles Edmond decided to cancel his abdication, which of course has absolutely no precedent. This made two camps in the family. Today, of the Dutch branch, only my younger sister Amelie and I remain in our generation, but thankfully I have two sons and three grandsons to carry on the name. My brother has one son who will also carry on the name. Of the males in the French branch, there only remains my cousin Charles Edmond and his son, Huques, born while his father was still married to his first wife and thus not in the dynastic line.

The Court case that Charles had started in France went nowhere because he was banished, and therefore could not return back to plead his case. The widow and her sons, together with Amelié and Gruau de la Barre, however, took up the gauntlet again in 1851.

Jules Favre, who later became the famous Foreign Minister of France, pleaded the case to have the birth certificate of June 8, 1795 set aside. The argument was that there were many irregularities, but the Court found that it was properly drawn and registered so the suit failed. An appeal was filed in 1874, again by Jules Favre and, for the same reasons, it failed again. However, one son in the French branch had not been part of these proceedings and his family continued to pay a yearly fee to hold the Court case appeal open to him. The French courts heard another appeal in 1954, but the case was again lost because the basis continued to be the badly drawn certificate rather than the wrong body.

The Dutch branch never was part of any of these court proceedings. We always felt that the cases as presented to the courts were badly drawn and we reserved the right to bring our own case, and that we will do.

We sorely need the 202 missing papers confiscated in 1836, because without them a solid case remains very difficult. But now there is DNA and we hope to solve this case once and for all with the research of the DNA of Louis XVII.

In 1866 the family came into a strange inheritance by way of Mr. Bremond who had died in Switzerland. At the beginning of the revolution, Mr. Bremond's friend and superior, the Marquis of Monciel, Minister of the Interior under Louis XVI, had received some very detailed information about a platinum mine in Colombia. It was said to contain enough platinum to pay for all the national debt of France. Louis XVI had previous knowledge of this mine, as did the King of Spain, and he instructed the Marquis to keep the information until the revolution was over and, only then, to bring the matter up again, or, if he did not survive, to try again with Louis XVII. This the Marquis had done, but during and after the revolution he could not find Louis XVII so he left the envelope and the instructions with Mr. Bremond. Now Mr. Bremond had died and the envelope went to his son who contacted Charles' family, because he knew from his father that these were the descendants of Louis XVII. The Bremond son made an arrangement with the lawyer Gruau de la Barre that, when they found the treasure, Bremont would be reimbursed for the 60,000 francs that his father had given to Charles,

Thus over the next few years, Gruau de la Barre, still acting for the family, tried a search for the treasure. He first dealt with the Colombian Government and offered them the plans in return for 1,300,000 Dutch guilders—an enormous fortune at the time. The President of Colombia placed a bill before his Parliament but, because there was a great shortage of funds, it did not pass. Then in 1872 a pair of Dutch entrepreneurs showed up and made a deal with the family to exploit the mine. When this news arrived in Columbia there was a big uproar and a Mr. Saravia-Ferro was sent to Holland to negotiate with the family. Mr. Saravia-Ferro lived near the mine and was therefore in a much better position to survey and exploit it. Now a new deal was struck between the new partner, the two old ones and the family.

However, the work was much harder than first thought. The partners just could not get it done and soon abandoned the project. Gruau de la Barre gave up on his management and shortly after that he died. He had worked for his Royal Family for over fifty years and his only belongings, which he left to Amelié, were his shares in the platinum mine—the mine that was never found. Surviving his master by forty years, Charles' nine children all considered him their stepfather and called him by that title.

In 1871 the lawyer in France for the family, Jules Favre, became the Foreign Minister and as such, along with the German Chancellor Bismarck, had to sign the Peace Treaty of Versailles. After the documents were duly signed, Bismarck produced the seal of the state of Germany and affixed it in the proper place over his signature. He then turned to Jules Favre and asked him to attach his seal, but Favre had not brought one.

Bismark replied: "Then use the ring on your finger!"

Favre: "Very well, but do you know whose ring this is?"

Bismark: "No, but it really does not matter."

Favre: "The ring was a gift from a client who could not pay his lawyer's bills."

Favre went on: "My client was Louis XVII and his ring will now seal the Treaty of Versailles."

Jules Favre was a strong Republican and greatly opposed to the Monarchy, but he felt very strongly about the rights that anyone has to carry his own name; and therefore he stayed a friend of the family until the day that he died. As Foreign Minister he saw papers that existed in his Ministry which fully proved that Charles was Louis XVII. Still, he could not use these papers because he would have been in a conflict of interest, yet it shows that the Government knew and still today knows the truth.

In 1904 it was necessary to move the grave in Delft and to replace the stone. The Dutch Government then assumed the upkeep of the grave, installed a metal rail around the stone and placed gold-colored lilies on its corners.

General de Bas, President of the Dutch Association of Archaeology, spoke and said:

"It is to the eternal honor of King Wilhelm of Holland to have been the only Sovereign of his time to have acknowledged Louis XVII."

The same year the Commission for Old Paris dug again for the grave of Louis XVII in the St. Marquerite cemetery, and once more they found nothing.

In 1913 the French branch of the family brought an action in the Correctional Tribunal of the Seine against the newspaper "La Patrie" because of an article which stated that the family did not have the right to the name de Bourbon. The court found for the family as it had legally received this name from the Government of

Holland, and this act is fully recognized and legal in France.

In 1951 interest in the family flared up again for two reasons.

First the family received a notarized statement from Charles Eduard of Saxe Cobourg Gotha in which he stated that after World War I, August Wilhelm of Prussia had told him that, while searching through the archives, he had happened to find the dossier on Naundorff. In it were Naundorffs' letters to Le Coq, to Prince Hardenberg, to the King of Prussia, and he states that the dossier definitely proves that Naundorff was Louis XVII.

We are still searching for this dossier, because two years later we received confirmation of its existence from Professor M. Baldenspergen of the University of the Sorbonne in Paris, who confirms that the historian George Pariget interviewed Chancellor Bulow who in turn confirmed that these papers existed in Berlin. Now a war and a Russian occupation have passed over Berlin, and whether these papers still exist and where they are today is our next quest.

The second reason is that Mr. Carl Begeer, a friend of my father asked for a second exhumation and thanks to the work of Dr. Hulst, the forensic expert of the time, we now know that the theory that Naundorff was Charles Werg, a lover of Mrs. Sonnenberg was false. Naundorff had indeed stayed in the Sonnenberg rooming house at about the same time as a Prussian soldier called Werg. Several writers have insisted that the two were one and the same. Dr. Hulst proved that Naundorff was too young to have been Werg and also that Naundorff was too short to have been in the army where Werg was a soldier. We also know that the wounds of the two assassination attempts were not self-inflicted.

The exhumation does have a negative effect, in that through it we lose two well-known historians who have written excellent books in favour of Louis XVII. They are Alain Decaux, a Minister in the Government under Mitterand, whose book on Louis XVII is among the very best and his friend André Castelot who wrote a very interesting book in 1949 that ended with a new theory based on the hair comparison between the Dauphin and Naundorff. Castelot managed to get a lock of hair that had belonged to Louis XVII when he was only a child, and he also obtained some hair from Naundorff. An expert studied them both and claimed that hair samples could identify people as did their fingerprints. He found that the hair from both samples had the same characteristic off-center channel. There could be no argument Charles was Louis XVII.

Unfortunately, when the exhumation provided some more hair and they tested it again, the case fell apart. This hair did not show the same similarity and the two historians changed their minds. Experts have since established that hair changes over the years, and that regretfully it cannot be proven that certain hair came from a certain person some thirty years later. Thus the hair experiment is invalid for the moment, yet both historians had far more proof than just the hair. The DNA research on hair hopefully will show a result.

In the 1950s the French branch in Paris consisted of a René Tschoeberlé, whose father, Louis Charles de Bourbon, waited until he was on his deathbed before adopting this son.

René was an outright scoundrel who lived on his name and who managed to damage our name almost beyond repair. This then made it no wonder that some of our supporters turned away. René managed to accumulate all the papers that belonged to the French branch of the family. First, of course, he inherited all the papers from his father and those of my cousin, Charles Edmond who, at the age of fourteen, lost his father. René soon had the papers from that branch, and took over the upbringing of Charles Edmond who, as a result, had a very miserable youth. Then René also managed to contact my cousin, Madeleine —the only daughter of the oldest son of Adelberth. She was a dear lady and my great-aunt and I, when I was young and before I moved to Canada, spent some time with her and her mother. Her father had also settled in France. Whenever I could return to Europe, Madeleine was always an essential visit for me. She promised me all the papers that her father had gathered over the years would eventually, come to me. She was aware of the arrangement that my father had made with my uncle Henri. Henri had promised that the papers of his French branch would come to me on his death.

Suddenly Madeleine disappeared into a nursing home where strict instructions had been given that nobody could approach her, and where her mail was not to be addressed to "Princess Madeleine". She was a charity ward and her position had become very delicate. It was not until after her death that I found out that this was all the work of uncle René.

The same happened with uncle Henri. When he had become really ill, close to his end and out of funds he was "saved" by René who took all that there was. Unfortunately René had only a daughter when he died, and she hated the family. Why this was the case I never did find out. They knew her in Paris as the "Red Princess" and she refused all my correspondence and telephone calls. She had a great auction after the death of her father and the papers of the family are now spread all over the country. It is interesting to note that the French Government reserved several lots for itself, and, under the laws of France, these had to be handed over and are now in its archives. Why would the Government be interested in the papers of a man they consider to be an impostor? Or are these also going to be "lost"?

My father wrote a poem when the last exhumation took place on September 27, 1951.

TO HIS GRAVE IN DELFT

Again the fall, again those dull gray skies

Again that little park, to which my dreams return, in pain

again the mist, when summer's heat has gone

the flowers have wilted and I alone remain.

The tombstone is slid from its vault

and with steel chains they lift the heavy burden.

Between the mourners and those that reject your claim

stand your earthly remains, a silent sentinel.

It is written on a simple ribbon "The unlucky Prince"
and all the sadness, all the pain and smart
of your existence, of your few years on earth
hurt deeply as an arrow, the center of my heart.

Hungry, chased, cheated and expelled
but looking for happiness like each of us
no peace, no home were ever yours to enjoy
even your name belonged to someone else.

Nothing much has changed down here
Karl Wilhelm Naundorff, France's poorest subject
the earth, where rights are trampled by so many
still offers your kin no peace, no respect.

I carry it forward; the torch of these lost ones
I share your uncertainty; I share your lonely lot
but I know that this road of darkness, of thorns
ends in the unending right, in God.

Chapter 16.   PROOF GALORE

Emile Zola : "J'Accuse"

I believe that this mystery can be solved and I have been working on it for nearly thirty years. For my family I would just like it to be done. Certainly, we could throw in the towel but that is not our way. It must be a concrete proof to satisfy us. There are two items that would satisfy us. First item is the recovery of the body of Louis XVII and the second the disclosure of who Naundorff really was. The official burial took place in the cemetery of Ste. Marquerite. We have seen how the Bertrancourt, the gravedigger confessed to his wife and his friend, that he moved the body up against the wall of the church. That was outside the cemetery! There has been a body found there and that body showed all the signs of being that Dr. Pelletan and his colleagues autopsied. It was not Louis XVII.

We have seen how Napoleon was the first to dig in the cemetery and then found an empty coffin. We know why, the gravedigger only dug to the coffin and then opened it and took out the body. No need to dig up the whole thing, that would take at least double the effort and then try to take out the whole coffin. A major job even for someone used to this work. No he had a stack of caskets in the church and the body that was found was in a lead casket. We cannot even get permission to test that body for DNA because the French government says this has been proven NOT to be the body of Louis XVII. Why then did they allow the heart that belonged to that body be buried as Louis XVII? The decisions of the Government are hard to understand and of course the large group objecting to our existence is influencing them.

The late Count of Paris testified on television that he believed that the body in Ste. Marquerite was not that of Louis XVII. He added that he believed that Louis XVII now was dead. Almost 200 years later I also agree with him there.

So if that was not Louis XVII where is he then? He was not the Baron de Richemont, the most famous of the false dauphins because he had brown eyes. So was he one of the other false dauphins? There are more than 50, some say over 100 but all except Naundorff have been unmasked. That only leaves Karl Wilhelm Naundorff. The problem could be instantly solved if someone was able to prove that Naundorff was just Naundorff. But no one has ever found a sign of him, not a birth date, not a parent or sister or brother. No trace of him and many, many have tried.

The kingdom of Prussia tried very hard when the Dutch king asked them to find out if Naundorff was an imposter. The court in Brandenburg tried, his future son-in-law tried and travelled all over Germany to find out about his prospective father-in-law. George de Manteyer tried; he worked for the Spanish branch of the de Bourbon's, so there would have been a nice bonus. He never succeeded but he did write a book about Naundorff in which he claimed Naundorff and Werg were the same person. We have shown how Dr. Hulst solved that myth in 1951 and yet in 1999 another writer comes back with the same story.

Then was he Hervagault, who had a large following. No, Hervagault was born Hervagault. He was unmasked. How about Charles de Navarre, another very successful impostor. No he was born Mathurin Bruneau. And so the list goes on. Everyone unmasked except one, Naundorff.

And how do all the stories get started? There was a writer who wrote that Naundorff had bought a leather easy chair from the Temple and there in the folds of the seat he had found all the papers that he possessed. And with those papers he became Louis XVII. The government had auctioned off all the belongings of the Temple when it was demolished. Unfortunately for the writer there still exists a list of the goods auctioned off and no chair. But still someone had to make an effort to disprove that tale. And "historians" still copy that story and it gets new life.

Andre Pillet wrote three books about Naundorff. He visited almost all the town halls and parish halls in Germany and Prussia but never found a trace of Naundorffs background. Louis-Philippe, King of the French, a member of the Orleans, family ordered Naundorff out of the country and ordered a full investigation into his background which turned up nothing.

Maurice Garcon was the lawyer for the de Bourbon-Parma's in the court appeal in 1954. He claimed that the Naundorff family should not win this case since they could not come up with a single paper to back up their case. This was a really low, blow. The papers hidden from us and destroyed run into the thousands. I have already mentioned that Naundorff had 202 papers, which he had to surrender when he was thrown out of the country and exiled to England. He had the receipt but the papers were lost (?). There is the report that Dr. Desault made to the Committee of Public Security on May 31, 1795 and numbered 263. The records of the Temple given to and signed for by Minister Benezech on April 10, 1796, when he took over have been gone since. The laundry lists are in good order as we have seen. But anything that might have given us some idea of what really went on is missing.

The official file that the French government had in the Quay Dorsay, a dossier called "Le Dossier Rouge", was seen by Clemenceau, Jules Favre and by Pierre Laval, President of the Cabinet, Minister of the Interior, is missing. The last will and testament of Marie Therese, Louis XVII's sister is missing. It was to be opened 100 years after her death when she felt her secrets could be revealed. This document was in a box eighteen by twenty inches covered in crimson velvet, with two ribbons and sealed by twelve seals from the Vatican. It was seen and fully described by the Count of Pins in 1949. He told our partisans Bourmont-Coucy and the Marquis de Castellane that he had seen the box in the Ministry of Foreign Affairs, Quai d'Orsay. He asked his chef Mr. de Ribier what was in this box. But in 1950 when it was to be opened it was gone. My father travelled to Paris and asked to be present for the opening. The government said it had no such box or testament.

The papers that Naundorff gave to the police inspector Le Coq in Berlin and then forwarded to Prince Hardenberg in Prussia were last seen just before the Second World War. These papers are now gone.

Then there were the papers of:

a) The town official Pezold in Crossen, Prussia taken and missing since his death.

b) The General Barras confiscated and destroyed by Louis XVIII.

c) Robespierre, taken and probably destroyed by Louis XVIII.

d) Louis XVIII, his testament thrown in the fire by Charles X in front of several witnesses. He disclosed therein the existence of Louis XVII and his right to the throne but it was thought Charles X was a better monarch since he was brought up in the court.

It is true we do not have as many papers as we ought to, but is it any wonder?

Many writers among the 300 or so books about Louis XVII write that he could speak no French when he returned to France He had trouble with words because since he was ten years old he had been forced to speak only German and he spoke French as a ten year old. After 30 years it did not come easy for him and I know what I am talking about. After 50 years in Canada I have sometimes trouble with my Dutch, I fall over words, I throw in English when I am stuck although I have been back many times and I have a good ear for languages. Some people do not have an easy time with a language they haven't spoken for awhile.

Another complaint against Naundorff was that he did not contact anyone for years untill 1831. But he did contact police chief Le Coq and thought that he was looking out for him. He wrote constantly to his sister Marie Therese, a letter dated September 4th 1819 explains that his first-born daughter now has the name Amelie, which is the name carried by Marie Therese on the trip to Varennes. Frankly he was tired of running. He had settled down in Germany, was happily married, had a good job and a wonderful family. Why would he risk all that for a name. He probably would never have gone back if he had not been constantly harassed, thrown in jail, falsely accused and defiled. Had they left him alone we, his family might still live in Germany. But when Pezold was warned that a new attack would take place he finally decided he had had enough.

Charles made many mistakes and he did silly things, especially when he was broke and at his wits end. He was very depressed that his sister would not write him or see him. They had been very close, only children with all they went through. But she had been warned to stay away from him by Louis XVIII and she would not take a chance. She went to the trial of Mathurin Bruneau to testify that he was a fraud. She asked him a list of things but he could not answer. However Naundorff knew the answer to all of them. But she never saw her brother and if he had been a fraud, she could have destroyed him in five minutes. Louis XVIII desperately needed her inheritance and he forced her to marry her cousin, the son of Charles X.

There exists another mystery. It is believed by many people that the guards in the Temple prison violated Marie Therese and that she was mentally destroyed by this action. That after her exchange for some French officers, she was substituted by Ernestine de Lambriquet, a girl almost the same age who had been brought up by Marie Antoinette after her mother died. The girls were very much alike. If that is so then the story goes that Marie Therese was moved into a small castle in Germany in Hildburghausen where indeed an unknown lady lived for many years. It is the mystery of "Die Dunkel Grafin" or the "Dark Duchess". This story however does not agree with the marriage of "Ernestine de Lambriquet" who was married in Paris in 1810 and died in 1813.

Now for some of the proofs in Naundorff's favour. Most of all there were his memories of his youth and the things he remembered of the court, the trip to Varennes and his time in prison. He remembered the roofs on the way back from Varennes when he noticed that the pattern of the tiles was an S. He won over Madame Rambaud when he remembered the little suit he should have worn but which had become too snug. She had kept it and he remembered it. He won over the Minister of Finance under his father Mr. Joly when he told him about the metal bars on the window when they were hiding from the riot at the Louvre. Mr. Bremond knew instantly he was Louis XVII when he told the story of the hidden box that the father had shown him, a secret only four people in the whole world knew.

He won over Mrs Marco de Saint-Hilaire with a description of the music instruments that his mother had used when he was a little boy. Several had been smashed during the revolution but he knew them all. He convinced the Abbot Alpert when he told him about the small billiard table they had played on and about the recitals that he used to give. Charles was the second boy and his older brother was Louis. Many false dauphins called themselves Louis, which was wrong. Louis had been the older brother and he was always Charles and not Louis. The real Charles knew that.

Besides the memories there are also the physical markings that are so amazing. Certainly there are many blondes with blue eyes but not too many in France. When Naundorff died in Holland the doctors made a list of the markings on the body:

1) On the forehead— a scar two centimeters above the nose at the centre line of the forehead to the right side downwards as a half moon on about one cen timeter.

2) Backside of the head—a scar on the upper right side.

3) On the face:

A) A small scar on the centreline of the upper lip

B) The two centre teeth of the lower jaw stand forward

C) On the outside of the center of the chin—a one centimeter scar

4) On the chest—two centimeters left of the breast bone a scar in the shape of a hook, difficult to see since the body has already started to swell up with gases

5) On the arms—on the back of the left shoulder a scar of one centimeter. On the left upper arm about one third of the total length down on the inside three scars of inoculation in the shape of a triangle.

6)On the legs—on the inside in the middle of the left thigh a large birthmark.

From this list we can take four items that we know were present on the body on the young Dauphin before his imprisonment. First is the scar on the upper lip. When young Louis XVII was playing with his rabbit it bit him on the lip. This story is well known.

The second mark is the inoculation mark on his left arm, as testified to by Madame Rambaud. Inoculations were very rare in those days and the young children of the king were amongst the very first to receive them. They were inoculated on both arms but the scar on the right arm was not visible. The body had started to swell and the right side might have had a small scar that disappeared. Reactions were always stronger in one side or another.

The third and most important scar was the birthmark in the middle of the left thigh, recognized by both Madame de Rambaud and Dr. Jeanroy, who said:

"By this mark alone one can identify the Prince out of a million."

The fourth item, which was also quite pronounced were the two teeth that were set slightly forward and ahead of the others. They are called "rabbit teeth".

Beyond that there was the blond hair, the blue eyes, the way of walking and the short wrinkled neck that Madame de Rambaud had mentioned.

The chances that two people with those same markings and of the same age would walk on this earth are more than one in a million. That they would claim to be the same person is one in a billion.

Mr. Carl Begeer of the famous Begeer Silver Factories in Holland published a huge book named "Genealogie de Bourbon" in which he compares many family traits and likenesses based on portraits, paintings and sketches and the similarity is profound.

Then there is the work of Dr. Silvassy over which more is written in the next chapter. And finally there are the handwriting experts who worked on this case. One of them at the request of Alain Decaux, a former Minister of France and a well-known writer, whose book on Louis XVII is one of the better ones. He hired Roger le Noble a director of the Bureau of Studies on Synthography. His report says that the writing of Naundorff and Louis XVII is identical and close to that of Louis XVI who studied with his son Louis XVII before his death.

The second handwriting expert was Mr. De Rochetal in 1911. He studied the handwriting of the young prince and of Naundorff and claimed it was identical and came from the same person. Mr. De Rochetal was president of the French Association of Graphology.

In total an overwhelming amount of proof and yet our enemies continue to fight us from all sides. Last of all I would like to point out some strange coincidences, some may be just that, but some show a definite pattern of suspicious behaviour.

1) The death of Dr Desault just after he has seen Louis XVII the first time and has reported to the Government that he does not recognize this boy. The death of two more doctors within a two-week period, the flight of a fourth doctor to the United States. Dr. Desault had talked to all three doctors prior to his death.

2) January 21, 1824 Naundorff writes Louis XVIII that he is coming to France to clear his name. Before he receives an answer and gets a chance to leave in June 1824, he is charged with setting fire in the theatre. In July 1824 Louis XVIII dies after having changed his will. In July 1824 Naundorff is charged with passing false money. He is acquitted but thrown in prison for three years because he gave a wrong answer to the judge about his background.

3) May 23, 1814 Josephine de Beauharnais, former wife of Napoleon tells the Czar Alexander I that Louis XVII is still alive. May 29, 1814 she dies from poisoning. May 30, 1814 Alexander and the allies declare the Comte de Provence, King of France for a two-year tryout period only.

4) March 1832 Pezold, the town notary in Crossen has a visit from the Prince of Carolath and his secretary the Baron de Senden, who questions him severely on his support of Naundorff. The following day he dies of poisoning. His successor Lauriscus who has promised to continue his support dies suddenly four weeks later. Two months later Naundorff receives a message that the King of Prussia has ordered that he must be arrested and imprisoned. Naundorff leaves the following morning for Paris.

Chapter 17,   THE LAST YEARS

"Justice delayed is Justice denied."

–William Gladstone

From now on our two stories are side by side. My ancestor lies in Delft waiting for his descendant to finally put an end to this story. He keeps quiet but still he may help us with what he has left behind.

After our first trip by boat to Florida the real estate market is still poor and we decide to go to Europe to see our friends. A high school teacher in Holland has asked if he can write a story about the family. He has an idea that DNA research could give us a positive answer. He claims that he is totally neutral and will consider both sides of the story. I know that an unbiased person will soon see our side and with my friend Stephan Schoor we promise to help him. Stephan's parents were good friends of my parents since the Second World War and we two have remained great friends. He has been my representative in Holland, keeping his eyes on what is happening there. Stephan had already earlier brought up the case for a DNA research. He wrote to the British head office of Madame Tussaud, the famous wax museum that has branches all over the world. They have death masks of Louis XVII and Marie Antoinette which show some dark spots which could well be blood caught by the mask which was supposedly made after the quilotine had done it's work. But the managers at Madame Tussaud were not convinced that the masques were genuine and so that avenue closed for us.

In 1989 Arline and I visit a dear friend, the Marquise Marthe de la Hamaide in Bruxelles and she lets me have her summer residence for a reunion with my friends from France, Holland and Belgium. We have come together to discuss our plans and to meet one another. There is my long time friend from France Philippe Mac'Rel and his wife and daughter. My representative in France the lively Andre Fages and his friend Count Alain de Brett D'Avray. Also from France the famous writer Jacqueline Monsigne and her husband the American actor Edward Meeks and from Belgium the Marquise Marthe de la Hamaide. It is a wonderful group and we have an excellent day. On the second day I receive some horrible news. The island of Montserrat has been hard hit by the hurricane Hugo; the devastation is tremendous. We try to phone but all the lines are dead. We had exchanged our home for an apartment in Paris owned by a young lady from England and she is there with a Canadian girl friend. We do not know what has happened, as the reports are very vague.

It takes several days before we finally get in touch. The two girls have put a mattress down in the hall as the storm starts; they put another mattress over themselves and wait it out. Suddenly the roof above them gives way. They decide to run downstairs where there is a whole floor empty with a whole house above it. The drawings show a lower level, which was supposed to be the basement, but the builder constructed it as a main floor. It was never finished but it kept the girls safe. The roof is gone from most of the house, only the kitchen and one bedroom are still covered. The previous owner had bought much metal furniture and tables made of pressed wood products. What has not rusted is impregnated with water. The bedding and beds are almost all destroyed, all the doors and floors are pretty well ruined.

We rush back to Canada and prepare to go to our little island. We bring sausages made by real butchers that will last in the hot climate and we bring lanterns and dried foods. We arrive there three days after the disaster and find that the girls are gone and the man looking after our property has given up and says it cannot be saved and we should destroy it. But we work like beavers to get things sorted out. Our grapefruit trees give the neighbours and us enough fruit for the first few weeks. The rubbish is burned, we try to get supplies but there are tremendous shortages. When it rains we get out a squeegee on a long pole and run through the rain bare naked pushing the rain down the steps. We are a sight to be seen and we keep laughing. We make a long list of all the supplies we need. Friends are going to Florida to fetch some supplies and we beg to come along. We decide to share a container and I get my first introduction to Home Depot. We need beds and bedding, doors, roof shingles and roofing boards, hardware and lots of lumber. When we arrive back to the island all the locals have become carpenters. My friend brings an extra container of mattresses, which he distributes, to the locals. Many have been completely left without housing or bedding.

From September to February we live without electricity except for a noisy generator that gives us one hour of refrigeration per day. At Xmas time a kind neighbour drops by with a present: two ice cubes for a Xmas drink. Slowly we resurrect the house, the new doors are much better, and the asphalt tile floor is now a beautiful ceramic tile. All is fresh and new, we have built a strong arch in the dining room, which opens the living room up much better and stronger. The roof is new and all is well. The insurance has covered most of our losses and we are actually better off now. We head back to Canada but find the real estate market still very poorly. The Re/Max franchise I sold has gone under. The new owner over extended during the last days of the boom and was caught with a pile of bills when the market turned.

So in 1990 we pack the boat once more and head again to Florida. Thank heavens we are making a solid ten percent on our little retirement fund and manage to live without touching much of the fund itself. Living aboard is rather economical with little to pay in rent, taxes, electricity or water. We now know the way and the trip is uneventful. When we return in the spring we find everyone looking forward to a good season and several agents ask if I would like to open another Re/Max franchise. I test the waters and indeed there is some interest. I decide if these agents are so eager perhaps they would like to share the franchise with me. I have always liked working with people instead of for people. I should have realised that owning a real estate brokerage and being an agent runs contra to each other and it soon becomes a problem for the business. The agents are looking out for themselves while I try to have a good brokerage. But we start out at a gallop.

The "esprit de corps" is just great as all the top agents in Markham are with me, with few exceptions and my agents bombard them. In no time we have the lion share of the business in town. After two years we are the fifth largest brokerage of the Toronto Real Estate Board. We have great socials where we raise money for charitable causes. We need a huge hall to get everyone in. The second year is better than the first. The third year we start to have problems, the agent/owners want to have a free ride and I want a strong company. Their small investment has more than tripled in value and they have an almost free ride. There are now over seventy-five agents and many are strong personalities. Life is interesting but not a bowl of cherries. When I ask for an extension to my contract for one year they turn me down and I am a free soul again. It is time to retire.

Meanwhile in Holland the DNA research is standing still. After six years the teacher turns out to have had questions about my family from day one and for six years he has corrupted the doctor doing the research. We have given the doctor hair that came out of the coffin from an earlier exhumation in 1950. He has done over 60 tests but has not been able to get a mitochondria DNA formula. He turns to a very dubious bone, which has a different DNA formula than the hair and bases his results on it, unless I let him exhume my great-great grandfather again. I do not like to give in to blackmail and I begin to doubt the doctor. The results are published but are totally inconclusive. The French doctor who shares the work will not sign the report. When the notice for the news conference goes out his copy is marked "Do not deliver until _____" that is the day of the press conference and obviously he cannot get there and object. The report states that the samples from the Queen of Romania and her brother (both related to the Austrian family of Marie Antoinette) also do not match with the DNA of Marie Antoinette and there must be a flaw in that family or an adoption. It of no consequence at this time but it is vital in a later test.

A group flies to Austria because in a cloister there is a chain of medallions from the Austrian Royal family made up of lockets with hair of Marie Antoinette and her mother and two sisters. The samples are notarized and taken back to Belgium for tests. There is also a lock of the hair belonging to Marie Antoinette in France and my cousin has been able to obtain a sample. Then in a museum in Nijmegen we find a picture with samples of hair of Marie Antoinette and her son Louis XVII. This is a fabulous discovery as now we have hair from Louis XVII as a young man and of the body in Delft. They should be the same. In his final report, Dr. Cassiman does not even mention the hair from the young king. He has completed sixty four tests on the hair from the coffin. I do not know how many tests on the dubious bone, but enough so that not a speck remains in case we want to test it. Yet the results of the hair of the young Louis XVII are not even mentioned. This is a very suspicious omission.

The teacher publishes his book and claims that my family has a disease, which makes us, want to be kings. A friend who knows our story inside out needs sixty pages to point out the errors in the book, but the University accepts it and he is "promoted". He claims our ancestors were ordinary Germans and we should never be de Bourbons. Then he sends me a copy addressed to: "His Royal Highness Prince Charles de Bourbon". I think the word is hypocrite.

But from some tragedies some good comes and in this case, it is a call from a young eager Dutch lawyer. He is Dominique Rijnbout and he wants to be of service. In the following years he turns out to be a great help. We finally are on the right track. Dominique and Stephan Schoor incorporate the Foundation de Bourbon with members Maarten Koning, my nephew and Felix Hes.

In 1995 I receive an invitation to make a pilgrimage to Medjugorje where five children have seen the Holy Mary on a mountain. It is a very controversial site but Arline and I would like to see it. I can be talked into making a trip anytime. We fly into Switzerland and motor through some really devastated countryside to Medjugorje in Bosnia/Herzegovina. The damage from the war is devastating; there are whole villages burned to the ground. Apartment buildings are still standing but are completely pockmarked with bullet holes. Arline who has never seen war and cannot believe her eyes is very upset. She is usually strong but this really affects her. Any idiot that starts a war should be hanged. There is no excuse at anytime for anyone to begin a war. This is craziness. There is no excuse. Such destruction strengthens our opinions about the senselessness of war and its damage to mankind in every way.

We are very impressed with the devotion of the people in Medjugorje. There is a Mass every hour on the hour, 24 hours a day. In every possible language. And the church is full at all times. Arline and I are put through a very heavy schedule and I have caught a nasty cold.

We are lucky to be staying with friends when we return to France because between the cold and the stress I have a minor heart attack. A Quebec doctor owns the French hospital where I end up and the services are wonderful, they specialize in heart problems and after nine days I am allowed to go back to Canada.

Our friend who invited us to Medjugorje has a fabulous idea. He contacts Dr. Johann Silvassy in Austria. As Dean of Forensic Anthropology and a court accepted expert, he is highly regarded for his studies in Genetic Population and Historical Anthropology. He is the doctor that has established that a skull found in Austria is indeed the skull of Mozart. He accepts the task of proving our claims.

He examines the features of the heads, the faces, the features of the profiles, the features of the foreheads, of the eye region, of the chin, of the nose and of the ear of Louis XVI and Marie Antoinette and Naundorff/Louis XVII. His certificate shows two PROBABLES, one VERY PROBABLE, four HIGHLY PROBABLES and one HIGHEST DEGREE PROBABLE OF A RELATIONSHIP BETWEEN THESE THREE PEOPLE. His end result states that in criminal law high levels of similarity is proof for identity. Therefore alias Karl Wilhelm Naundorff is the son of Marie Antoinette and Louis XVI. Finally scientific proof. But will it be accepted. He does a second set of tests called the SUPERPROJECTION in which he compares portraits, photos and half profiles. The results are again a full statement that Naundorff was the child of Marie Antoinette and Louis XVI. A full scientific statement from a court appointed expert!

Only after we arrive home do we hear that the volcano on Montserrat has become active. The last explosion was 400 years ago and made the wonderful valley where our house is. Now it is the first area declared out of bounds. Our insurance company sends us a letter that the insurance now will only cover 60% of the value. We do not think that is nice after 19 years of paying premiums but the company explains it: "Would you insure something, which has caught fire?" Since we can no longer stay in the house we cancel our plans to go there and soon thereafter a pyroclastic flow comes down the mountain at a speed of over 100 kilometres an hour. Most of our area is covered but our house escapes.

However we no longer have water or electricity to the house and most of the roads are impassable. We file a claim for total destruction. A couple of months later a new flow covers our area altogether, including the airport and the little town called Farms, which is located next to our subdivision. Nineteen locals have refused to move and their houses are completely covered since they live in a small valley. No one gets out alive. You cannot even see where our roads were. Ours is a two-story home made of solid concrete. After this second run not even one block can be seen. Our 8 feet tall concrete pillars are gone; the site looks like a moonscape. It takes the insurance two years to settle with us and then we are offered 40% of the insurance policy, which we must accept. We have no backbone left to stand up against them. We have some lovely lots for sale at a good price.

In 1999 we receive word that my father who died in 1975, has been awarded the decoration Yad Vashem from the State of Israel. He was town mayor at the beginning of the war and has helped several Jewish families escape from the Germans. Bob Zadok Blok who was a young boy at the time was helped along with his brother and mother. He has never forgotten and has asked for this honour. I go to Holland with my wife and daughter and we visit Oss where my father was town mayor. We are very well received and the reception is excellent. The Ambassador of Israel is surprised at the large gathering but my father was obviously well thought of. I meet some old school friends; it has been 50 years since I lived there. The following year I am asked to come back and listen to a musical that the local theatre group has made about my fathers life. It also is a great success and because of the interest, they have to put on an extra performance.

Now we have a new obstacle, a friend in France tells us that the Spanish branch of the de Bourbons have come up with a new bright idea. They have tried for over 150 years to upset the Dutch branch because with us out of the way, they claim that they are the legal inheritors of the French throne. An Italian member of the aristocracy tells me he once had lunch with the Spanish branch where the subject of Naundorff came up. All were aware that he was the true Louis XVII but they were told to never mention this in public. That is what hurts the most is the knowledge that they know the truth! Their representative in France is the Duc de Beauffremont. He is the guardian of the royal graves in the church of St. Denis. Twenty-five years ago he accepted the heart of the boy who died in the Temple, the boy that Dr. Pelletan autopsied. The heart that Louis XVIII and Louis XVII's sister Marie Therese refused to accept. That heart has made its rounds and at one time was in the study of the Archbishop of Paris, sitting next to the heart of his older brother who had died at an early age. The revolutionaries ransacked this study and later the son of Dr. Pelletan was able to find ONE heart and assumed it was the one his father had saved.

This heart then made the rounds and over a hundred years later was offered to the Duc de Beauffremont, who accepted it as being from Louis XVII. This then is the heart of the body that lies in the churchyard of Ste Marquerite in Paris. That is IF it is the heart that belonged to Dr. Pelletan. A heart was then offered to the same doctor who had already made a mess of the research on the hair of my great, great grandfather in Delft, the hair that did not match the bone. He accepted the bone as being from my great, great grandfather. We were sure of the hair but refuse to accept a bone that did not match with his hair.

His report states that this heart has a DNA that is related to the family of the Queen Anne of Romania and her brother. They in turn may be related to Marie Antoinette, but NOT SO in the earlier DNA report of my great, great grandfather. It states: "Queen Anne and her brother Andre de Bourbon-Parma are the descendants of a female adopted several generations earlier". Their DNA did not match with that of Marie Antoinette. The doctor did mention now there was no proof of identity only the fact that this heart was related to the family of Marie Antoinette and it was up to the historians to prove whose heart this was.

It did not take long to find such an historian because one of the members of the group that started this examination was Mr. Delorme who had written a book against my family. Thus the heart that was buried with much pomp and circumstance on the 8th of June 2004 may have been the heart of the older brother in which case he also belonged to the family of Queen Anne and a family with an adopted female or it may be a heart found in the caves of St. Denis that was known to have belonged to the family at some time. We have asked the Government of France if we could open for the tenth time the grave of the boy buried in Ste. Marquerite to see if indeed this heart belonged to that boy. The Government responded with: "It has long been known that this body could not be the body of Louis XVII and thus it is needless to test it again." There we are, the body of the heart is not Louis XVII!

There exists a photo of the heart in its urn dated 1894. It was at that time examined by doctors Chevassus, Siredey and Jouin Mertelliere. They reported that the heart was absolutely dry, it measured 8x3 cm the left ventricle of 25 mm long and which constituted the mayor part of the organ and a right ventricle, which was flat and deformed, and of minor size. In 1999 however the heart was dry and only 6x3 and the left ventricle was only 2mm with the right being 1 mm. The opening of each ventricle was large and dilated. These two hearts are completely different and no further drying could have done that, as they were dry to begin with.

The sad part is that the press that attended this farce in droves never questioned any of it, with perhaps one or two exceptions. Thus the world has received the wrong message that Louis XVII died as a young boy and his heart is now in St. Denis.

My experiences with the media over the years have been a very mixed bag and I guess I am not alone in complaining that often any reports and interviews come out the way the interviewer wants it to come out and sometimes not the truth at all. One day a T.V. crew came to do an interview for a program on DNA. I should have known that it was their intention to make the DNA researcher look good and even though I gave an interview of at least half an hour, the results barely showed me and only the doctor's explanations were shown. He had made a mess of his research and the scientific magazine "Nature" had turned it down. Still they accepted it completely even after my explanation.

And often with the media it is not what they show but what they leave out that is important. I have had very bad experiences for instance with the group Life-Time-People. My father did a large program with Life; they took him to Paris and Versailles. I have some beautiful photos but the story was never printed. A Canadian writer proposed an article to People magazine in New York and they were very excited. Arline and I were planning a trip to France and so we met him and his photographer in Paris. The article was very interesting and New York liked it but the wanted to pass it by the editor in France. He was a friend of the Orleans family and you know where the article ended up, nowhere. Then Time published a story on the burial of the false heart in June 2004. They accepted the false story hook line and sinker and published it with a photo of a painting of Louis XVII. But they are so ignorant of the story that they published a picture of the false Dauphin.

My cousin who lives in France and I then decided that we must do a final test for the elusive DNA and this can only be done by opening the grave in Delft. We made application to the mayor of Delft who has severe reservations because he believes that the previous tests were done properly. I had to convince him how badly the last lot was handled and four years later we finally received permission. My cousin found many ways to delay the completion of the protocol required by the Town of Delft. This time we hope to have Dr. Oliver Pascal from France again as well as the well known DNA specialist from the University of Leiden, Dr. P. de Knijff and to make sure we have a unquestionable result we have asked Dr. Brandt of the University of Lausanne, Switzerland. Dr. Pascal has worked with the United States Laboratory of the Army and we hope to get them involved as well. We must be sure this time. Dr. de Knijff has promised to bring Dr. Maat a forensic specialist from Leiden.

It is difficult to do DNA tests in my family. I am enclosing a genealogy of the various branches of the de Bourbons. The Spanish branch has accepted as a male member a boy delivered to the Queen, which is the result of an alliance with the Minister of Foreign Affairs (no this was not a foreign affair). This is the end of the de Bourbon bloodline even though the King and the Cortez have accepted the boy. DNA research would not find any de Bourbon blood. Then there is the Orleans branch; they have switched a girl for the son of a jailor. Thus here again we cannot find any de Bourbon blood. Both these houses are claiming rights to the French throne; their claims are extremely fragile.

We have tried five different dates on the three doctors and none is acceptable. My cousin also keeps objecting but we finally settle on October 27, 2004. The Dutch team is available and they are the only ones that must attend, according to the protocol agreed to by our lawyer Dominique Rijnbout and the Town of Delft. Dominique has done a wonderful job of getting everything lined up. We have two tents, one for the doctors and one for the other staff and the coffee and sandwiches. Even a portable washroom has been ordered. Arline and I arrive ten days ahead to help with last minute problems but all goes well till the night before. At four p.m. the town and Dominique receive e-mails and letters from a lawyer who claims to act for my cousin and wishes the exhumation stopped. A Vice President of the Institute Louis XVII also calls but Dominique can only take instructions from my cousin or me and my cousin is not available. The town and Dominique check to see that all conditions in the protocol are met. The town will only take instructions from Dominique and it is decided to go ahead, the tradesmen have all gone home and would not be available till the following day. The trades would want their fees and my cousin has not sent us his half of the cost. At the last moment we find out they have no funds.

The following day is beautiful and we are all on hand at 8 a.m. My friend Dr. Rudy Meganck has driven all the way from Antwerp, Belgium. Dominique has brought a pair of photographers to record all the proceedings. The gravel around the stone is soon removed and the workmen remove the cement around the stone. They then pry the lid up and soon the large crane has removed it. Dominique has arranged everything so that the work can be done without removing the wrought iron gate around the grave. The chief in charge of National Monuments is happy there will be no damage to the Monument. The gravestone covered a brick cave in the ground and at about one foot above the bottom are 2 steel bars on which the casket rests. Now a messenger brings news that again notices have been received to halt the work. It is too late, and we continue. The weather continues to be beautiful, what a difference from that rainy day in September 1950. I am the only person to have been at both exhumations. This one is so much more professional and well arranged. When the casket is raised we see that water has attacked the bottom of the casket even though it was a foot above the floor of the cave. The wooden casket is taken apart and saved. The top is still in good shape. The inner zinc casket is now sawn open and the original lead casket is all broken up but it is enclosed.

The doctors have now arrived with their assistants and Dr. Maat starts by checking all the bones to see what is missing and the conditions of each. The upper arm bone is not there but we know it was removed at the previous exhumation. Only two small finger bones are missing, there are no extra bones or bones that do not match this skeleton. Cuts are then made to two bones to help in estimating the age of the person. Then four portions of bone are enclosed in separate containers and four teeth are also put in separate containers. Now units of bone and tooth are put in containers and sealed and signed by the lawyer and the bailiff in attendance. The attending police officer and the doctors also sign each box covering the samples. Dr. Maat now explains to all of us just how he has found the skeleton and the whole body is now put in a new zinc liner inside a new casket and all is sealed and put back in the cemetery cave. We are all done by three pm and everyone is very impressed. Now the waiting starts.

The results are going to take some time, since the other doctors have not yet made arrangements to pick up their samples, which are now kept in a refrigerated container at the University of Leiden. We will now have to make arrangements with the French group to see how they can raise funds to pay their share. The first item we will test is to see if the body in Delft is indeed a forefather of my cousin and me. My cousin, my brother Henri and I have all given blood samples to the doctor for comparison.

I will wait for the results before making any plans for the future.

PHOTOS & CHARTS

302

"King Louis XVI says goodbye to his family the night before his execution, January 21, 1793. Queen Marie-Antoinette, his daughter Madame Royale (later Duchess of Angouleme) and his son Louis XVII. At the extreme right is the sister of the King, Madame Elizabeth and at the left is the King's manservant Clery.

Louis XVII as a young man

Louis XVII in 1859.

de Bourbon family portrait.

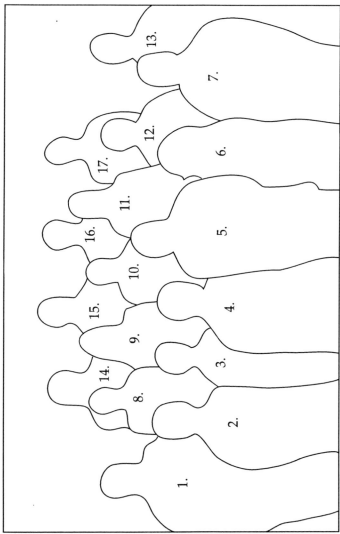

1. Dauphin Michael Henri 2. Jacqueline 3. Sebastian Koning 4. Princess Arline 5. Prince Charles Louis 6. Princess Louise 7. Prince Edmond 8. Princess Michelle Lys 9. Jaana Koning 10. Princess Julie Anne 11. Saskia Koning 12. Princess Amelie Koning-de Bourbon 13. Laura linda Rudy 14. Prince Marc 15. Peter Koning 16. Maarten Koning 17. Steven Koning

Prince Charles Michael, the author and Princess Arline.

From Left: The author, Prince Andre, Prince Edmond, Prince Michael, and Princess Caroline.

309

From Left: Our lawyer Dominique Rijnbout, Baliff Ms D.J Vermeulen, The author, Sargeant of Police B.J Horvath, Town Mayor G.A.A Verkerk, Princess Arline, Photographer Martin Boekhout, Town lawyer Ms. Rosalie Buise.

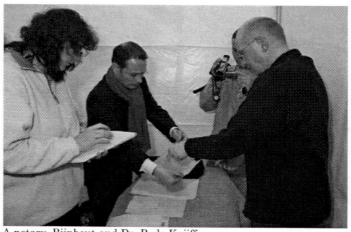

A notary, Rijnbout and Dr. P. de Knijff.

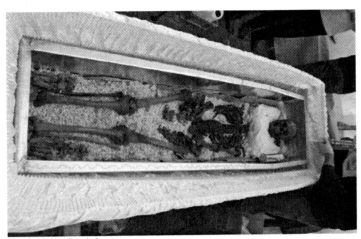

Ready for reburial.

The grave stone.

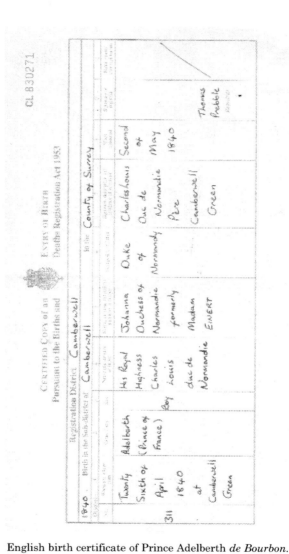

English birth certificate of Prince Adelberth *de Bourbon*.

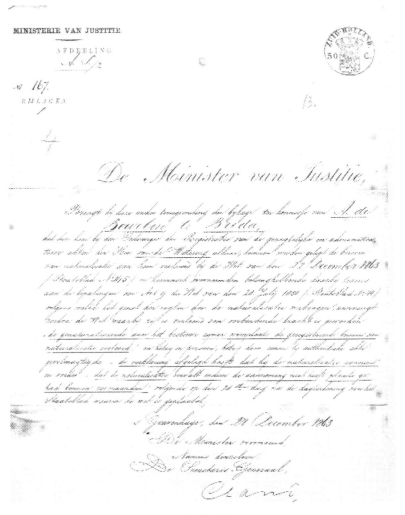

Dutch naturalization of Adelberth *de Bourbon*.

Official registered abdication of the french branch in favour of Prince Adelberth.

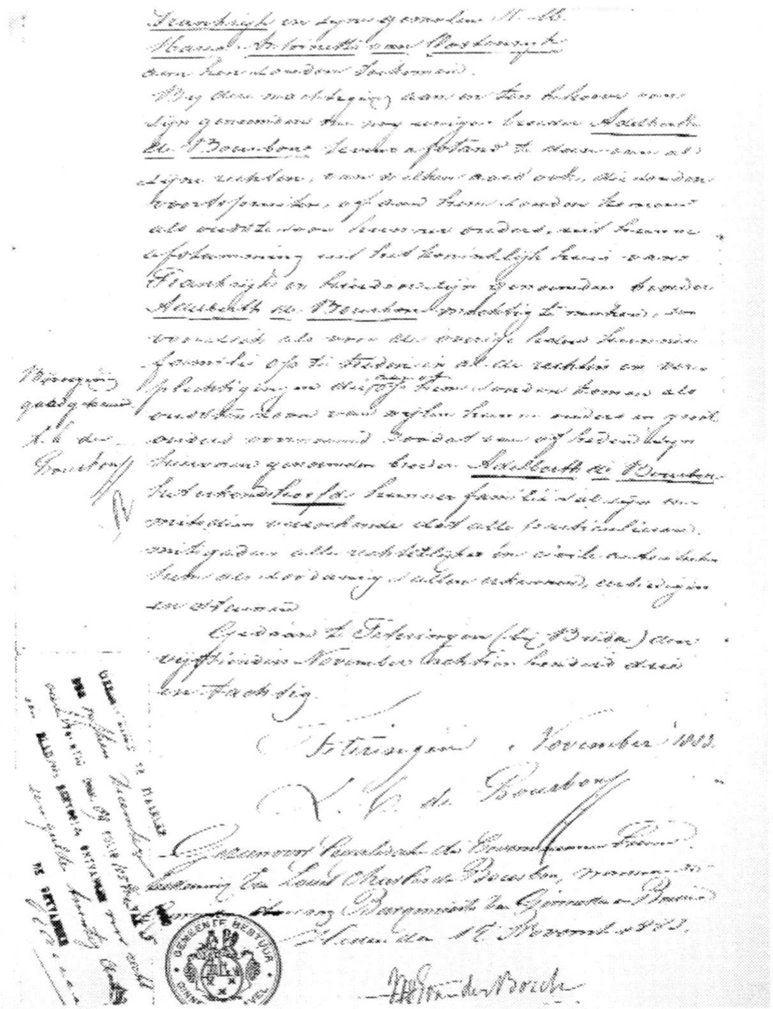

Descendants of Louis Charles - Louis XVII

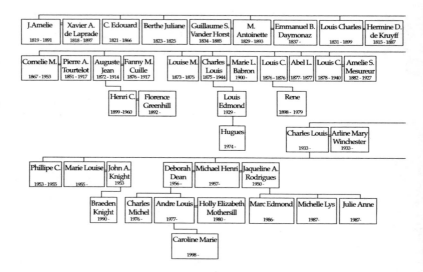

Louis XVII and his descendants.

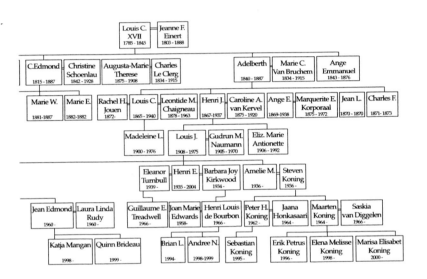

Louis C. XVII 1785 - 1845 = Jeanne F. Einert 1803 - 1888

C.Edmond 1815 - 1887 — Christine Schoenlau 1842 - 1928 | Augusta-Marie Therese 1875 - 1908 | Charles Le Clerg 1834 - 1915 | Adelberth 1840 - 1887 | Marie C. Van Bruchem 1834 - 1915 | Ange Emmanuel 1843 - 1876

Marie W. 1881-1887 | Marie E. 1882-1882 | Rachel H. Jouen 1872- | Louis C. 1865 - 1940 | Leontide M. Chaigneau 1878 - 1963 | Henri J. 1867-1937 | Caroline A. van Kervel 1875 - 1920 | Ange E. 1869-1938 | Marguerite E. Korporaal 1875 - 1972 | Jean L. 1870 - 1870 | Charles F. 1871- 1873

Madeleine L. 1900 - 1976 | Louis J. 1908 - 1975 | Gudrun M. Naumann 1905 - 1970 | Eliz. Marie Antionette 1906 - 1992

Eleanor Turnbull 1939 - | Henri E. 1935 - 2004 | Barbara Joy Kirkwood 1934 - | Amelie M. 1936 - | Steven Koning 1936 -

Jean Edmond 1960 - | Laura Linda Rudy 1960 - | Guillaume E. Treadwell 1966- | Joan Marie Edwards 1958- | Henri Louis de Bourbon 1966- | Peter H. Koning 1962 - | Jaana Honkasaari 1964 - | Maarten Koning 1964 - | Saskia van Diggelen 1966 -

Katja Mangan 1998 - | Quinn Brideau 1999 - | Brian L. 1994- | Andree N. 1998-1999 | Sebastian Koning 1995 - | Erik Petrus Koning 1996 - | Elena Melisse Koning 1998 - | Marisa Elisabet Koning 2000 -

317

Ordre Légitime de Succession au Trone de France

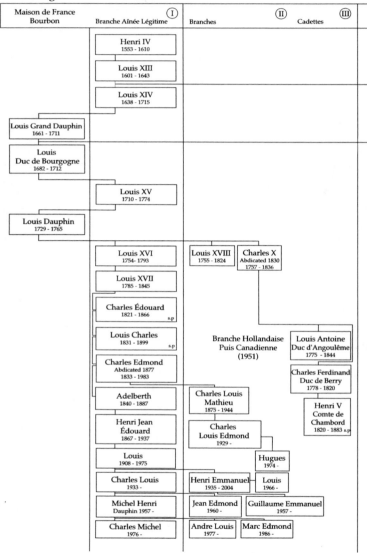

The Royal family de Bourbon and its branches.

Maison d'Espagne Bourbon (IV)	Ducs de Seville Bourbon-Castell VI (V)	Duc de Sancta Helena (VI)	Bourbons des deux-siciles (VII)	Bourbon-Parme (VIII)	Bourbon-Orléans (IX)
					Phillipe dit Monsieur Duc d'Orléans 1640 - 1701
					Phillippe dit le Régent Duc d'Orléans 1674 - 1723
Philippe V d'Espagne 1683 - 1746					Louis Duc d'Orléans 1603 - 1752
Ferdinand VI 1683 - 1746					Louis-Phillippe Duc d'Orléans 1674 - 1723
Charles III 1716 - 1788				Phillipe Duc de Parme 1751 - 1825	Louis-Philippe Joseph dit Phillippe Égalité régicide partisan de la Revolution Française 1747 - 1793
Charles IV 1748 - 1819 ∞ Marie-Louise de Parme			Ferdinand I 1751 - 1825		Under the name of the Count of Joinville he exchanged his daughter Maria Stella for the son of the prison guard Italiann Lorenzo Chiappini.
CARLOS parti Carliste — adultery with			Branche des Bourbons des deux-siciles		
Ferdinand VII 1784 - 1819 fait modifier la loi par les cortès: les femmes peuvent régner en Espagne	Don Manuel Godoy 1er Ministre de Charles IV d'où François de Paule				Louis-Phillippe 1er 1773 - 1850 Branche du Comte de Paris non dynaste
	recognized son by FVII and the government				
Isabelle oo François d'Assise	Henri Duc de Séville 1823 - 1870				
Alphonse XII 1857 - 1885					
Alphonse XIII 1886 - 1931	Branche des Ducs de Séville, non dynastes pour la France comme Louis DIT XXX CAR Également issus de Don Manuel Godoy, Donc d'une Liaison adultère reconnue telle	Albert 1er Duc de Sancta Helena 1823 - 1870			
Jaime Enrique 1908 - 1975 — Jean Comte de Barcelone 1908 - 1975		Branche des Ducs de Sancta Helena non dynastes pour la France comme les Bourbon d'Espagne et les			
Alphonse 1936 - 1989 — Juan Carlos I 1935 -					
Louis DIT XX 1974 - — Felipe infant 1968 -			Postérité actuelle (2 lignes)	Branche de Duc de Parme, des grands Ducs de Luxembourg et des branches Cadettes de Parme (Nombreux descendants)	

319

COLOPHON

This first printing consists of
300 books Numbered 1 to 300
Signed by the author

This is number _____

ISBN 1-41205299-8